GHOSTS OF DREAMS

A NOVEL

BOOKS BY THE AUTHOR

AUTHORED BOOKS
The Psychoanalysis of Symptoms
Dictionary of Psychopathology
Group Psychotherapy and Personality: Intersecting Structures (lst edition, 1979)
    (Reprinted edition, 2015—Group Psychotherapy and Personality: A Theoretical
    Model)
Sleep Disorders: Insomnia and Narcolepsy
The 4 Steps to Peace of Mind: The Simple Effective Way to Cure Our Emotional
    Symptoms (Romanian edition, 2008; Japanese edition, 2011)
Love Is Not Enough: What It Takes to Make It Work
Haggadah: A Passover Seder for the Rest of Us
Greedy, Cowardly, and Weak: Hollywood's Jewish Stereotypes
Hollywood Movies on the Couch: A Psychoanalyst Examines 15 Famous Films
Personality: How it Forms (Korean edition, 2015)
The Discovery of God: A Psycho/Evolutionary Perspective
Anatomy of Delusion
There's No Handle on My Door: Stories of Patients in Mental Hospitals
Psychoanalysis of Evil: Perspectives on Destructive Behavior
A Consilience of Natural and Social Sciences: A Memoir of Original Contributions
The Making of Ghosts: A Novel
Ghosts of Dreams: A Novel

CO-AUTHORED BOOKS   (with Anthony Burry, Ph.D.)
Psychopathology and Differential Diagnosis: A Primer
    Volume 1: History of Psychopathology
    Volume 2: Diagnostic Primer
Handbook of Psychodiagnostic Testing: Analysis of Personality in the Psychological
    Report (1st edition, 1981; 2nd edition, 1991; 3rd edition, 1997; 4th edition,
    2007; Japanese edition, 2011)

EDITED BOOKS
Group Cohesion: Theoretical and Clinical Perspectives
The Nightmare: Psychological and Biological Foundations

CO-EDITED BOOKS   (with Robert Plutchik, Ph.D.)
Emotion: Theory, Research, and Experience. Volume1: Theories of Emotion
Emotion: Theory, Research, and Experience. Volume 2: Emotions in Early Development
Emotion: Theory, Research, and Experience. Volume 3: Biological Foundations of
    Emotion
Emotion: Theory, Research, and Experience. Volume 4: The Measurement of Emotion.
Emotion: Theory, Research, and Experience. Volume 5: Emotion, Psychopathology,
    and Psychotherapy

GHOSTS OF DREAMS

A NOVEL

HENRY KELLERMAN

Published by Barricade Books Inc.
Fort Lee, N.J. 07024
www.barricadebooks.com

Library of Congress Cataloging-in-Publication Data

Kellerman, Henry.
Ghosts of dreams : a novel / by Henry Kellerman.
    pages ; cm
  ISBN 978-1-56980-103-1 (alk. paper)
1. Psychological fiction. I. Title.
  PS3611.E435G48 2015
  813'.6--dc23
                                                          2015012550

            10 9 8 7 6 5 4 3 2 1
    Manufactured in the United States of America

To
My beautiful granddaughters
Esther, Sam, Mira

CONTENTS

PART 1

THE GHOST IN MY DREAM

· 1 ·

THE GHOST

It took many years for me to realize that I was actually, at unexpected and hazy moments, confused about where I was, or even who I was. Such a feeling would take me by surprise and would also disappear as instantly as it appeared. No, let me change that. I need to fine-tune it. It wasn't so much confusion about where I was. It was more specifically a strange and distant, even ambiguous feeling about which my personal reality seemed to be in a state of confusion. That's it. I would feel momentarily confused insofar as I suddenly felt that I had done something, somewhere and some time ago, and I could feel the feeling but without any memory attached to the feeling. The feeling, I think, was a combination of some vague guilt as well as a sense of danger or even a kind of impending peril mixed with a pulsating anticipatory anxiety generated by this peril. Whenever that particular feeling hit me, it would be disorienting, but would only, thank God, last a split second.

After careful thought, and without knowing quite what it was I was feeling, I came to the conclusion that that sort of disorienting moment reminded me of a kind of clandestine personality change of roles — along with something like what would be in a novel or movie regarding — regarding something like — like an assassin's mission. I know it sounds adolescent. I mean, here I am, college professor Dr. Alex Cole, who teaches the psychology of abnormal thinking along with its partner, skewed behavior, and teaching it in a graduate doctoral psychology program, so, you know, I'm sure I don't change names, dress differently, and travel to other countries like a CIA operative. Thinking *that* would be delusional and, certainly for me, actually *being that*, would be preposterous. Nonetheless, I can't help noticing that in the moment of considering this strange feeling that does, in fact come over me, it immediately creates an association about myself as though I'm something—actually like a CIA operative, one who spies or does some such clandestine dangerous thing. Yes, a dangerous thing that could generate bona fide peril.

No, I'm realistic, so it actually doesn't feel as though I'm James Bond. That would have positive feelings attached to it. My dilemma is that the stuff I'm thinking and mostly feeling has distinct negatives attached to it. I actually have this remote, vague feeling that I may have—and I hate to say this—shot and killed someone. It's fleeting. Yes, I do feel it's squalid. I can tell it's something deliberate and motivated and when it happens, I get the urgent need to escape. It's the need to escape peril and I know it creates in me a sense of desperation.

I've never told a soul about it, and although I should have the memory of it all, I don't.

It would be more or less psychotic to think that I'm a 007 Bond swashbuckler, primarily because I avoid any kind of dangerous situation. I confess I'm more Clark Kent and not even close to being Superman. And, to boot, here where we're about to enter the 1980s, I'm a forty-one-year-old year old Clark Kent. Yet, the truth is that every once in a while I would awaken from a dream and sometimes have a flash of this vague reminiscence of myself in a kind of another way. This other way actually includes danger, aggression, and I'll even say rectification—getting even, making things right, perhaps something like revenge? All in all, it's like feeling there's a ghost in my dreams.

Yes, I think that's it. But the ghost—that feeling of another me—is also closer to that getting-even thing. It's as if the ghost needs a gratifying sense of vengeance. This precise kind of a disturbing moment would sometimes appear when I would awaken from a nightmare. It didn't have to be a nightmare of terror. It could be an awakening based upon any intense emotion that turned the dream into a nightmare.

That's what happened to me last night. I awoke with a nightmare. Something in the dream woke me out of it. The "something" surprised me, startled me. But I know it was the scene in the dream where I said to someone or maybe I asked someone—I don't know which—or actually maybe I said it to myself:

What's in a book?

Or maybe it wasn't a question, maybe it was
something declarative and emphatic, like:

It's in a book!

In either case it kind of feels to me as though
it's part of a dialogue with someone.

That's when I woke up surprised. I woke up completely awake like I was never even sleeping. I knew that a nightmare is the result of any emotion that wakes you up. That's the first thought that hit me. That's me. I always go to the analysis of something. It's only then that I go back to the feeling. It's my need to figure it out. That comes first. But now I remembered that in the dream, before it became a nightmare, and immediately before I said or heard someone else say the phrase about *a book*, I recall walking down a street—I think I was in another country—passing by a man. As I was passing him I took out a pistol with a silencer from my raincoat pocket and shot the man—killed him. I then felt the urgency of escaping, of keeping myself entirely hidden—actually invisible. I believe the point was to erase any evidence that I had been in this other country at all and especially at the time of the killing.

My sense of it is that I accomplished my disappearance by driving a car a long distance from the murder scene into a neighboring country. I had the thought that the point of this type of escape was not to buy plane tickets. That could be traced. Then I wondered: What does that mean—*it could be traced?* I instantly knew that the question was unnecessary because indeed I did know what it meant. In a moment I knew that I needed not to buy airline tickets because if I was habitually and serially doing that sort of thing and then boarding a plane some genius detective would eventually piece it all together; figuring out that one specific individual consistently flew out of the country immediately following the killing of someone. The whole thing—especially how I think about it—reminds me of the theme in my favorite book, *The Day of the Jackal* by Frederick Forsyth, published in the early 1970's. It's a story about a hired assassin who could not be identified. Obviously, it's really a story about the issue of *anonymity*. I have to admit it's my favorite kind of story. What scares me is that the *Jackal* story resonates just about perfectly with my whole dilemma — my concern with *assassination* and with *anonymity*.

I guess the dream/nightmare was a visitation of this exact vague memory where I did some terrible thing and then needed to escape, never to be discovered. But it was the element of the dream concerning the *book* that actually awakened me from the dream. It wasn't the shooting that awakened me. It was the intense emotion that accompanied the issue of the *book*. Well, actually it was the *book* thing as well as the *escape* that carried the emotion.

*   *   *

It was at that moment that I knew I needed to start a log. I needed to make sure from this moment on I would have a running dialogue with myself. It would be the start of a diary. I was not going to be inert about it the way I had been about *it* for over I don't know how many years. The "it" is that I would have these same flashes of memory in the past but would let it go. It was the flashes of a memory that I had done something wrong, something terrible. That was no longer going to happen. No, I'm now committed to, so to speak, making it all flesh. In other words I'm no longer going to let myself forget the bad feeling until it hits me again and then I forget it again and then, sometime later, it hits me again. Now, I think I can see that it's this thing with the "book" and how it turned into the nightmare that apparently shook me out of my inertia and out of my rumination about it all.

I could see that the diary would unfold as the story of my life reflecting my deepest concern about these unrepressed yet vague dream memories. And these dream memories seem to repeatedly lobby in my emotional life, inching me closer to an awareness that something is indeed, wrong. It all specifically includes the entire thing of self-doubt that shakes me because in no uncertain terms it almost insists that yes, I have done something wrong.

I'm naming the diary "*The Night of the Jackal: A Cynegetic Investigation*." I liked the subtitled adjective *cynegetic* because it means a hunt. And that's what I'm after here—a psychic investigation, a hunt for what I've been vaguely feeling and, at least in the past, such a feeling and memory was safely tucked away in my psyche, in my unconscious. But this is not the past, and for the first time this "something" will no longer be safely hidden. I've gotten access to it even though this access with respect to content is, in the present, inchoate. But I'm determined to dig it out. Call it an archeological dig. The basic question is: 'Am I a jackal and don't really know it?'

I immediately went to my supply closet and removed my briefcase. I filled it with several file folders and yellow pads, and I dated it. The first idea I jotted down of this, my psychic investigation, was the instruction to myself to follow the emotion. So, no, it's not solely the emotion of terror that makes the nightmare. That's ridiculous. It's obvious that any strong emotion can shake the dreamer out of the dream. When I was only seventeen years old, my first so-called nightmare was a sexual dream, and, when I had the orgasm, it was the orgasm that woke me. I once had a dream where someone told a joke, the punch-line was funny, and I started laughing, and the laughing woke me. So, no, a nightmare is any dream that wakes up the dreamer because of a strong emotion. Period.

So, why am I thinking about the definition of a nightmare and not about the surprise that woke me up? I've known the answer to that for years. It started twenty years after the war. It started about 1965. The war ended in 1945. All during that twenty year span I would have flashes of a memory. Well, not really a memory. It was more like a distant feeling. It's like I said, like I did something wrong, but that it was covered up so I couldn't figure out what it was—is. I think it was all connected to that emotion of surprise that shook me out of the dream last night. When I awakened, I quickly noticed my stream of consciousness especially about the particular verbatim quote in the dream—*What's in a book?* or, *It's in a book!*

It was my stream of consciousness after I awakened—what I was immediately thinking upon awakening that anchored my memory of the quote. It felt as though this quote had bored a hole directly into my heart so that all of it seemed to connect and reinforce this guilty feeling, this feeling that suggested I might have done something wrong—terribly wrong.

The dream into the nightmare was so vivid that it had the feel of what's known as a hypnagogic hallucination. That's the kind of dream that feels so real that when you awaken you really have trouble distinguishing the real from the unreal—almost like a hallucination encased in some hypnotic trance. So that the question that remains is: Did it really happen? Have I ever really killed anyone? At such times, the answer comes back to me as: I'm not sure.

*   *   *

Let me start from the beginning. Almost ten years ago, in the wee, small hours of a misty, cold winter morning, my friend Rowan Quinn (nickname Rowdy) and I, after partying at an all-nighter, were walking down Fifth Avenue in New York City. At the corner of Fifth Avenue and 20th Street was the bank where I had a checking account along with a safe-deposit box. As we turned the corner into 20th Street we were passing by the street side alley of this bank when something at the deep end of this narrow alley next to the trash-disposal sidedoor of the bank caught my eye. I asked Rowdy what he thought was in the very large canvas bag sitting beside all the trash bags that were stacked and awaiting the next garbage truck? Rowdy looked, stopped in his tracks, and without a word we both made a beeline into the alley, sensing a distinct possibility. We went right for the bag.

It was a lot! We tried to be furtive about it but couldn't.

The bag was extremely heavy and, as fate would have it, awkward to lift and, at the same time, awkward to open. We squatted, pried apart the horizontal clasp on the canvas bag while also looking around to see if anyone had spotted us, and then pulled it open. At first crack we glimpsed two shiny gold bars obviously genuine, plus stacks of hundred dollar bills bundled in wrapper strips. Reflexively, we closed the bag. Rowdy pulled off his raincoat and each of us holding one of the handles of the bag carried it out of the alley, with Rowdy's raincoat draped over, concealing what we were carrying. We tried to look casual walking down the street talking to one another, trying of course to appear inconspicuous—despite the fact that we were obviously lugging something that, if not requiring strength, certainly required endurance.

Rowdy lived on 20th Street east of Third Avenue, so we were only a few blocks away. He lived in a four-story walk-up. There was no doorman to worry about so there would be no one saying: "Yeah, we saw them carrying something heavy. The raincoat was covering it."

We arrived at Rowdy's apartment. Because it was so early in the morning we hadn't encountered a soul. Of course, the first thing we did was to rifle the bag. Exactly two gold bars and, after counting the money, exactly one hundred thousand dollars ($100,000) in fifty stacks of two thousand dollars each. We quickly consulted the encyclopedia and discovered that usually gold bars weigh about 400 troy ounces each, which translated to about thirty-seven to thirty-eight pounds per bar. We figured both bars together weighed about seventy-four to seventy-six pounds, and a bar was estimated to be worth about a quarter of a million dollars.

We were now sitting with a lot of money; two gold bars together worth about a half-million dollars along with another one hundred thousand dollars in cash. Let's call it an even half-million. Wow. We were excited, more like bewildered, but most of all, we were scared.

What to do? Return it? Keep it?

Neither of us had ever been involved with anything like this or had stolen anything—or ever did anything remotely close to the level of a felony. At least that was true of me and I was sure it was true of Rowdy as well.

Rowdy says it: "Is this stealing?" He answers his own question, and then wonders: "Definitely it is! Probably. Maybe" Or, "maybe," he says, "finder's keepers!" He looks at me, then looks away and keeps talking. "The bank's insured." Finally, looking directly at me, he says: "We keep it." Then he says: "Where do we store it all?"

I'm in a quandary. What are we getting into? But Rowdy goes off on a riff as though he's been doing this for years. "We split the cash and hole it up in our apartments." He hesitates momentarily, thinks, and then, as he's imagining it, says:

> "We keep the cash in secret places in our apartments and only use it when we need it. It should take us a lot of years to use it up. We keep the bars in a safe deposit box in a bank—and we let it sit there for a long time till this whole thing blows over. By then, if gold soars we'll have much more then than it's now worth. We're going to need to figure out how to unload the bars and how to justify the half-million or even much more than we're now figuring. Also, no one can know anything about this. No one! We'll each have a key to the box and we stipulate that the

box cannot be opened by only one of us. We both need to be there when the box is opened."

Rowdy says this without a moment's hesitation. Then for a few moments we're silent, looking at each other, then turning away thinking.

"It needs something more," I say. "I mean what if one of us dies? How does the survivor open the box? Can't keep that much cash in the house. We keep some in the house and when it runs out we both go to the box and take another sum. And whenever we go we'll get a chance to look at those bars. We'll need a large box and we need to open an account at some bank, but not this bank, because I have both a checking account and a safe deposit box here. We'll wait two months and then open the account at some other bank. Let's not make our opening of a box too close to the event of a missing canvas-bag-bonanza. Meanwhile we keep the bag with all of it here."

"No good, Al," Rowdy says. "You take the first batch, let's say about fifteen thousand and keep it at your place. I'll put the bars in my conked-off fireplace and intermingle them with the other bricks that are stacked there. They'll be covered by the other bricks. I'll stash the cash in the back of the shelves of my bookcase. The shelves are deep so the books will hide what's behind them."

Then, after Rowdy says all that, I feel an instant change of heart. "That's it then." I paused. "I mean, what the hell have we gotten ourselves into? I'm really nervous, Rowd. And you are too. Let's face it. Maybe we should can the whole thing and return everything."

"Relax Al," he answers. "Let's see what the papers say tomorrow — if anything. OK?"

Rowdy says that with confidence, and it does in fact relax me.

"OK," I say. "In that case I'm going into the bank tomorrow afternoon to make a deposit. It's a check I got from the insurance company for a visit to my ophthalmologist. It's for $64.71. It's an innocuous amount. Not noticeable. Talk about noticeable — I'll wait a bit to see if there's any noticeable uproar about the missing bag or something."

* * *

When I had the nightmare about *What's in a book?* or *It's in a book*, along with the element of the shooting, I woke up and instantly thought about the canvas bag and the money and Rowdy and me finding it. Then I held my head and it felt like a meteor hit me because I suddenly realized that the entire episode of the canvas bag had never happened. It was a dream I had forgotten, but had over the years haunted me without my quite knowing what it was that was gnawing at me. Apparently, I had been going around for years with the vague feeling that something was wrong. From time to time it felt like I was afflicted with an amorphous bombardment of something underlying or hidden in my vague memory storage, something that was serious — but something that I couldn't put my finger on.

Apparently, it was all under the surface of my consciousness and, like I said, every now and then this concern would surface, and I was left asking what it was all about — what was it that was continuing to bother me? What memory couldn't I access? And, more, I now suddenly also remembered that I'd had the Rowdy dream with the canvas bag before. When I had the dream before, or some variation of the same dream, I remember that it was in these other times that Rowdy and I decided to rent a safe deposit box in another bank we chose as the place to keep the loot. I now was sure that I'd had this same dream several times before, but had forgotten it each time. It was clear to me that my feeling in all these same dreams concerned the motive for our visits. We were always checking to see whether the gold bars and stacks of hundreds were still there. In these dreams we would open the box and just stand there staring at its contents, reassuring ourselves that it was all still real.

But there's more. You see, Rowdy is a close friend, but it was sometimes difficult for me to be with him because although he is a warm and decent person, he is intensely competitive. It's clear that he needs admiration—inordinately. It was all palpable. Once you knew Rowdy, this other persona of his came through. He compared himself to others and his rating scale that measured who was better was always in his favor.

Rowdy's need for such acclimation seemed to stem from a commonplace inferiority feeling. I believe that in his consciousness it was really a hope he lived with that assured him he wasn't inferior. Rowdy was not a dull person, but although bright, not a genius. He collected books. He was also full of clichés and frequently not so cool. Height-wise he was a lanky six foot two or three but weighed maybe only 160 pounds. Skin and bones would not be an inaccurate description, and he was wedded to his physical awkwardness. He had some kind of skeletal disorder, and a resulting stooped gait. This somewhat hunched position always made him feel uncomfortable, a feeling he couldn't ever shake. Nevertheless, he was also always, and without fail, striving for success and would practically vibrate in his single-minded ambition for some kind of fame. He was to most people the quintessential go-getter.

Rowdy's stuff, this compensatory striving, was, I'm sure, a result of the fact that he never had a job, never did his homework—even in our early years in high school—and then only lasted half of one semester in college. None of us who knew him ever understood how he supported himself. I had the impression that he had inherited some money and that's what kept him going. He never talked about it, including never telling me what his father's job was. I could sense not to ask him about it, and never did. The bottom line however is that, despite it all, I always liked him, and we were good friends. I think he trusted me and considered me his best pal. Oh yes, his grandfather lived with them for a while and his grandfather's work, or whatever he did was also never mentioned. Rowdy also once mentioned that his grandfather's favorite thing was to tell him great war stories.

The question for me became: given his personality, why was he in my dream? I believe the answer is that I needed to represent something about myself in the dream so that, in casting Rowdy, that particular something about Rowdy's personality could be symbolic and therefore could satisfy something about my own motives—about my own personality. Of course, the key would need to be something about me that was similarly competitive because if Rowdy could be reduced to one thing, one characteristic only, it would necessarily have to be this specific competitiveness—that is, he had an aching need to win. To win at what didn't matter. To win at everything was always the answer. I used to thank goodness that it was at this juncture where I parted with him. Competitive yes. But crazy competitive, no. It was the one thing about Rowdy that made it difficult for anyone who knew him to be with him for any extended period of time.

Rowdy is only his nickname. His actual name is Charles Rostmann Quinn. He hated all three designations: Charles, Rostmann, and Quinn—especially when people naturally called him Charlie or Quinn—and he didn't at all like his unusual middle Rostmann name, which he claimed had no identifiable historical antecedent. It may have been someone's surname, but he had no idea whose it might be. So, he named himself Rowdy. He thought it was cool.

It should be remembered that I teach abnormal psychology courses to graduate students. And, to top it off, I'm immersed in psychodynamic psychology as the so-called infrastructural dictionary for abnormal behavior. That means I'm kind of like a Freudian shrink, a Freudian junkie. In my own terms I consider myself an eclectic Freudian, meaning that I utilize Freudian ideas cobbled together with threads of my own insights.

As a Freudian shrink, of course, I was thinking about Rowdy as a symbol of competitiveness. I was obviously thinking about my own competitiveness—but also, and in a Freudian psychoanalytic sense—about my early life and my memories of my mother and father. I suddenly had an insight. I knew why I unconsciously selected Rowdy as a symbol in my dream. It was because of the good old Oedipus complex. It concerned that competition issue and Rowdy, because of his competitive nature was a good symbol of it.

You see, my father was a great guy. He was handsome and strong, but not particularly competitive. My mother was a can-do person. She was beautiful and very talented. To say she was on fire would not be an exaggeration. I was an only son and was good at most things and she always took pride in me. My father was also proud of me, but it was my mother who was more demonstrative and obviously derived pleasure from my achievements.

Both my parents were affectionate and I always tried to please them. I also believed that I was my mother's favorite. So, if I were to describe this as a competition then the favorite is the winner. In contrast, it was also clear that my mother was deeply in love with my father and, her love for me was of course different—parent to child. It was my youthful sensibility that confused caring with competition. But, despite this confusion, and perhaps, rather because of it, a light bulb lit up.

This connection to my mother explained why, when I was in my late teens to mid-twenties, I was mostly attracted to married women and in fact had many affairs with married women. I eventually began thinking about this as a peculiarity. Still, I was not always the one to start it. I found that many of these women had approached me first. It was this unusual special circumstance regarding married women that illuminated what my motive really was. It gradually dawned on me that I was always acting-out the scenario of being my mother's favorite. Interestingly, once I recognized what was motivating this behavior I never again had any romantic or sexual contact with a married woman. In a sense, I had been keeping myself in the dark—unconscious of the true meaning of my acting-out. In other words *knowing* it absolutely eliminated my need to *do* it. I had worked it out consciously as in *consciousness is curative.*

Remembering and understanding it all was satisfying but I realized I was getting away from my quest to understand a more immediate problem—that of figuring out the meaning of:

What's in a book? or, *It's in a book!*

I wondered: Is the whole thing really in a book? Which book? Or is the so-called book really a symbol for something else?

And here is where it gets complicated. It's about another story. Not a dream. A real thing. We came from Germany. We were German Jews living in Berlin. It was 1943, and I was five years old. The Gestapo burst into our apartment building and started rounding up all the residents who were Jewish. I was sitting at the kitchen table when they actually kicked the door in. They instructed the landlady to keep me until they sent someone to get me. They marched my screaming parents out of the apartment. That's the last time I ever saw them. I was gasping and didn't know what to do. I was screaming for my mother. The landlady was a very good friend of ours. She wasn't Jewish, but it made no difference to her that we were. She loved me, and I loved her. She quickly gathered some of my clothes and spirited me out of the building. We boarded a bus, and I have a vague memory of arriving at a farmhouse. I remember that the bus let us out a far distance from the farm house. We walked a long way before we arrived at our destination.

Frau Franken was a woman my family knew and she agreed to keep me at the farmhouse. The landlady told Frau Franken that she would say I ran away. The point I'm getting to here is that I believe all of my sick dreams and vague feelings about doing something wrong are maybe about how angry I still am. I believe the trauma of having my parents torn from me will never leave my raging sobbing soul. The worst of it is that in my childish anger I may even have blamed my parents—irrational though that thought might seem. However, as a psychoanalyst I also realize that such anger would always be a result of feeling abandoned—rather distraught for losing my family.

At the end of the war I was sent to my cousins in America. It was my uncle who shortened my name from Alexander Coleman to Alex Cole. I do, of course remember my wonderful parents, my wonderful landlady, and my dear Frau Franken. There are good people in the world.

I'm not sure I'm one of them.

· 2 ·

PENETRATING THE DREAM

My *Night of the Jackal* diary, with its cynegetic investigation, was growing larger. It was already loaded with notes of my psychological ruminations. I began to consider that because of all this mess of my dreams, my dream-ghosts, that my personality had been contaminated with, I think, hatred. Yet I was searching for the truth—like I was obsessed that the quote in the dream had something to do with something awful. I had been acting-out—been *doing* something in place of *knowing* something. That's what acting-out's all about. I knew from my research into the psychoanalytic engineering of the psyche that if I had been acting-out then I must be angry. It necessarily followed that I must be angry with someone—a person, a *who*.

So that's where it leaves me—in the dark. I kind of knew something was bothering me, and I felt bad about it. It was as if I did something that was sordid, dishonorable, or simply just corrupt. Yes, I definitely felt bad about it, and usually in shrink lingo this "kind of something" relates to feeling that a bad thing was done. It's diagnosed as an *enosiophobia*; it has seven syllables, en-o-si-o-pho-bi-a. Etymologically its root *enosio* means restricted or even entombed.

This seven syllable word means that such a person believes he has committed an unforgivable sin and, in addition, because of this belief, is usually terribly afraid of "accusation"—of consequences. It's like the person is entombed in this dark bad place and can't get out. The reality is that this "something bad" usually isn't true and never actually happened. Those who believe that it *has* happened, and even feel it has happened—yet know that it hasn't—are diagnosed as suffering with a *pseudomania*; that is, *pretending* that something bad happened. It's like feigning an illness.

Personally, I wouldn't want to live or die on the difference between these esoteric diagnoses, so that, as far as I was concerned, I had both fused into one. However, the truth is that I feel more like the enosiophobic; that is, I'm not feigning anything. I need to say it, to get it off my chest: I *do* feel I've done something wrong and I do feel entombed in the wrongness.

And because of this presumed enosiophobia, I'm actually gripped by an intrusive thought: Did I do something wrong? Or again, specifically: What did I do that was wrong that I could be punished for? I can't escape my need to retrace my tracks. And, to do that, I'm back to the nightmare of *What's in a book?* Or *It's in a book!* What does it mean? Why am I feeling guilty?

So this enosiophobia, that I consider to be my psychological symptom, about which I have no memory, but still feel a guilt that I'd done some bad thing—was it real?

I decided that if I could understand the dream that would decisively lead me to a place and a person, both of which would tell me what the bad thing was. Of course I knew I needed to let my mind freely wander. Perhaps this would lead me to discover what this *book* element meant. I needed to let myself relax into what's known as the flow of a "stream of consciousness."

I expected that the first clear notion that would pop into my mind could be an important link to the *book* thing. So I did just that—I let my mind wander. In a few seconds the phrase that occurred to me was: *A book is a box of facts.* I don't know if that's true (that "*a book is,*"—in fact—*a box of facts*), but I'm not sure that it's not true. Of course a book is much more than a *box of facts*, but, nevertheless, that was my first association.

I examined the *box of facts* phrase carefully and decided to fix on the word *box.* I asked myself about whether I had any kind of *box* that might lead to something significant. The answer came almost instantly. Of course! I had that safe deposit box in the bank where I held all my important papers—deeds to several properties I owned, insurance policies, and other things. And, of course, the "box" association is what Rowdy and I worried about and debated in the dream.

* * *

So now in 1979—thirty-four years after World War II—I went to see a shrink. I had known about him because he had published several professional papers on dreams and nightmares and was also an expert on hypnagogic phenomena including dissociative disorders such as amnesia and fugue. Fugue interested me because the diagnostic focus of fugue related to individuals who could wander away from home—frequently far away, even to another country—and not know how they got there. They might not even remember who they were when they got there. The hypnagogic part of it all—that is, a kind of dream where it becomes impossible to distinguish fantasy from reality—in combination with a fugue experience interested me even more because I'd had several other dreams that definitely seemed to be hypnagogic. In those dreams the story line was so vivid that I was never sure whether what happened in the dream actually happened *in* the dream, or had actually happened.

The shrink was Dr. Richard Martin. He was a psychologist/psychoanalyst/author. He was easy to talk to and was very welcoming. He asked what brought me to see him. I told him that for the longest time I had feelings that I'd been elsewhere but couldn't put my finger on where this was and then again felt as though it might be a recurring dream I was having but not remembering. Dr. Martin answered that even though I'd had these questions about such vague feelings, and apparently had them for a long time, the main point was that I called him for the appointment the previous week never having called him before.

"What made you call now?" he asked, emphasizing the *now.*

I told him I had a dream about something about a "book," and to it I associated a "box." I had figured out what it was, but also remembered, or rather only tentatively recalled, that I'd had that dream probably several times before. Along with the dream element of "book" and the associated element of "box," I remembered I had shot and killed someone—I think—in the dream.

I told Dr. Martin that my nagging suspicion was that either it was a hypnagogic experience in the dream or perhaps I was subject to fugue behavior and while in such a state actually shot and killed someone. I added that my vague feelings concerned a pressure of discomfort and also a definite sense of guilt. Dr. Martin then affirmed that I must be suffering from a possible enosiophobia. Apparently, because of my professional work, he assumed I would know what that meant.

Before I knew it, he had me lie on the couch, and, in typical psychoanalytic mode, he sat behind the couch. He knew I would be amenable to this kind of work. It gave me confidence that we were already working, even though we were more or less only twenty minutes into the first session. He didn't ask me the usual introductory questions about my date of birth, didn't set a fee with me, and didn't, didn't, didn't. He just went to it.

"Tell me, Dr. Cole, where did the element of *the box* lead you?"

I told him where and how I figured it out and that the bottom line was that *the box* led me to the location of the key to my safe deposit box, which I had inadvertently misplaced and then couldn't find.

"Dr. Cole, it wasn't inadvertent, was it? You know better. We both know that misplacing an important item like the key means something correspondingly important that you needed not to know." He waited. "Agreed?"

"Yes," I hesitatingly answered. I was hesitant because I found myself fixed and preoccupied with his comment.

"So that the dream itself was, it seems, your attempt to undo your acting-out of misplacing the key. You wanted to know what it meant rather than keep yourself in the dark and, therefore, to continue to perhaps do things that eventually got you to the point of worrying about it — that is, worrying about whether you've actually done something wrong. It's the enosiophobia. Therefore," he continued, "the dream was a retrieval attempt on your part to get to the bottom of it and to ultimately retrieve the all-important *key*. We both know that the *key* as a noun can also be the verb we're looking for. In other words, you misplaced the noun, and now we're searching for the verb — as in *keying* it in — meaning the action of finding the answer to the entire puzzle."

"Yes, that's right. I also was originally considering it an enosiophobia; that is, feeling guilty about some felony or that perhaps, God forbid, I murdered someone. I know that sounds ridiculous, but that's what it feels like and that's what comes to mind. It's the killing business that really bothers me more than the entire context of being fuzzy about things."

We went on like that for a while and all the time we were circling the issue of some fugue experience with which I was possibly afflicted and, in addition, the possibility about me existing in another guise—a me who was perhaps acting in the role of an assassin—even, heavens forbid, perhaps a serial killer. Was it in a dream or was it actually happening? And, if so, where was this somewhere? On top of that, why was I doing whatever it was I was doing?

But the question that was really eating away at me concerned what I then asked him.

"What would be my reason, my motive, either in a dream or in real life that would bring me to the point of doing such things?"

As I said that to him, I immediately had the thought about my parents. Before I had a chance to talk about it, he continued.

"Well, tell me those things that are important to you in life—especially those things that have happened to you in life that you consider to be not just unfair, but more than that, like something vile or evil."

"I'm always infuriated by genocides. I hate the idea of helpless beings being tortured or killed. If it were up to me the entire world would be vegetarian. That's why I'm against abortion—because it's killing something that's helpless. I'm against any kind of oppression. Yet I know if I were inadvertently to make a woman pregnant I would insist on the abortion despite how I'm against it. It's my living with contradictions. I know I live with contradictions. But mostly it's about my parents." Then I told him the story.

"On a ten-point scale it sounds to me that genocide is ten," he said.

"Right," I answered. "And, despite my stance against capital punishment, I do in fact believe in personal retribution. Getting even, one on one, is not out of the question for me. If someone takes advantage of you and hurts you, then I firmly believe you have a right to strike back. If they kill one of yours, then you should kill two of theirs. One is not enough. I know this is a very rageful position, so it's clear to me that I'm always in a potential rage against any sort of power violation."

"OK, Dr. Cole, we're onto something here. You're clearly full of righteous indignation that can bring you to a boil. The question is, does the fruit of such indignation lead to acting-out? Or do you swallow the anger and let it therefore attack the self—as in you attacking you. As we know, anger is either externalized or it's internalized. So which is it with you?"

"I would say it's typically, but not always, definitely internalized. Then again I would also say it's possibly occasionally expostulated. And in one way that might be possible if there are actually two mes."

"Let's call it a day now," Martin announced, "and, if it's agreeable to you, we'll continue in three days here in the office. Then we'll decide on the fee and I'll also take down pertinent personal information. I do have your phone number."

I thanked him and left the office. In the street I had the feeling of: Wow! My own comment of "if there are two mes," floored me. It hit me dead on, and I knew in my gut that I was entering another world, the world of considering if there are, in fact, two of me. I was eager to be entering this new world accompanied by Dr. Martin.

I could see that, as a result of my dreams, I might question whether in another guise it could be that I actually *was* an assassin? Somewhat humorously speaking, I think I was comforted by the thought that Dr. Martin was a fellow assassin. His motive however, was not born in the gestation of righteous indignation. Rather, his mission was to assassinate pathology — sickness, fugue, pseudomania, enosiophobia, and, of course, rage — and, as far as Dr. Martin's work as an assassin of pathology is concerned, I could sense that the pathology, the sickness, would know it.

I put it all in my *Jackal* notes.

*   *   *

The nagging thought I had but that I had not mentioned to Dr. Martin was something that kept staring at me. The fact was that over the past ten years or so, since I was in my mid twenties, I had been to Europe about twice each year for scientific and clinical papers that I delivered at conferences on the subject of abnormal psychology and all of its vicissitudes — sleep disorders, split personality (known as multiple personality or as dissociative identity disorder) and on the structure of emotional/ psychological symptoms. I became known in the field of abnormal psychology because, at the tender age of twenty-six, I had published my first book, *The Psychoanalysis of Symptoms*. So I wasn't a CIA operative or a covert agent. Rather, I made my bones as a writer and also as a knowledgeable professional psychologist/psychoanalyst in the broad field of psychopathology. Part of my yearly income was based on lecturing assignments.

I also knew that some of the dozen or more former Nazis who had escaped prison terms had been shot and killed over a protracted period of time, in several different countries. The German police, along with Interpol, had noted that these were not random shootings. Rather, it seemed like a mission of revenge. I could not overlook the possibility that the authorities in these various countries would think that some kind of Jewish plot to murder former Nazis was not just brewing, but was actually happening. I was always checking the newspapers for noteworthy items regarding these stories. I would check them when I traveled to Paris, London, or Berlin, or, several times, also to the Soviet Union—or even when I visited Argentina or Paraguay. Argentina seemed like a reasonable destination for a scholarly presentation at a university, but does Paraguay? The memory of my trip to Paraguay made me feel uncomfortable. My question was: What was I doing in Paraguay and why did I accept the invitation to lecture there?

What scared me was that these stories of killings—possibly assassinations—never were reported in the tabloids when I was in those countries. It invariably happened that the stories appeared several days later, after I had returned to New York City. These connections or correlations seemed more like facts and not mere suppositions or even dreams! One bald fact that couldn't be refuted was that I had visited all the countries where these killings had occurred.

I was certainly aware that former Nazis like Eichmann and Mengele had escaped to Argentina and, yes, to Paraguay—shuttling surreptitiously into these countries by the Vatican's so-called Odessa underground priesthood railroad. Others of the most notorious of Hitler's SS men escaped to these countries and were welcomed by Juan Peron—and his celebrated wife, Eva Peron.

I knew some of the other names of those Nazis. They included Freidrich Sommer, Werner Best, Horst Kopkow, and Erich Traub. Traub was one of the ones that always interested me and whom I would consider a perfect target for assassination. I knew why I thought of assassination with respect to these Nazis, and such thoughts would enter my mind whenever I heard or read the name Erich Traub. I knew that Traub was a Nazi virologist who, it was rumored, used children in some of his experiments. The idea of hurting children was the thing that got me. What troubled me was that Traub escaped punishment and became a successful businessman. I actually had the thought that Traub's got to go soon or he'll probably die of natural causes in a not so distant day because now, in the late 1970s he was already beginning to age. Even if he had fifteen or twenty years left—what's fifteen or twenty years? It's one or two blinks.

And this brings me to Bishop Alois Hudal in Rome. Hudal was a Vatican favorite. Yet he was rumored to be a vital cog in the Odessa underground railroad. Some called it a fact, not a rumor. Then there was the community in the foothills of the Andean mountains of Chile named Villa Baviera or Colonia Dignidad (Dignity Colony). This so-called dignity colony of former Nazis and their families was populated solely by those who escaped to Chile via Hudal's Odessa. Therefore assassination would be out of the question, primarily because the colony was heavily guarded. But, I thought, a small atomic weapon on the tippy-tip nose of a guided missile would do the job just fine. The fact that there are children living there who had nothing to do with the Nazi era did in fact enter my mind, but the truth is that even that didn't bother me. I did actually notice it, and it did bother me that I made a distinction between those children who were traumatized and persecuted because they were Jewish and those children who were the offspring of Nazis in Colonia Dignidad in Chile, for whom I had absolutely no concern even if a bomb were to explode all over Colonia Dignidad. Again, I admit to having blatant contradictions in my life.

My main fantasy target however, was Joseph Mengele, the so-called doctor/angel of Auschwitz. He was never apprehended and finally settled in Bertioga, Sao Paulo, Brazil. He ostensibly died this year, 1979, because of a reported massive stroke while swimming. I didn't believe it, or didn't want to believe it. My thought was: Save Mengele for me. I'll take care of it.

Mengele was my main preoccupation because, among other atrocities, he used children in unmentionable experiments. He was the one who someone definitely should have targeted for assassination. I'm sure the Israelis were after him. "One bullet to the head!" And that thought always gave me pleasure. No other way to say it! In my mind's eye, and while thinking about Mengele's deserved and hoped-for assassination, and not at all to my horror, I actually saw myself doing it—the assassination. What also made me nauseous was the truth that many of these Nazis made it to America—facilitated for one reason or another by the American government. I almost can't say it.

Dr. Martin commented that to say I was angry at such people and about such things would be a gross understatement. He contemplated that the intensity of such fury can be equivalent to delirium — to mind-altering delirium. And that statement more than interested me. It fascinated me because I believe it corresponded to my vague sensibility about my possible dual personas.

"Wait a minute," I said to him. "You're implying that I could make myself delirious as in fugue delirium and you're indirectly suggesting that it's possible that I'm an assassin?" I quickly recovered and continued: "Of course that's pure speculation. Am I a *closet assassin?*"

I added notes to the diary.

*   *   *

A book is a box of facts. All of this thinking about these possible correlations jogged my memory about the dream, and I suddenly remembered another element. In the dream it was my mother who said to me: "Look in the *closet.*" Then I almost simultaneously forgot that particular element of the dream at just about almost the exact moment I remembered it. Yes, it occurred to me that my mother was the ghost of the dream. She mentioned "*closet.*" She said: "Look in the *closet.*" And that's what I said to Martin: "I'm a *closet* assassin. Putting the two together it seems to come out as:

> *Closet* and *assassin* go together, and since a book might in one way be a box of facts, then *closet* and the *key* to the box might also go together. What I did figure out was that *what's in a book* or *it's in a book* related to my association to a book as *a box of facts*; and, therefore, something that ties it all together might be certain facts that are in the box.

What happened and how I figured it all out was this: the night of my session with Dr. Martin I had another dream. In that dream my box of tax receipts and records popped into my head. Then, I knew. The *box of facts* was the box I use to store all my tax records for the current year, and it was the kind of box one is given in a copy shop — a standard 8 ½ x 11 letter-size box. It's in this same kind of box that I keep the facts, the data that my accountant eventually gets.

I remembered that I must have kept the key in last year's box along with last year's data, rather than switching the key to the current box. My mother's comment in the dream to look in the closet was absolutely right. I jumped out of bed, ran to the closet, but the closet was full. I then remembered I stored last year's tax records and receipts in my bedroom closet, lowest shelf, left-hand side. I ran back to the bedroom and into the closet. Sure enough it was there. I knew as I opened it that the key would be staring at me in its vertical position standing up in the little envelope at the back of the box. It was.

Now that I had the key I decided to check out the safe deposit box the very next day. I hadn't been to the box in more than three years. I knew I wouldn't find any gold bars and certainly no hundred thousand dollars stacked and bundled in the wrapper strips that in my dream Rowdy and I absconded with. But what else would I find other than varied and sundry things—anything really of interest?

At the next session Dr. Martin asked me to tell him another dream, any other dream. I did, and the content of this other dream really interested me. Dr. Martin's request was easy because I'd had a dream some time ago in which I was walking past an alleyway (there's the *alleyway* again that I had dreamed at another time when Rowdy and I netted the canvas bag with all the money and gold bars in it). In that dream it was dusk, and, as I was walking past the alleyway, lurking there was a panther or a leopard.

This menacing big cat was about to bound at me. I instantly woke up with a scare. Dr. Martin asked me how I saw the dream, how I understood it, or whether I understood it. I told him that obviously the leopard was my anger that I had externalized and projected onto the menacing leopard. "And?" he asked waiting. "And," I said: "It means that I don't want to own my anger and need to distance myself from it." That was evident to me after I thought about it for a moment. It also told me that there are things about me (actually about us all) that we just don't want to know, so we find ways of not knowing them. I continued, "If such forgetting or repressing or obliterating memory of different things about ourselves persists, it can become habit forming, and over time can become our fate." And that's a frightening prospect—to have your fate depend on a life of repression, of not-knowing.

"So, Dr. Martin," I asked, " what do you think? Do you think I'm someone who can split off part of me and go about being a different person? Like having a fugue and doing something angry or aggressive and then believe that someone else did it — pawning it off, so to speak, on the leopard? It would be like putting distance between me and the aggression. As you can see, I obviously, have great doubt as well as confusion about what I might be capable of doing.

"And by the way, I know my mother in the dream is me. The ghost is me. It was my unconscious doing the talking to me and telling me where to look. You see, when I was growing up — even at age 5 — I looked more like my mother and my personality was also like hers. Later on, as I got older, I realized I was looking more like how I remembered my father looked as well as showing more of what I remembered of his personality. But I think the key is that the person in the dream that will represent the self is the one who you represented as a child more than the one you represent as an adult. Therefore, it would be mother over father. My mother in the dream was me.

*   *   *

His name was Gerhardt Eisler. Long after the war, maybe twenty years after the war, he was on trial in Germany for Nazi war crimes. The clamor, the demand for his trial was deafening, so the issue of the elapsed time became a nonissue. He was accused of ordering the execution of thirty-two people in a little town in Greece. The order of execution allegedly attributed to Eisler was in reprisal for an attack on a Nazi location by Greek partisans. The partisans blew up the barracks, and six Nazi soldiers were killed while another three were wounded. Eisler was exonerated because of scant evidence. One woman who was known to be mentally unbalanced testified against him, but her testimony was at best seen to be unreliable. The trial was held in 1965, and Eisler was set free, although the general sense of it was that he was truly guilty of the grim command to execute all of those people.

Years later, on a winter's night in Berlin, Eisler was walking with his wife from a night at the theater. He was summarily executed with a bullet to the head as his wife was walking with her arm in his. She was horrified, screamed for help, but no witness and no perpetrator could be identified and there was no one else in the street to witness the execution. I call it an execution because the shot from the gun was muffled, there was no robbery, and his wife was not touched. It was an assassination.

*   *   *

"Dr. Martin, I can see you're getting more and more interested in this whole assassination thing. You're thinking that I'm a modern-day Scarlet Pimpernel. You're contemplating that I might do the nasty thing and disappear; therefore it's ingeniously done and then I'm invisible. Yes, I believe you're becoming intrigued. I think it would be better for us to try working on my enosiophobia instead of getting caught up in some delusion about me as an assassin. And, speaking of delusion, as you know, to cure a delusion—whether it's mine or yours—requires getting to the delusional person's basic wish. That means you have to cure it from the inside rather than trying to talk or persuade the delusional person out of the delusion from the outside. Right? For the delusional person, logic has no power. If either of us is delusional about my having an alternate personality based upon some kind of fugue, some kind of multiple or split personality, or about some hypnagogic state, this would necessarily mean that we have to understand what the basic wish is. Mine would probably concern something about the wish to get even—some kind of retribution involving a righteous indignation that's burning a hole in my brain. But your basic wish would be for me to actually have all that psycho stuff because for you it's simply fascinating were that actually to be the case. Dr. Martin, I think you're a so-called vicariouser—living through other people's dramas—and loving it. In my case it gives you a chance to be a covert operator, like a sanctioned assassin, so that you can experience what it feels like to be a 007. We've got to be careful because our job together is to get me out of this psychological strait-jacket and not to reinforce and validate it."

I'm going to say all that to Dr. Martin in our next session—after my next class at the college. In my next class I'm discussing the anatomy of delusion, and several of my students have been assigned the task of researching various components of a delusion and to be prepared to discuss it in class. Later, when I see Dr. Martin I'm also going to discuss my next trip to Austria. I've been invited by the *International Conference on Psychopathology* to give a paper on how personality is formed. It will be a keynote address based upon my published book of the same name—*Personality: How It Forms.* The touchy problem in discussing it all is that it is widely known that Vienna, Austria was a typical drop-off place for many Nazis who were, so to speak, hiding in plain sight after the war. So, for me, simply being in Austria was never easy.

Dr. Martin is going to want to see whether anyone will be named as a former Nazi (even though now probably seventy-five years old or even older) who, in one way or another, was killed while I was there, but whose body was discovered some days after I returned to New York City. The fact is that I, too, will be especially interested in that answer.

When I get ready for a trip, my first order of business is to plan my itinerary, get all the details taken care of, and, of course, not to forget my passport. I needed to visit the bank to retrieve my passport which was safely sheltered in my safe deposit box.

It was a bright Monday morning. It was not very busy at the bank. One of the managers accompanied me down to the subgrade lower level where the S-D boxes were located. He signed me in, and I took the box into one of the private cubicles. I opened it and searched through various papers until I found my passport. Then, while searching for all my spare keys at the bottom of the box, I found another passport seemingly hidden between a thick stack of neatly arranged papers. It was a passport in the name of a Mr. Roland Bremen. Mr. Bremen's photo was missing, but the notation of his age was of a man in his seventies. The city *Paris* was stamped on it. I had no idea who that man was, and, for the life of me, I couldn't understand how such a passport wound up in my safe deposit box.

More notes for my *Jackal.*

* * *

Bremen's address was listed as 491-3 Rue Coquilliere, 75001, Paris, France. I could actually picture the street. Rue Coquilliere is a main boulevard, and I knew it because whenever I visited Paris I would frequent a little café not far from there. I knew the approximate location of the 400 to 500 addresses, and his was 491-3. But who the hell was he? I couldn't help thinking about it even though I was almost entirely preoccupied with my coming trip to Vienna.

I figured it was about five-hundred or so miles from Vienna to Milan and another five-hundred or so from Milan to Paris. I wanted to make the intermediate trip to Milan because a small psychoanalytic institute there had an archive related to Stomersee Castle near Riga, Latvia. The archive was of a Baroness Alexandra Wolff, who had married the Prince of Lampedusa, Giuseppe Tomasi di Lampedusa. Lampedusa was a small Mediterranean island considered a gateway to Europe.

At the time of the Lampedusa/Baroness Alexandra Wolff's relationship, the Baroness was then situated in Sicily, in Palermo, but, for whatever reason, her archive was housed in Milan, at the Psychoanalytic Institute. I had heard that the archive was a treasure trove of psychoanalytical material, some of which concerned phenomena of mind such as fugues, hypnagogic episodes, as well as a variety of other mind-altering personality states. Just what I was dying to see. However, I had the nagging thought that I was feeling impelled to eventually wind up in Paris, mostly as a double coda: first as my workshops were completed at the University in Vienna and, second, after my stopover in Milan to examine the archive; then, finally, to Paris, primarily of course because I needed to investigate this business with Roland Bremen—whoever and wherever he was—and it seemed that he was in Paris. His passport jolted my heart. It was littered with stamped entries for every country I'd visited, including France, and apparently he had been traveling like that in a time span that paralleled my own. That one really shocked me. I couldn't help but think that for sure this was more than just a coincidence. Who was he? I began wandering in my thoughts, and out of the blue it hit me:

Was I him?

It cannot be easily dismissed that at times, I, might be a depersonalized individual— someone who at least in a part-time sense has experiences of being detached and feeling as though I was actually *in* a dream or can't really tell the difference between reality and dreaming. This sort of an even part-time depersonalization can produce in the sufferer behavior that would not be in keeping with the person's typical patterns of behavior. In such a case it could mean that this kind of person could actually be in thrall to his other personas—the ghosts of his dreams—with elements of the dream that seem to be of another world. And this other world correspondingly is apparently populated, so that there seems to exist a knowing of specific others, who, at the same time, one really doesn't specifically know.

Could that be true of Roland Bremen? Is Roland Bremen someone I know that I also don't know? I then was eager to arrange it so that I would be able to approach him, and finally see whether he recognizes me. If he does recognize me, then that would give me a chance, on the one hand, to further examine what in the world was or is happening to my psyche and, on the other, how that was affecting my conscious life. I would then be able to ask him the important question:

Mr. Bremen, how do we know one another?

I will go from Vienna to Paris by way of Milan. Ultimately, I must see if I can meet him—if I can meet Roland Bremen—assuming he's not me.

These were important notes. My *Jackal* was acquiring a body of work.

PART 2

SEARCHING FOR THE JACKAL

· 3 ·

VIENNA, MILAN, PARIS

I was off to Vienna. I packed one suitcase, one carry-on, and, of course, my precious briefcase containing all of what I began referring to as my *Jackal* notes. I would be gone for two weeks: four days in Vienna, then three in Milan, and the last week in Paris. I planned on spending the largest portion of time in Paris. I was hell-bent on finding Bremen, and perhaps also uncovering or connecting other, let's say, situations, that generally might shed more light on my life — and, more important, perhaps specifically uncover some information that would let me know if, you know, I'm really all there.

Actually, in one way I felt normal in all respects except for my doubts regarding some fugue possibility along with the palpable experience of a probable enosiophobia. In another way, I didn't feel quite normal — really because of my resistance to marriage. I couldn't quite ever put my finger on why I had such resistance, because I always marveled at the terrific relationship my parents had, at least how I remembered it. Yet, I knew that this resistance was caused by some deep-rooted trauma harkening back to my five-year-old self who watched helplessly as my parents were wrenched away from me screaming. I have considered how my mantra became "Don't have children." It seems to me that this mantra may have unconsciously led me away from marriage. *Go it alone. Don't be destroyed and don't destroy children.* It could be that's what my early trauma engendered.

In any event, on the plane I was seated next to a very attractive woman who appeared to be in her mid forties or so. Whenever I meet such a woman, I'm always feeling regretful even before getting to know her. I'm sure it's that, despite the decades of having tons of liaisons, I never married. And "tons" means a lot. And now, in my early forties, there's been a lot of time for it to be defined less as numbers of relationships and rather more as the count of accumulations! Most were based on sexual, and at times, romantic interest. I believe they never worked because of this quirk of mine related to the ghosts of my dreams, especially to my intermittent ostensible disappearances, as well as to my reluctance to marry. It's very clear to me that being a professor of psychology—specifically teaching courses in abnormal psychology, does not at all guarantee a clean bill of mental health. And yet, in the face of it all, in one way I felt normal.

At this point in my life I've begun assigning meaning to these failure-experiences of mine including asking myself whether these failures can be attributed to fugues, to hypnagogic states, to enosiophobia, as well as now also to my putative and conjectural characterization as someone "depersonalized." What woman wants to deal with that? So what I have typically done, is to break off the relationship myself before it gains any traction. I guess I firmly believe that I'd better do it before she does.

OK, this woman on the plane, her name was Jeannie. She was gregarious and friendly, and we spoke almost nonstop across the Atlantic. Actually she spoke nonstop. Originally, she was sitting somewhere several rows in back of me but asked the stewardess if she could possibly occupy the unoccupied window seat next to me. The stewardess asked me, and, of course I agreed.

I almost immediately regretted my acquiescence because of Jeannie's nonstop talking. She just looked at me as though expecting me to continue—so I did. Yes, she was articulate and other than her need to justify her existence by such nonstop talking, she might even have qualified as satisfying the five important qualities in a person I or anyone else might want to marry. Here's my list:

1. Is what she says and how she says it, interesting and original, and does it all hold your attention?
2. Is your eye nourished looking at her?

3. Does your heart feel loved?
4. In your gut, does she feel trustworthy?
5. Is her behavior good?

Experience reveals the most important of the five. It's behavior. If the behavior is not good the relationship will not work. Except for her incessant patter, Jeannie might have been the one to satisfy all five. But, of course it was still only a single encounter. In my case, my, let's say, "encounters," all fell down on at least two of the five. I was afraid to think of how many of the five I fell down on. Of course I also know that it's my perfectionism that I use as a defense against acknowledging what is, so to speak, *good enough*, so that it ultimately becomes clear—as it does in my case—that the perfect is always the enemy of the good. In that sense, if I'm honest with myself, I think I fall down on about three of the five. My eye will always be satisfied because I have what might be humorously called eye disease. I love looking at what I consider beautiful. My heart will usually feel loved by whoever she is because my romantic soul craves rapture. If I don't feel the rhapsody, I will probably find something to be critical about regarding whether she is trustworthy, whether her behavior merits a badge, and whether she can hold my wandering and sometimes withering attention with whatever it is she says. On these last three of the five criteria, Jeannie fails to persuade me, and, because of how I judge it all, I obviously fail to give it a chance. I already sensed that there was no possibility of anything rhapsodic with Jeannie.

So here I was, looking at, and listening to her, and only here and there luckily, was I able to insert a comment or two. Jeannie was talking a blue streak and it was all in her apparent certainty of inviting my attention by the way she was looking at me—smiling, laughing, and being strikingly flirtatious.

At one moment, it just popped out of me, and I said it to her directly.

"You need to justify your existence!"

It was perhaps socially inappropriate for me to say this so abruptly. It must have seemed to her that "it," itself, came out of the blue. But I needed to shift the conversation to something interesting like her personality or mine. It surprised her but she didn't skip a beat:

"My, aren't you the critical one? Please, explain yourself!" And she stopped! She actually stopped talking.

"Look, you're beautiful and you're eloquent. But you're what's known as a hypomanic talker. *Hypo*, means "less than." And that implies that you're not quite manic, but close. I'm guessing that you're in your forties, so you're not a child. Yet you continue to identify yourself as Jeannie rather than Jean. I can imagine that you think I'm in a desperate condition and clutching at straws—all in the service of criticizing you. But the truth is that the desperation is in your need to justify your existence by nonstop talking. A psychoanalyst would simply seek to know who it was in your early life that made you feel desperate regarding your very existence so that you found yourself running in front of that proverbial freight-train and can't stop running for fear of being run over and flattened. The inexorable running is the inexorable talking.

"I'm trying to persuade you. I'm trying to tell you that this feeling of desperation that I surmise you had as a child—about protecting your very existence—and that I'm presuming you continue to have felt all your growing-up years—even to this very day—is no longer a real, true force in your life. Sure, I'm predicting it was a powerful force that you experienced then, but it's not one now, in the present, even though you're behaving as though the past and the present are indistinguishable."

Now it was an appropriate time for me to discontinue my soliloquy—maybe my own hypomanic polemic—but I didn't. I needed to include some kind of finishing peroration.

"In my not so humble opinion, it would be exceedingly helpful to you if you were to make a sharp distinction between the past and the present. And, believe me, I know I'm being presumptuous!"

She was about to say something, but I had turned the tables so that now she was prevented from going off on who knows how many tangents and needed rather to listen.

"Listen, Jean, trust me," (I called her Jean), "I notice that when you're on a verbal riff you will incorporate any material whatsoever into what I would characterize as your pseudo and facile run-on sentences. I can't call it a conversation because it's really a monologue, not a dialogue, and therefore it can't be defined strictly as conversation. I noticed it in the first five minutes. You would incorporate any stimulus in immediate earshot or anything that was immediately visible and almost seamlessly knit it into whatever it was you were saying. It's an amazing talent and, in the absence of a trained eye, probably just about unnoticeable—even though

I'm fairly certain that the other person will leave your presence feeling toxic and angry.

"Let me say this one more thing. As far as I'm concerned, yes, I get critical about it because I see it as pure exploitation. It's unfair, as though the other person doesn't exist and that's why I needed to stop you so abruptly and maybe even rudely—for which I apologize. I can feel that it's your motive—unconsciously designed—to control the other person. It's what's called passive-aggressive behavior. In your case it would be diagnosed as passive-aggressive, aggressive type; that is, you do something directly and it ends up making the other person angry. I think that when I confront it like I'm doing now it can seem cruel. And, by the way, I still like you despite what I'm saying—I think—because, among other things, I'm usually held captive by beauty and your beauty weakens my resolve.

"But I'm not letting you off the hook. You see, you have virtuosity as a talker but it's nullified with the compulsive nature of it. I would call it a defective gift. Let me explain that. When a person is gifted with some kind of virtuoso talent like with great artistic talent of one kind or another—let's say like in reading stories to children, or even to adults, and they read the material with interest and passion and great feeling, the listener or listeners will be nourished by it because that's what gifts are all about—especially those given with virtuosity. This is what could be called uncontaminated giving. But when the gift becomes contaminated because the giver holds it back so that the listener can't even hear the story well, or that the giver of the gift can't stop talking, then that needs to be corrected. The problem is that there are those who are listening, but who in the guise of what I consider to be bourgeoisie fence-sitting don't correct the situation because they consider it good manners not to correct it. That's something I can't do. I refuse to fence sit. That's what most Germans did and it allowed Hitler to do what he did—that Nazi thing. Most Germans sat on that damn bourgeoisie fence not saying a word. I'm never going to sit on that fence in the guise of good manners. You, Jean, have a gift of eloquence but you refuse to deliver it as a gift and that's an example of my not sitting for it. Sorry. Call it rude if you wish. In my opinion, fence sitters just never grew up. Again, sorry I have to say it that way."

Now, I had finished. The silence seemed deafening, and, when I wondered how I sounded, I instantly knew that I sounded pedantic. If she had parried and said; "Who's the manic talker now?" I would have agreed. But she surprised me by telling me she appreciated my, as she said, "Getting on top of me."

My God, I thought, she really didn't appreciate or understand what she just said. She said: "I appreciate your *getting on top of me*." Of course she meant that she appreciated that I stopped her and offered her an impassioned entreaty. Or maybe it was the other thing that she really meant: both underneath it all as well as "on top" of it.

We talked some more, and Jean continued to be friendly, although she seemed a bit depressed. She was no longer flirtatious, and I could see that her interest in me was entirely different. I knew that I had extinguished the flame. I also could see an example of how in psychoanalysis (which is probably what I was doing poorly), one thing just leads to another, then to another, and so on. Jean's entire need for attention gradually evaporated. I, on the other hand realized that her passive-aggressive stuff made me angry and that's why I went on my own riff. I was responding in kind.

I slowly drifted off to sleep. When I awakened, she was sleeping. I kind of regretted the entire episode, and the remainder of the trip continued to be a bit awkward for us both. I could have again asked for us to try and clear the air, but I decided it was, at least for me, and I'm sorry to say, essentially unimportant. I knew that because my encounter with Jean was really unimportant to me, I then felt relieved, at least in this case, not to be such a prisoner to my *Jackal Diary* entries, not to be so controlled as to need to put every single thing into the accumulating notes about my search, my hunt, my need to unravel everything about myself that needed unraveling.

Instead, I removed my book from my carry-on and began to read. The book was on the essence of acting-out; that is, *doing* something rather than *knowing* something. Chapters in the book focused on what, of course, I already knew and then I saw it. The author was quoting me verbatim: about the unconscious mind, instructing the person's psyche to engineer what the psyche tells the conscious mind to think and to do — the purpose of which is to satisfy the person's basic wish. It's the basic *wish* that is the person's algorithmic essence. That's it. That's the basic structural dynamic of personality. It's what psychoanalysis understands perfectly. Everyone wants to satisfy their wish.

We landed at Vienna International Airport. Poof, Jean was gone.

* * *

I admit I felt bad about my behavior, but thinking of living in a hotel was always good. Yes, I've always loved hotel living. I could easily live in a hotel permanently. Not knowing anyone there always gives me a sense of anonymity. And, of course, I now understand that anonymity and aloneness are intrinsic, one to the other. It all fits.

After checking in, I showered, dressed, and couldn't wait to have dinner. I was famished. After dinner, I returned to my room. I chose the Hotel Regina because I loved its old world charm and yet I also was very pleased with the updated modern rooms. Of course, it was in close proximity to the University of Vienna so that everything woud be convenient. It was all very comfortable, the food served in its dining room was well prepared, and the service was excellent. But, perhaps I needed to undo it all like I did with Jean on the plane; that is, I couldn't help thinking the bad thought: Leave it to those Austrian/Germans. Perfectionism in everything—including genocide! Yes, I had to sully it. It was character assassination in subtle form, and I did it with an exquisite and even capricious incision. I did it with Jean, too. That's how I've always recognized the sequence of my thinking and how I convey what it is I'm thinking sequentially—first nice and then not nice. And the nub of it for me is that if there's one thing I hate in people it would be the tendency to assassinate someone's character. So, here I was, out of character, doing what I hate in others. So, instead of brooding, I began to plan the format for the seminar I was about to conduct at the university.

I had the faculty of the seminar distribute assignments to all the students asking them to research any question that interested them with regard to anything at all concerning altered states of consciousness. I offered examples such as fugue, split personality, enosiophobia, even pseudomania or anything else that could be related to altered states.

The workshop lasted two days of four-hour sessions per presentation. It turned out that participants had prepared a full smorgasbord of analyses largely covering the entire field of altered states. The truth is that none of the presentations lit my fire. They were tedious to the point of being moribund. Not a trace of life could be found in any of the presentations. Students just repeated known symptoms or variations of altered states.

During the coffee break on the second day, there were five or six students bunched together in the stairwell near the coffee machine seeming to be having fun and laughing. I was nearby and asked them what the joke

was. One of the young women suddenly answered that it would be important for people to realize that we all understand what was done to the Jews
but that now nothing is off limits and even the macabre can be turned into
a joke that might seem disparaging but not really so.

"Well, what's the macabre joke that's OK to tell?" I asked curiously.

"OK," she said, "here's what was so funny. It's largely because we can
stare into the horror of it all and minimize it or dismiss it as not in any
way being related to us here and now. In this way, for us, it means we don't
own it. In a sense it becomes meaningless and even points out that we are
all beyond it—that we didn't do it and therefore we can turn it into something banal. The stupid joke is in answering the question about how one
can get a hundred Jews into a Volkswagen. And the answer is by incinerat-
ing them and spreading the ashes into the car."

I was silent. They were looking at me. Two or three of them were not
laughing. The others thought it was clearly not anti-Jewish but that it was
the kind of humor akin to one being freed from the worry of guilt. The
young woman who told the joke also seemed to try to short-circuit what
probably appeared to be my astonishment, maybe disgust.

She said: "Look, it's kind of like how black people in the United States
use the derogatory term *nigger* and turn it into an expression of solidarity.
I think you're taking it very seriously," she boldly said.

She was right. I had the immediate thought that the wrong country was
targeted for the two atomic bombs dropped in 1945. But I let it go and
tried to appear nonplussed. But, for sure, Germany/Austria was not my
cup of tea. I couldn't wait to leave. Then again, I couldn't let it go. I interrupted her atavistic antediluvian humor and asked:

"Are the sons responsible for the sins of the father?"

She immediately answered: "Of course not. That's ridiculous."

I said, "it might not be ridiculous if you think about it this way: The
sons are indeed responsible for the sins of the father insofar as the sons are
responsible not to repeat the sins of the father."

They all looked at me in silence, and she didn't say another word. The
implication of what I said did not fall on deaf ears, because I was really
asking whether, in contrast to how their fathers' supported Hitler and the
Nazis and did those murderous things, have they themselves reached a
place very different in understanding than the place their fathers' were in?

OK, I got the last word in, and it probably slammed them. I guess I meant to slam them, although I didn't think it was done with the least antipathy or any evidence of loathing. Ha!

The final two days at the workshop were devoted to a Q & A and each lasted about two hours. It was one of the discussions in the last day of the Q & A that was actually only a remnant of some discussion of the previous two days, but it was that particular remnant that caught my attention—actually gripped me.

So there it was. And, wouldn't you know it, only on the last day of the workshops, during the last discussion in the question/answer period, did I get the only exciting lead about a remnant, a residual of something that might be important in my persistent but sometimes fractious search for myself.

The question was: "What was the remnant?"

* * *

It was easy to decide not to comment in my *Jackal* notes about my interaction with the students, but I was definitely going to do so regarding the remnant. The remnant was a piece of something only parenthetically referred to by one of the faculty members. This faculty member happened to mention a paper written by one of the students. This student had decided to investigate a particular concept cited in professional and theoretical psychoanalytic literature. The idea was *the observing-ego*. It means that, to one extent or another, we all have something in us that enables us to see ourselves as though we're looking at ourselves from the outside—from the outside in.

Of course I knew what *observing-ego* meant. The question is why that was the something that struck me and suddenly came alive. The answer is: I believe it struck me this way because it instantly occurred to me that if indeed I had some "observer" doing its job—like the observing-ego—then whatever it was that troubled me, that confused me, that perhaps identified my diagnosis at least as having enosiophobic tendencies, or that implied that I was intermittently fuguelike, or even that I had some sort of strange split-behavior, wouldn't it stand to reason that my observing-ego would know about it, would have seen it—how about "observed" it? For example, even if I had been the one to place Roland Bremen's passport in my own safe deposit box (which I still can't believe I did), wouldn't my own *observing-ego* have witnessed it? The answer seems to be an irresistible, unwavering, and resounding Yes!

Now, the further question becomes: How do I access what might be thought of as the brain and memory of my observing-ego? How do I get to it? Then again, where is the observing-ego located? Is it stored in the very core of my personality? Is it in my unconscious mind? Is it in my psyche or perhaps, in the brain in my gut? It's certainly not in my consciousness where I would have access to it. I wondered if I could be hypnotized, would this covert so-called observing-ego be animated, vitalized, and reconstituted and so brought from ghostliness into the light as a viable, shall I say, "discussant?" Then could I talk to it? It's what Freud said about talking things out in place of doing things willy-nilly. He actually said that that which is not spoken is reenacted instead. Another genius added that if it becomes reenacted, as I referred to before—it becomes your fate. The point of it all was that, no more, no less, Freud was warning us about acting-out.

Talk it out so you might begin to *know* it and therefore not need to act-it out. That's what he was getting at. That's the wisdom. And, of course, if it's true that I'm really involved in some apparitional activity, in some out-of-body unconscious behavior, then talking rather than *doing* will lead to *knowing*—and *knowing* might get me to the mystery of it all. To what mystery? To the mystery of not knowing whether I was doing something wrong; whether or not I have an enosiophobic condition based on some real acting-out.

At rock bottom the true mystery is not the item of the Bremen passport in my safe deposit box. That's important and, of course, it needs to be solved. The most important issue is the one that's been troubling me for years. It concerns my nagging suspicion that I've been doing something wrong, something dangerous, and something loaded with tension and I don't know if it's a figment of my traumatized imagination or if it's real.

At this point I'm actually doing my own investigation so that my work with my good working shrink, Dr. Martin, almost seems secondary. He's working on investigating my psyche and my unconscious mind. I'm doing actual Dick Tracy stuff, and despite the fact that I was quite familiar with the psychoanalytic concept of observing-ego I decided to dig out what the late Dr. Louis Ormont, the psychoanalytic group theorist and group psychotherapy specialist, said about the observing-ego. He said:

The observing-ego is that part of the self that has no affects [meaning no emotion], engages in no actions, and makes no decisions. It functions in conflict-free states to merely witness what it sees. It is like a camera that records without judgment. It is never weighing any thought, gesture or action on the scale of right and wrong, sane or insane, good or bad. It is a psychic entity that is intact and separate from what is taking place.

Ormont's definition was perfect. It explains it beautifully—especially the part where he says it "merely witnesses what it sees." I think it's necessary to add that because it has no emotion and, as Ormont says, is "separate from what is taking place," whatever anxiety the person feels does not affect it—is not at all affecting the observing-ego. Therefore, I mused, no matter how much difficulty I may have with respect to what my conscience finds unacceptable, nevertheless, my observing-ego still should know what it's all about—and let's get down to it—especially what it's all about with respect to anything concerning assassinations. My basic question to myself becomes: Is it necessary for me to exert extreme repressive mechanisms to keep my ostensible bad behavior from entering my consciousness, and, again, even if I felt that the assassination was deserved, none of it would matter at all to my observing-ego. My observing-ego would simply be as Ormont says: "like a camera that records without judgment."

Therefore—and here is the bomb:

> Getting in touch with my observing-ego would replay for me my entire script—no matter the implication. And, as a bonus, I also felt it would tell me how Bremen's passport found its way into my safe deposit box—assuming, of course, that it was I who put it there. My observing-ego would simply, dispassionately, and faithfully report how it all happened—what it observed.

And here's the perplexing question: How am I to get in touch with my observing-ego? Of course I couldn't help but continue thinking about it, and it felt as though I was practically dissecting my brain for an answer. I was thinking: *You can't talk to it, you can't press a button and call it forth, nor can you ask someone else about it.* Then gradually it crept up on me. It hit me. Yes, I thought, you do need to talk to it, but first, here's bomb number two:

You need to have it talk to you.

That's it! And how might you get your observing-ego to talk to you?' I pondered it. Then I automatically knew. The answer has to be one that implicates your dreams. Actually, I thought, the observing-ego is one's constant ghost in dreams. Yes, one must access the observing-ego through the language of one's dreams. This thought energized me, actually electrified me. Then I was exhilarated by the prospect of sitting down and, one by one, carefully analyzing my dreams. I could feel how it all might happen; that is, my work with my own dream would be an encounter with my unconscious mind, the end result of which would be that my *wish* for my observing-ego to contact me (and talk to me) could then be possibly realized.

Thus I was thinking about communicating with my observing-ego or rather, perhaps, having it communicate with me. In this sense, my deliberate conscious message to my unconscious mind would implicitly instruct my unconscious mind to create the story line of the dream that would necessarily contain the material revealing what my observing-ego had observed!

I was praying for such a dream, but, at the same time, thinking about Milan. I had a vague intuitive feeling that the Baroness Alexandra Wolff's material on a variety of mental phenomena was going to yield other key elements that I might be able to piece together to help form a basic synthesis of my entire personal dilemma.

I was going to summarize it all on my little pad with code words that would remind me of each event. I kept this little pad in my jacket side pocket so that I could easily access it and quickly jot down a reminder of any event. Too tired at the moment to tackle the actual *Jackal Diary* notes, I was about to go to sleep when another bolt of lightning struck me.

Wait a minute, I thought. W-a-i-t a m-i-n-u-t-e! In my dream in which I was trying to figure out the saying "What's in a book?" my mother spoke to me. She said: "Look in the closet." Now I was sure that it was my mother's voice that was the proxy for my observing-ego. She was my observing-ego talking to me and telling me where to look for what I needed. And she was able to instruct me because as the observing-ego my behavior was fully observed, not to be redundant, by my observing-ego. And of course my observing-ego knew what I did. But in the dream my observing-ego was telling me, through my mother, where to find the key. But, I thought: why did I choose my mother to be my observing-ego in the dream, the purpose of which would be to let me know what I actually did with the key, which my observing-ego of course, witnessed? The answer was instantly apparent.

Even though she was taken from me when I was five, nevertheless I had a fairly clear memory that whenever I needed to find an article of clothing, or something else that I needed, I would always ask her where it was, and she would unfailingly tell me. She always knew. So, I anointed my mother to be my observing-ego, because in my early life that's what she was.

And I wondered whether in future dreams, if I needed to communicate with my observing-ego, would she always be the one to appear. It's a pretty wonderful idea: not only will she remind me of where to find something but it will also give me the chance to see her again.

· 4 ·

OBSERVING-EGO AND THE DREAM

That night I had what seemed like a long dream and I think I remembered just about all of it. In the dream

> I was sitting on a fire escape of an apartment in a large residential building. It was in The Bronx. Something was happening in the next apartment that I knew I shouldn't be seeing and I also knew a bad thing was happening. I knew it was risky to look, but I couldn't help but lean toward a second window to try to see what was going on. I think a woman was in trouble. I felt torn between not being seen and helping the woman. It gave me a sick feeling. It woke me up. It was a nightmare.

This dream/nightmare was tailor made. I understood its meaning in a flash and yet I had various associations to elements of the dream. For example, given the things I was doing or what I was thinking about the day before—led me to associate to the passport I found in my safe deposit box. And that gave me the feeling that I was ambivalent about knowing how the passport got there or, who was the *who* who put it there. In this case, my observing-ego was me. I then had the sensation that all my nightmares were in one way or another always referring to my trauma when I was five years old when my parents were torn from me by those Nazi soldiers. In fact, if we boil down the elements of the dream, we perhaps get the sense that the dream does indeed reflect my observing-ego, that partitioned hovering part of my psyche that observed it all, and now this observing-ego of mine could be considered to be actually talking to me. I suspect it was telling me that I shouldn't have what I wanted. Therefore, it was a strong superego dream—my conscience operating; that is, that natural partitions in life should not be breached—like mother belongs to father, or, Europe is Europe and America is America. Therefore, don't invade and do bad things like assassinations.

I didn't like what my observing-ego was saying to me, meaning that what I didn't like must relate to a *who*—to a person. I guess it could mean that I didn't want to know who the *who* was. Nothing short of fantastic! I was the *who*.

That was my global sense of the dream. But I needed to decipher it in more detail. You know, the seeming redundancy which is not at all redundant is that *details need to be specific*. Could I derive more from the dream was my question.

Here are some details, some clues perhaps of my musings:

1. The idea of a *fire escape* contains two elements. First is the idea of a *fire*, which means "danger." Second, the *escape* issue resonates with my vague fantasy or sensation that in my dreams I think I needed to always *escape* something I did that was wrong.
2. The idea that I couldn't *see* something, but that I wanted to, directly relates to my obsession about wanting to have an insight (wanting to *see*) what in the world was happening to me.
3. Thus, something was probably happening that was *bad*, and that my looking really meant wanting to know what it was that was not to be tolerated.
4. The second window represents what that something is that I wanted to *see* but that, at the same time, might be "*risky*" for me to *see*.
5. I felt "torn" between looking and not looking, which means between knowing and not knowing. The question is not knowing what? It could mean having the satisfaction of retrieving my mother along with the satisfaction perhaps of getting closure by killing Nazis.

6. A woman was in trouble, and I felt I needed to help her. I believe the feeling I had in the dream about helping her but not being able to reminds me of the helplessness I felt when I saw them manhandle my mother and father.

7. The idea that I needed not to be seen (rather to be invisible) is, I believe, my desire to rescue them, or to rescue the *who,* and, yes, here it is—by killing those Nazi soldiers—by actually being a Scarlet Pimpernel. It appears to me that in this case I myself am resisting my own observing-ego—keeping it from reporting to me exactly what happened or what it is that I don't want to know. Could it be that I don't want to know what my true illegal motive is? Am I the *who?*

8. And, finally, my *sick feeling* was undoubtedly my fury against the Nazi perpetrators that I wanted to kill—and perhaps still want to kill. It's the psychoanalytic truth that behind the fear is the wish.

Despite all this speculation and associations to the dream, I think the dream was possibly a narration of what my observing-ego observed, that I resisted. Therefore, I needed to try to have another reciprocal communication with my observing-ego (if possible) in order to ascertain whether my desire to kill all those Nazis is only a reflection of my wish system or whether I'm really doing it or, ultimately, whether the whole thing becomes a reference to some other current person in some kind of current situation.

It's no wonder that I now understand my actual diagnosis better. The diagnosis is post-traumatic stress disorder (PTSD). This is a new diagnosis that's to appear next year in 1980 as part of the latest version of the *Diagnostic and Statistical Manual* of the *American Psychiatric Association.* I've been studying these newer diagnostic classifications in a preview that was given to a variety of shrinks all over the country. PTSD is the umbrella diagnosis under which is subsumed all the other stuff—the possible depersonalization, the possible enosiophobia, the possible split, and even the possible fugue. And the woman in the dream, as perhaps me, or my mother representing me, was, in fact, in trouble. Now I know that one aspect of my enosiophobia concerns an inner conflict that has me stuck! Stuck in a historical problem and stuck in a current problem. I do understand the historical problem, but not the current one. And my delving into the interpretation of the dream tells me that not only don't I understand the current problem, but in fact I don't want to know something about the current one. I also know that not wanting to know it means it's about a person that I don't want to know. It's never about a table or a chair. It's always about a person—a *who*. Is the *who* is me?

I'd begun referring to these visitors in my dreams as the *ghosts of dreams*. In this case I wouldn't permit my ghost (my observing-ego mother, or me, or whomever) to breathe—to talk to me, to tell me what happened, even though such revelation would surely help open and expose the inner cause and effect of my post-traumatic stress of then and now that housed my enosiophobia.

My first association was to the Baroness Alexandra Wolff. The Baroness and her tantalizing archive about such phenomena instantly came to mind. My thought was that no matter how much I resisted the ghost of my dream's ability to reveal everything that had happened in the formation of my enosiophobia, nevertheless, with respect to the psychology of dissociative phenomena, if in the Baroness' archive there existed the answer to such a phenomenon as enosiophobia, then I wouldn't be able to keep myself from seeing it. And, despite my ostensible not wanting to see it, fearful of what I would find, that response was superseded by the urgent sense that I would indeed want to see it.

* * *

I was thinking about Milan because I wanted to investigate whether the Baroness had collected materials that could shed light on typical or even atypical stimuli that preceded the onset of fugue or split personality. I knew that in split personality, or multiple personality, findings in the psychiatric literature suggest that when trancing into the alter personality the host personality would first trance into an angry persona. This angry persona was materialized by the host's *wish* for something, whenever the gratification of that *wish* was thwarted by another person—blocked by that other person. This, of course, again verified to me that one's *wishes* are crucial elements of the person's psyche. Of course I knew that my *wish* to rescue my parents was nonsense because I was only a child who though fighting, was helpless to the whole world of insanity.

The question then becomes: Is it possible that, decades later, as an adult, I can trance into an angry persona whenever I'm in Europe so that being there becomes the stimulus for a fugue reaction that then in turn enables me to do something terrible like assassinate someone—someone I hold symbolically responsible for my PTSD—for my original trauma, for the murder of my parents?' If that were true, it would be akin to a psychological repetitive action that satisfies how my father's values and mine are basically unified. He would not truck any miscarriage of justice or any unfairness. I'm like that too.

The last thing I remember when we were screaming for each other was my father turning his head toward me as they were dragging him out of the room. Our eyes met and then he was gone. My father was a gentleman and a respectful person. But he was physically strong and not afraid of physical contact. I remember him well, even though I was only five years old when I last saw those Nazi vermin dragging them screaming. Like I said, my father would never tolerate unfairness and always responded to it strongly. Since that's where I take after him, then getting even or getting revenge is something I've never gotten over. But, alas, what we know is almost never more compelling than what we feel!

The result of such a unified alliance with my father—would be to punish the guilty. This might be the only way that I reflexively behave, enabling me to believe that my post-traumatic stress could be relieved—resolved. But what does that mean—be "relieved," be "resolved?"

I think that what it would take to be relieved and have my PTSD resolved would be to undo what happened to my parents and to me—as well as to all of the six million Jews that were murdered by those swine—and all their fellow travelers.

It's now pretty clear to me that my enosiophobia relates to my need to get even. It's the enosiophobia that defines my sense that I think I've done something wrong. I can sense the "wrongness" of it even though I've never had any evidence of what it is that I might have actually done that was wrong. But maybe that's what happens when I'm in Europe. Maybe I look up these guilty Nazis who were let go and I complete the job so that whoever it is will get what they deserve.

In my ruminations about this, I was also thinking about this true story—about this guy Kovner who organized a group of survivor Jews who after the war decided to kill six million Germans. They were called *The Avengers*. Their first goal was to poison the water supply of four German cities. I believe Nuremberg was one of the cities. I don't remember what exactly happened, but I know that various obstacles prevented it. I remember another true story where another group of Jewish survivors got together and obtained employment in a bakery that provided loaves of bread to German prisoners. These prisoners were high-value Nazi officers specifically involved in personally murdering Jews. Unfortunately, various obstacles prevented them from almost concluding what I would consider justifiable homicide; six million for six million. But what does "almost" mean? What it means is that six million Jews was one-third of the entire Jewish population. Therefore true justification should be proportional. One-third of the entire German population of let's say sixty million is twenty million, not the six million that was determined by Kovner's group. Kovner was not working with ratios. In my feelings, yes, twenty million is the better number. Then again, how about sixty million?

So I'm thinking that maybe I'm the one doing the actual assassinations. The PTSD is the stimulus that boils my blood, puts me in a fugue state, and then my unconscious takes over and permits me to play one of Kovner's Avengers—perhaps the chief Avenger.

I considered Freud's prediction that early trauma could establish what he called the repetition compulsion. This is the compulsion to continue to repeat the same behavior as an ostensible way to master the original trauma. It was a perfect explanation for me, provided of course that I was actually a serial killer, specifically an assassin of Nazi war criminals. In a way I *wish* I was that person, that Avenger. Freud also said that this repetition compulsion will never actually resolve the original trauma and therefore, the perpetrator of this compulsion to repeat, needs to continue the slaughter over and over. Good God, I thought, was that me?

But it's becoming gradually clearer to me that PTSD is the issue. That's what might be happening to me when I'm in Europe. I get PTSD when I'm in Europe. Despite the fact that I'm visiting Europe twice a year for lectures and presentations, it could very well be that Europe itself is so contaminated for me—especially Germany and Austria—that, when visiting I'm overcome with a post-traumatic stress syndrome that puts me in an alternate state, an alternate reality—one in which I become someone with whom I'm not really familiar.

This is what I need to analyze with Dr. Martin.

* * *

The trip to Milan was uneventful, and I was thankful to finally arrive at my charming hotel in the heart of Milan and a five-minute stroll to the Psychoanalytic Institute and the archive of the Baroness Alexandra Wolff. I had dinner and went right to bed early as I planned to rise early in order to arrive at the institute as soon as it opened.

By 10 a.m. the next morning, I was already on my way to the institute. Crowds of people were walking in all directions. I crossed the street corner with the rest; as we approached the middle of the street we were met by the opposite throng crossing toward us. I noticed a tall man in the crowd crossing with us. He was somewhat ahead of me. It seemed to me he was with a woman walking along to his right, but I couldn't swear to it. As I kept walking, among the people coming toward me was a medium-size man with his mouth wide open and his head tilted upward as though in pain. It stopped me in my tracks because not only were we face to face, but apparently he had just been stabbed with a knife, the blade of which had entirely penetrated into his stomach. All that was visible was its handle.

Blood was awash all over him, and also pooling on the street. The accumulation of the blood looked like disgusting black liquid that was slowly forming into some amoeba-like random shape. People walking with me starting screaming, and both crowds—those coming as well as going—encircled him. Traffic slowed to a crawl and stopped. Police appeared, and one policeman asked who the person was closest to the victim when the incident occurred. Several people pointed at me.

I was flabbergasted because the truth was that immediately prior to the stabbing, it was the tall man with a lady who seemed to be with him who was precisely the one closest to the victim. Wouldn't it be therefore, that the tall man was the killer? But before I knew it, the police ushered me into their car and we drove off. I instantly realized that this was like the dream I'd had about using a silencer to kill someone walking toward me in the street.

At the police station I was questioned by the authorities who could speak English. At one point, the victim's name was mentioned. Astonishingly, his name was Hans Milch. The chief at the station, a tall Italian by the name of Aldo Tancredi who spoke English as though he came from Hell's Kitchen in New York City handed me Milch's file. It included Milch's photo and key issues of his past. It revealed that Herr Milch was the same Milch who was acquitted of crimes against humanity at one of the special tribunals that were hastily organized after the war. The accusation against him concerned his participation in a mass shooting in a gully on the edge of the western coast of the Crimean Peninsula—on the black sea coast of Ukraine—in a place called Yevpatoriya, near the city of Simferopol. There, twelve-thousand Jews were murdered. It became known as the massacre by Nazis at a place that further became known as The *Yevpatoriya Ditch*. The Soviet poet Andrei Voznesensky wrote the classic poem, *Rov*, translated as: *The Ditch*, about the massacre—how the machine guns never stopped and then, in the following few days, the surrounding population dug up this mass funerary ground in order to take anything of value from the twelve-thousand dead Jewish men, Jewish women, and Jewish children.

Milch was exonerated largely because the one witness to the massacre thought he might have been one of the commandants but couldn't or wouldn't swear to it. Milch's military record indicated that during the war he was assigned to a contingent of soldiers guarding a bank in a town somewhere in the north of Germany.

I couldn't have been more astonished than I was already. That is to say that right smack-dab into my pathological vortex about Nazis and assassinations, there, practically in front of my eyes, was an assassination in broad daylight. I knew for sure that I didn't do it. It was that tallish man. I was sure he did it! I kept telling the police that I didn't actually see it go down. I even challenged them to take fingerprints off the handle of the knife, knowing full well that my prints wouldn't be there. Then again, I kind of expected that the killer's prints wouldn't be there either. In fact I had a quick postscript to myself: 'No one's prints would be on the handle.'

After half the day at the station, when the police had thoroughly questioned me they then released me. Before I left I asked Tancredi how he learned to speak English so well. Apparently from the age of four to fourteen he grew up in the Bensonhurst section of Brooklyn (a largely Italian section), after which his family moved back to Milan. My American chauvinism surfaced because I wondered why anyone would want to leave New York City in order to live in Europe. But then, I was an unreconstructed New York City nationalist!

By the time I arrived at the institute, the archivist was gone and my chance to work with her was dashed until the next day. But I couldn't stop thinking about the incident and that tallish man. Despite the truth that

I had nothing to do with the killing, I also could not shake the idea that it was no accident that the killing occurred when I was there and perhaps even *because* I was there. I even had a creeped-out paranoid sense that the killer, that tall man, made sure that it all happened just a few feet away from me. He timed it. I'm convinced of it.

Early the next morning, my plans to get to the institute were again interrupted by the police asking me to appear at the station in order to view a line-up of individuals who had been rounded up. They were all tall, but I couldn't identify anyone. I only had one more day in Milan, but they still wanted me to go over the entire event of the stabbing. Interestingly, I, too, felt a strong need to review it, especially to discuss that tallish guy who was part of the crowd and walking only a few feet in front of me at the exact moment of the bloody incident.

I was dreading possibly missing the opportunity to see Baroness Alexandra Wolff's archive, but at the same time I was about ready to give up on Milan and head straight to Paris when suddenly into the police station walked a very attractive woman—actually quite beautiful—asking for Police Chief Aldo Tancredi. Tancredi was the one interviewing me at a desk just inches away from the front vestibule where she had entered. She got right to it and announced her name: 'Dr. Katherine Tess McFarland.' She then named Tancredi as the person she wanted to see. Tancredi looked at me and without responding to beautiful Dr. McFarland, explained that after I had told them what I was doing in Milan he contacted the institute. The director phoned Dr. McFarland, setting an appointment for her to appear at the police station the next morning. So, there she was. And how! She looked to be about in her thirties. I couldn't take my eyes off of her. She was all woman—full bodied with that mature womanly aura. With a kind of cosmic velocity, I was thinking Tancredi would be right to insist I extend my Milan stay. Actually, my instantaneous thought was "McFarland in Paris."

We were introduced, and I commented that I was grateful to finally meet her. Tancredi made a few other comments and in a joking manner befitting a man who could see what was happening, he said:

"I'm granting Dr. Cole a temporary elopement into your custody."

I thought it was quite a flourish for a police chief in Milan to put it exactly that way. He simply could have said: "Dr. Cole, you're free to go, but do not leave Milan without informing me first," or something equally authoritative like "Dr. Cole, you're to remain in Milan for several more days." That would have pleased me. Instead, he said what he did and then laughed. Dr. McFarland smiled and looked at me. My reaction to her must have been very obvious. I was smitten. I also thought that Tancredi's term *elopement* is a term usually referring to two people secretly embarking on a lifelong marital commitment or that the term actually was also frequently used to characterize one's leaving as an *escape*. So *elopement* suited me perfectly insofar as I had never married, but who knows what could still happen. Also to me, escape also means disappearance connected to a wrongdoing. Tancredi hit it. I was apparently phobic about marriage, and then also enosiophobic about some possible wrongdoing from which I needed to escape, to disappear, and to disappear, no less, unscathed.

We both walked out of the station, and Dr. McFarland greeted me in perfect English with a mid-Western accent. Originally from Kansas City, she had been working at the institute in Milan on a psychoanalytic fellowship specializing in archival constructions — especially with respect to psychoanalytic collections on the subject matter of altered personalities. As she was bringing me up to date, I noticed the absence of a wedding band. She was giving me a sketch of her entire history doing this archival work.

She'd been in Milan for the past two years and spent the previous two doing archival research at Tavistock Clinic in London. I mentioned that I was quite familiar with Tavistock and certainly knew of the work of a variety of luminaries who were affiliated there. I also could instantly tell that I was trying to elevate myself in her estimation so that she might be a bit more personal. I dropped some Tavistock names: Wilfred Bion, John Bowlby, Michael Balint, and Mary Ainsworth, hoping to impress, but was met with her careful listening and nothing more. Without skipping a beat, she launched into her own history by describing her service at the New York Psychoanalytic Institute, and at the library of the Postgraduate Center for Mental Health, both in New York City, in sorting and classifying a great deal of material of psychoanalytic interest with respect to her focus on altered personality. In addition, it was obvious that she was familiar with the Baroness's specific archive and regaled me with some interesting stories as well as notes that were apparently voluminous and, thankfully, quite preserved in the archive.

I could clearly see she was all business and didn't behave in any way that might reveal any personal attraction to me. She was entirely different in personality than was Jean on the flight to Vienna. Yes, she was certainly beautiful, of that there was no doubt, but was she straight, was she gay? That, I couldn't tell. The only personal comment she gave was when she said her friends called her Tess.

We did finally wind up at the Psychoanalytic Institute of Milan, where Tess, Dr. Katherine Tess McFarland, introduced me to the entry switchboard operator, the elevator operator, and, finally, as we entered the library, the head librarian. Everyone there was on a first-name basis, and all were very friendly. The Institute was old-line and had a distinctly permeating gemutlich and quiet feeling about the place.

We entered a room with an engraved plaque on the door that read: Archival Collections. It was a room filled with file cabinets, filled with folders of case histories of this or that, bookcases with stacks of reference periodicals, and so forth. McFarland made a beeline to the far side of the room, went to the top two drawers of a large file cabinet, and pulled open the second drawer from the top. There she extracted a large binder that contained several folders. McFarland identified this file cabinet as the Baroness's entire archive. The title of the binder read: "Baroness Alexandra Wolff Stomersee (Lampedusa) — *Altered States*."

Here were the Baroness's files on various cases she had either treated or, instead, of patients for whom she was the supervisor, monitoring her psychoanalytic students who would have been the actual treatment personnel of these patients. Each case was an example of a patient who presented variations of what could be termed altered personality or altered state.

McFarland addressed this and told me that the Wolff file covered very interesting phenomena related to altered states of consciousness. These included hypnopompic and hypnogogic states, Kundalini Syndrome, dissociative as well as psychogenic fugue, depersonalization experiences, derealization experiences, paranoid systematized delusions, something called Mana Character Personality, and, as a postscript, she included the issue of "intrusive thoughts."

I mentioned that the enosiophobic state is something I had hoped the Baroness would have some notes on.

"Oh yes, she said, I'm certain I've seen that in her notes somewhere. I believe she connected it with a case of childhood trauma."

"That's it," I said. I'd love to see that. In the meantime, I knew what the hypnopompic state referred to. It was the specific part of sleep in which the subject comes out of the sleep state and instantly feels strongly and emotionally motivated to align the feelings and story line of the dream with what the subject knows is actual reality. In contrast, the person who experiences the hypnagogic state similarly needs to create coherence with respect to all the din and discombobulation of dream images as they begin to appear going into the dream. It's the initial process of the dreamer trying to insist on rational focus even though already asleep. Clearly the theoretical difference between the two seemed always to me to be insignificant, and I tended to see the difference as incidental and not particularly clinically useful. Therefore, I used *hypnagogic* as the term to reflect the same thing; that is, to define such dreaming as almost entirely successful in deconstructing the boundary between fantasy and reality.

McFarland was proud to show me that the Baroness's entire file was translated into neatly typed English. The file contained notes on several of the cases in which each of the dreamers awakened convinced that their dreams represented, and actually faithfully reflected, reportage of something that had actually happened. This was getting to the enosiophobic condition. I quickly became immersed in reading the Baroness's materials, and in my cursory distillation of her notes I could see that she felt such dreams were clear verifications of Freud's hypothesis that the dreamers were expressing their very seriously and overdetermined *wishes*. She actually stated that the *wishes* emerged in these dreams "as reflections of historical antecedents of the patient's history." That immediately captured my attention because it told me that my own dreams of this nature were both a throwback as well as a forward reference to what I had begun to see as my post-traumatic stress experience. It also confirmed for me that, in fact, I did have an impactful post-traumatic condition.

In addition, the Baroness's notes on patients who experienced what was known as a Kundalini Syndrome (a reference derived from Asian spiritual culture) were those apparently also suffering with a post-traumatic experience but usually because each of these patients had had a near-death experience. In other words, a near-death experience was necessary to consider Kundalini. This was not relevant to me. I had never experienced anything like near-death.

McFarland also leafed through the notes and lifted out comments by John Lilly, M.D. who was well known for his work with bottlenose dolphins (Tursiops truncatus), and at the moment, and to my pleasant surprise, it was this same John Lilly, the psychiatrist with whom I had worked in the summer of 1965, in his dolphin lab in Coconut Beach, Florida as well as in his sea lab in the United States Virgin Islands, on the Island of St. Thomas. I told McFarland that my work with Lilly concerned his request that I adapt an index (a test) of emotions, the *Emotions Profile Index,* that I and a Dr. Robert Plutchik had developed. I told her that Plutchik and I had worked together in the construction of this index for several years and that it was eventually published almost a decade later, in 1974.

I was about to get back to the Baroness's file when she asked me to tell her more about the dolphin work. I told her that when Lilly first got wind of our work he contacted us, and when he discovered we had not yet completed our project for this emotions index, but were nevertheless testing it out, he asked for a copy. After examining it, he implored us to adapt it for use with dolphins and then also invited us both to become associates in his lab with the title Senior Scientist. Plutchik was contracted elsewhere and couldn't make it, but I agreed to at least visit the lab.

I continued by telling her that our *Emotions Profile Index* was considered by many to be quite useful in the measurement of emotions, gradually being utilized by researchers and practitioners in a wide variety of clinical and scientific fields, and that before we knew it the Index also invited several translations. In short order it was translated into a half-dozen languages and literally used all over the world.

I wanted to shift to the Baroness's file, but McFarland wanted still to hear more about it all. I told her that after visiting Lilly's lab in Coconut Grove, I agreed to work there, but only for a few months. My task was to address what Lilly wanted—to adapt this index that measured the emotions of people to a version that could also assess the emotions of dolphins.

When I finished telling her all about the ins and outs of dolphins and how I eventually created a method to assess their emotions as Lilly had wanted, she seemed to like the story, and definitely became suddenly different in her attitude toward me.

"You're an interesting guy, Dr. Alex Cole," she said.

Yes, she said "guy." I knew I would need to either spend another few days in Milan or catch her on the way back from Paris before heading for New York. In any event, my stay in Milan will thankfully be, because of Dr. Katherine Tess McFarland, and obviously because of Chief Aldo

Tancredi, rather longer than I had expected. I did, however, notice that "Tess" was a bit standoffish or perhaps shy — or even a bit cold.

But I shifted. "Let's talk more about the Baroness's notes, OK?" She agreed, and we went right to it. Now it seemed that I was in the ascendancy, seemingly not too concerned about her, as she seemed more concerned (interested?) in me. I pretended not to see the shift.

In any event, Lilly's comments in the Baroness's notes also included his rumination about truth versus fantasy. He mused that fantasy might also be truth and that such distinction should not always remain enjoined. He meant that fantasy and reality are usually different, but at times need to be seen as possibly the same. For me this meant that my sense that I must have done something wrong, and feel guilty about this vague something, should tell me that "it" very well might be true. Of course I didn't need John Lilly to reinforce or strengthen my guilt-ridden hunches, so I passed it by and went onto the Baroness's notes on fugue and dissociation. My postscript here is that Lilly's contemplations were considered suspect because of his interest in experiments of "isolation" and LSD effects, using people as well as dolphins as his subjects. I had read these revelations in a publication some years after I had known him.

After several more hours of examining the Baroness's files, I could see that whatever was there was not new to me. My hope that something might appear to trigger a new idea for me simply was not realized. Other than the idea in her notes of "depersonalization" versus "derealization," which also didn't do much for me, my dream of entering Baroness Alexandra Wolff's world in order to find a key that would enable me to finally enter my own was at an unfortunate and rather inglorious end.

Of course I knew that derealization is technically defined as a personal subjective experience of something being real but not of this world. And that, I thought, didn't apply to me. In contrast, depersonalization experiences are those that focus on the sense that something is wrong within — that there is an unreality in the person's sense of self. My own insight or understanding of it told me that in either case intrusive thoughts will be characteristic. And, Lord knows, I certainly had, and continue to have, intrusive thoughts.

One of the last cases in the Baroness's folder almost rescued me from my pessimism. It was of a man who was suffering with what was obviously a profound enosiophobia – feeling guilty and personally convinced that he had killed his mother. The Baroness's notes confirmed that the mother was still extant and that the patient knew that his mother was still alive, and yet the enosiophobia was so strong that it transcended truth. In this man's case what was real and known didn't really count, but what he felt ruled his mind. That rang a bell for me. It told me that crazy or not, my particular enosiophobia does indeed motivate me to make a sharp distinction between Lilly's hypothesis of fantasy and reality possibly being one and the same and, in contrast, my problem as insisting (and hoping) that reality and fantasy are fundamentally different. My fantasy of feeling guilty about some wrongdoing was still in the realm of knowing that I needed absolute evidence to see whether my fantasy was the same as reality or not. In my case, it further clarified for me that I was still in the real world searching for answers, so that's why this particular case of the Baroness's almost but didn't quite rescue me.

"One more thing. Oh yes here it is," McFarland said. "The Baroness has still another case of someone who experienced years of enosiophobia. This was an analysis of a young man who was always being the so-called good boy to his parents. When he was eight years old, his parents were killed when flying their single-engine plane somewhere in Europe. There was no note in the file explaining why this eight-year-old son hadn't accompanied them on the flight."

This was the story that McFarland had mentioned that she thought had something to do with a case of enosiophobia. She started reading from the file: "The boy was analyzed as feeling deeply, but unconsciously angry at his parents for leaving him, for abandoning him. It didn't matter that, through no fault of their own, they were killed. It only mattered to this boy that he was now alone and that they were gone."

I took the file from her, and I could see that, according to the Baroness, the boy's anger toward his parents was unconscious. Further, she stated that because his grandiosity about always bringing good news was shattered, therefore it might have been that the only choice for him was to become the bad boy, the one who in his behavior became "oppositional." McFarland took the file back and flipped a couple of pages: "Here it is." She said: 'What this might mean is that he blames himself for the death of his parents. His grandiosity was given a terrible blow, and he was in a consistent condition of acting-in fantasies of violence toward others and then psychologically, and in fantasy, retrieving into life their dead bodies—

revitalizing them. The acting-in idea referred to his problem of torturing and befuddling *himself* rather than actually acting homicidally against others'."

This case told me very clearly what I had already essentially figured — that I was doing something similar. In my fantasies, woven into dreams, I was retrieving my parents by killing Nazis, and I was doing it in a compulsively repetitive way — the purpose of which was to actually regress in time so as to reverse it, and then save them. It was a prime example of what could be labeled *My Retrieval Project*, and reminded me of the interpretation of my observing-ego dream.

I was starting to feel better, primarily because I was getting an increased sense that in all likelihood I never killed anyone. It was only in my fantasies — the unconscious ones — and it all related to my *wish*, to my algorithm, but not to behavior. In other words, I *wished* to do it, but I probably never did. Of course, the operative term in that sentiment is "probably." And so, despite my increasing confidence that I had done nothing wrong, nevertheless, the whole thing was "probably" all still hanging there.

Thus, after all that searching and thinking and hoping, I was still fairly certain that the enosiophobia anchored in my psyche and in my guts was essentially not cured!

When we finished, I got ready to leave, but asked Tess whether she'd like to have dinner. I made it my business to call her "Tess." Quite naturally she responded "sure," and we arranged where and when. I arrived at my hotel and changed my travel arrangements in order to spend two more days in Milan. The concierge handed me a note from Police Chief Tancredi asking me to stop by to see him the next morning. In the note he mentioned that he was guessing I would be in Milan a bit longer than I had planned. By the tone of his note it was clear to me that, with respect to Tess, he definitely saw exactly what I saw, and that's why he knew I'd be in Milan, as he said: "a bit longer."

*   *   *

We had dinner and talked nonstop. I could see she was conflicted about herself, almost as if she needed to justify her existence. Not like Jean on the plane, yet with the same self-doubt concealed in a pose of scholarly objectivity. But she confessed to me that she was basically shy and, despite her looks, very unsure of herself. In turn I confessed and told her what I felt—that she'd instantly taken my life away and I felt as though I would do anything for her and really cared for her. It was the truth. It helped saying it. She just about metamorphosed in front of my eyes. We went to her apartment. We made love. Just fell into each other's arms. Afterwards, she was wearing flannel pajamas and I laughed.

"I feel comfortable in flannels," she unabashedly said.

I really liked Dr. Katherine Tess McFarland. I liked her in a way that I'd never before felt in a relationship. Other than her self-doubt, I couldn't detect a single thing about her that seemed anything but delightful. She was also obviously interested in things of substance rather than imitating the materialistic nature of so many people in my beloved America who were turning into bourgeois robots reaching always for the ten minutes of vacuous fame. No, Tess was all woman. Looked the part and acted it. She was apparently addressing something in me, in my history, that, as I told her, took my life away. And, yes, she took it away fast! I was experiencing a sui generis moment.

We were at it for about two hours without let-up. I was encouraging her, and she was responding and expressing how she was feeling. She was passionately involved. She was loving in all kinds of ways, and the really special thing for me was that she was a great kisser. That, for me was crucial. I always felt that sex is easy and that most people simply do it with a focus on the act, but, frequently neglect kissing. Maybe it's because they think that kissing is kid stuff and that sex is adult or that they're not really interested in relationship. In contrast, I've always felt that the secret is that kissing is arguably really the most intimate—plus it has art to it. Not that sex doesn't. But did we kiss! Don't ask! I was a bit worried that this acute onset of love might have a short life span while at the same time hoping that that was not to be the case.

We spent the night together—sleeping on and off—passionately touching and rapturously holding. Sex again, and then again, right through this blazing, ecstatic, and rhapsodic night. Oh yes, very loving. Tender, too.

I loved her flannel pajamas. Yes, I did.

The next morning we woke up at the same time. Tess dragged me out of bed and into the shower. We couldn't keep our hands off one another in the shower so Tess insisted that I shower first. After we ate breakfast, Tess accompanied me to Tancredi's office. She put her arm in mine and held me close to her as we walked. We arrived at about 10 a.m. The first thing Tancredi said was "Dr. McFarland, welcome." Then he shook my hand as well.

"The knife handle was clean. I kind of guessed that would be the case," he said.

Then Dick Tracy laid it on.

"About 3 a.m. this morning a Mr. Horst Kapkow, a German national who worked for the German embassy in Rome and who was vacationing in Milan—or whatever he was doing here—was stabbed in the stomach. He was found with the knife fully impaled. Apparently, and this might not surprise you, Dr. Cole, Herr Kapkow was once, about ten years ago, acquitted for ostensible war crimes. He was an assistant to the commandant of the Treblinka concentration camp and was accused of personally shooting several of the prisoners as they were doing their chores around the camp. Apparently, this was a common practice in the camps where certain Nazis would take pot shots at random—as you may or may not expect, just for the sport of it.

"Here's the surprise or maybe not the surprise. A tall man was spotted swiftly departing from the scene. Several couples were coming out of a party, heard some disturbance in the street, first saw the tall man scooting away, and then saw Kapkow lying on his back with only the knife handle visible. There was blood all over the place. By the way, Dr. Cole, could you vouch for your whereabouts in the middle of the night, like about 3 a.m.?"

"He was with me. We spent the night together," answered Tess, unconcerned. Without reacting, Tancredi looked at me, was not the least embarrassed, and said:

"Congratulations." He then went on to say that the people there all agreed that the man was at least six feet tall and had somewhat of an awkward gait.

"I'm still unable to shake the feeling that you, Dr. Cole, showing up in Milan for only a few days are here when both of these events took place. I mean there's no way to connect you, but my experience gives me the feeling, like an intuitive sense, that somehow it could be connected to your stay here. I'm not saying that a confederate of yours is doing the crime, nor am I accusing you of these crimes, nor do I believe that you're in any way guilty. I'm just noting the correlation of you here and two men, both ex-Nazis, dead. Despite my certainty that you didn't have anything to do with it, nevertheless I must ask whether you may have had some indirect or even remote connection to either of these men."

"Chief Tancredi, the truth is that in my heart I'm glad they were killed. But that's all I know about any connection—as you say. And yes, I, too, think, as well as feel, that it does in some way have something to do with my presence in Milan. However, I'm relieved that in these cases I didn't do a thing and yet the men are dead – were killed. I'm sure I'm innocent. No doubt. And to confess to you that I'm relieved to have such certainty doesn't bother me one bit. As a matter of fact, my psychoanalyst in New York City will be very interested in what happened here. He actually may be happy I didn't do any of it or, come to think of it, he may actually be disappointed. We'll see. I'm going to ask him."

"Alex, what do you mean you feel it may have something to do with your presence in Milan?" asked Tess concerned.

"Well," I answered, "here I am in Milan, and when it happened to the first one, I just about saw it the instant it happened, and I was the only one to have connected the tallish man with the deed done at the precise moment when he was passing the victim, as they crossed paths on the crosswalk in the middle of the street. I can't help but think that he knew I was walking behind the victim and that he planned it so I'd be in close proximity to the act. I think he even planned it so that because of this proximity, I would have an excellent vantage point enabling me to spot most of what happened. He planned it that way. I can feel it. What I don't understand is why he killed someone else, this Kapkow, and at a time when I wasn't there. That bewilders me because I feel, in contrast to the last time, he wanted to do it this time precisely when I wasn't there."

An attractive Italian woman walked over to us and handed Chief Tancredi a note, which he read on the spot.

"Oh look at this. We've been checking the airport and all passports and it's been reported that a tall man with an awkward gait was spotted and then seen boarding a plane at the airport here in Milan early this a.m. Destination, Paris."

PART 3

PARIS

· 5 ·

PARIS, AND BREMEN THE GHOST

I told Tancredi that in another day I'd be leaving—for Paris no less. He asked if that was part of my itinerary before all this happened—was it my plan to head to Paris? I told him it was and that I was looking for a man by the name of Roland Bremen who I believed lived in Paris on the Rue Coquilliere at the 491-3 address. Tancredi blurted out, "If you find him—and he's rather tall with an awkward gait—call me immediately," and he laughed in a way that was derisive—as though it was all absurd and basically irrelevant. I looked at Tess, and she at me, and we both knew that none of it was either amusing or irrelevant.

We left the station and walked in silence—not a word. Both in deep thought. I started: "I believe that if another one doesn't happen here in Milan that for sure it will happen in Paris."

"Good Lord," she responded, "what is going on?" She emphasized the "on." It was exasperation.

"You're angry," I said, looking at her. I could tell she was angry but I knew it was also something else.

"Right, I'm furious," she answered. We kept walking. Then it hit me. Dr. Katherine Tess McFarland gets furious when she's scared. So, I thought, you're really frightened. Still, we kept walking. Then it occurred to me that I didn't know whether she was frightened that the killer was coming after us—or maybe one of us—me? Or, she might be scared that the killer would be coming after her as well. Then the really scary thought hit me. No, she may feel that somehow it will all lead to me, and I might be indirectly in cahoots with the killer—even without my actually knowing it—maybe in a fugue state, and I'm not aware of it.

"You're deep in thought, Alex." Oh man, was she right. And the deep thought I was in concerned my usual sense of being in the wrong. I was thinking that she would eventually become aware of my belief I was involved with this killer. On an emotional level I would absolutely agree with her, even though, intellectually, I wouldn't agree. I knew it was my enosiophobia rearing its ugly head. This symptom of mine was banking on what I previously mentioned—that what one knows (as in thinking I'm guilty of something), is never as powerfully persuasive as what one feels. Therefore, what I felt would be agreeing with Tess's presumed doubt with respect to who I am or who I might be—whether I'm conscious of it or not or whether she's conscious of it or not.

"I'm thinking, Tess, that you're worried about getting involved with me because it would put you either in danger with the awkward tallish one or it's me myself that worries you—actually scares you. Or maybe it's both."

Smiling, she took a long look at me. "You've got a psychological problem that's beyond these events, Alex. I see it's got a hold on you. I also now think that's it's why you never married. Alex Cole always thinks he's in the wrong. I can feel it. And you're even thinking that I agree you're always in the wrong—and therefore it's justified that I should be afraid of you."

"Tess, what I think is that you're better at this shrink stuff than I am. Everything you've just said is absolutely right. I do have that kind of a symptom and I'm working on it with my analyst in New York. The symptom that you told me you knew about when we were reviewing the Baroness's notes—this enosiophobia or pseudomania—means I'm always vague about some kind of wrong thing of which I might be guilty. It's in my dreams but I can never put my finger on it. I'm also trying detective work myself; that's why I'm in Milan. The Baroness's archive of altered states is what I hoped would shed some light on all this craziness. Recently, I figured that I'm really in a condition of post-traumatic stress."

I told her about my history, how my childhood trauma may have affected me, and how I believed in the possibility that I could be the one killing these former Nazi war criminals. Yet if I thought logically, I knew it couldn't be me. I told her about the Bremen passport in my safe deposit box and everything I could bring to mind at the moment.

"Alex, I've never said this before, but I think I'm falling for you and you're right, it gives me those doubts you mentioned. Okay, I've only known you for a short time, but I sense you're a good person and that for sure you've never killed anyone. Yet I do have a foreboding, and maybe it connects to yours so that we're connecting unconsciously—sympathy pains."

Tess's had a bracing intelligence. I knew it even when we first met. Her thinking process was consistently crisp and incisive. There's not a trace of cliché in her. She's a bona fide original. In bed the previous night she told me she was thirty-five, never married, never engaged, and straight. I think I know why I hadn't married, but, for the life of me, I couldn't understand why she hadn't. I mean, there's no doubt that any man who would meet her would be immediately attracted to her. But there you have it – the mystery of life.

Then I knew. Thinking that all men would want her gave me the clue. It was that men probably fell at her feet and would want to do anything for her. That's how really beautiful she is. But there's the rub. She probably can't tolerate that kind of supplication or submission that comes over a man who meets her. Whoever the man is, he can't bring himself to be assertive in her presence. And she can't take the nice guys because they're overly deferent.

In that sense, my inclination to be assertive and not passive or supplicating is evident to others. I believe it's what attracted Tess McFarland to me. She also said I was cute and had great charm. She called me great, in her own charming manner as we made love the night before. It was then that I felt completely at one with her. And, yes, I did indeed fall in love with the compliment. It's also when I felt I could be with her—even uxoriously—for the rest of my life.

Milan, Milan—death and love.

*　*　*

Yes, she loved that I was assertive. We talked about it and she admitted she needed someone who could give her some "pushback"—someone who could say which movie he'd like to see instead of always deferring to her.

"One more thing," she continued, "when I was fifteen years old, I fell in the street on a broken piece of glass and sliced the palm of my right hand. In the hospital, a doctor stitched it and while he was tending to me I picked up that he was obviously extra-interested. I had had that kind of reaction from boys and also from men many times before—also furtive glances—so I trusted my instincts. He called my house to check on how I was doing, and my parents, in a moment of gratitude, invited him for dinner. They were impressed that the doctor would call. He was a man of about thirty, and here I was, an adolescent girl. He actually proposed and was serious about it. He even talked to my parents about it. I wanted to crawl into a hole somewhere. It scared the hell out of me. I made it my business never to see him again. Yes, he was assertive, but at that point I didn't need a stranger-daddy.

"And you're telling me about this because?"

"Because you're probably thinking I've decided, you're the one I want!" She said it with an exclamation point so that there could be no doubt. I didn't answer her directly.

"Tess, come with me to Paris. Take a week off and let's go."

She couldn't. She had meetings....other responsibilities at the institute. She smiled: "Let me see what I can do."

She went to work, and I went to the hotel and right to bed even though it was still afternoon. All of this had exhausted me—including this new phase of my life that was obviously starting. This new phase was called Tess.

The phone rang. I looked at the clock; it was early evening. I had slept for three hours. It was Tess calling from the lobby, insisting we have dinner. She arrived at my door promptly, having taken the LEM module at interstellar speed, directly to my door. She jumped into the shower with me, we dried each other off, and, because together we were absolutely combustible, we made love. Then showered again.

That night we slept together, and I mean nocturnal sleep. Out cold. In the morning I called Tancredi and left a message telling him we were on our way to Paris. Of course he would know that meant Tess and me. I gave him my forwarding number. It was at the Hotel de Rouen, a little place close to Roland Bremen's address at Rue Coquilliere 75001. I left the address of the hotel—42 Rue Croix des Petits Champs. I also left Bremen's address as the person I was looking for. If Tancredi needed me, he would know exactly where I was. Even though Tancredi figured that the killings in Milan were related to something about me, I believed him when he said he knew I was innocent. The trouble was, as might be expected, I, also felt the killings were somehow related to me.

The phone rang and Tess answered it. After several hellos she held the phone in one hand near but away from her ear, looked at me, and said: "No answer. There's no one there." I took the phone, called the hotel lobby operator and asked whether a phone call had just come in for me. She acknowledged it and said it was a man who asked for my room number and referred to me by name. She then connected him. I thanked her.

"That's no accident," I said to her. "That's definitely no accident. It's that someone who has had me in his sights, is following me, and probably has been following me all these years whenever I traveled in Europe. He's the one doing the killings. It's not me. I've done nothing wrong except in my fantasy life where to be honest, I do spin stories about how I would kill these Nazis, and then do my daring and brilliant escapes. I think about it – often. I also know it means I'm angry — maybe even furious. I know too it probably means that the anger is part of my post-traumatic stress regarding my parents. I haven't been able to shake it, I can't shake it."

We were sitting in bed and she was embracing me. The phone rang again. It was the hotel operator. She said it was the same male voice calling for me and that she had him on hold. I asked her to put the call through. Again, no one on the line.

"Dead," I said. "The line is dead. A hang up. It's already happening."

Tess said: He, or they know you're — rather we're here. I think you're right, you may be being tracked. Someone knows your itinerary. Who knows your itinerary?"

I thought about that one and all I could come up with was my travel agent and Tancredi. My students and colleagues know I would be giving workshops in Vienna, but they had no idea of the rest of my travel plans. Only my travel agent and Tancredi knew all of it — from New York to Vienna to Milan to Paris."

"Well, someone is tracking you, and that person knows exactly who you are and where you are, and I'll bet they've thought of you often, and even perhaps through the years — maybe even decades. I believe you have an enemy, Alex, and I can see that maybe you never considered it. We know one thing for sure, and you've convinced me of it — that the tall man staged the killing knowing full well that when the curtain opened and the performance actually unfolded, with the victim located stage center, and with that knife stuck all the way in, that you, Alex, at that very moment would be arriving also at stage center so that you and the victim would be a duet, a two-actor scene. And he worked it perfectly. He knows exactly what he's doing. Yes, that's it. He's taunting you and keeping you in a thrall with your own 'enoso' thing that you think you have. So, who is it, Alex that wants everything you have? I think that's what it might be. It's someone who covets everything you have and knows he can't be you so that in order to win, in order to be better than you, his genius is to make you lesser than he is. It could be that simple."

Tess had it right, and it hit me right. It offered me a clearer view of it all. It reminded me of what those theoretical mathematicians and astrophysicists say about the elegance of a theory insofar as its beauty alone almost verifies its validity. And in fact, it was put that beautiful way—by a beauty.

"I feel you're on to something, Tess. Not there yet, but close. I think you're right. But there's more to it. I can feel it."

"Alex," she said, "we're off to Paris."

*　　*　　*

There were a number of Nazi criminals who disappeared after the war and were never located. Then there were those who escaped punishment but were eventually found. One of them was Gerhard Sommer. Sommer interested me primarily because he was convicted of being involved in the murder of hundreds of people. He was convicted in absentia, but the German government refused to extradite him. I've often thought that some assassin needed to take care of it. I was ruminating that he would be in Paris and my double would do the taking care of. However, I knew Sommer was now protected by the German government and, in his advanced years, was secure in some safe house.

"You know, Tess, wherever we go, we need to be alert to who is around us. It's the tallish guy with the funny gait that very well might be shadowing us. We both know he's the one making those phone calls. Right? And, by the way, I believe he may have been with that woman who was walking next to him when Hans Milch was stabbed in Milan. The problem is the crowd was so thick people were all practically one piece. So I can't really be sure. I mean, he may have been working alone." I said "working" instead of "walking." I heard myself say it. It meant to me that I believed that the tallish man is on a specific project—one that requires planning, stalking, and then, obviously killing—assassinating. It also occurred to me that, for whatever reason, he actually knows what I would like to do and *he's* doing it instead. But I don't know what our connection is. Did he know me when I was a child in Berlin? Could it be that he went through a similar trauma and somehow connects it to mine? That would mean that he's also probably Jewish. Also, can it be that he might be blaming me for something? Yes, I think that's what it could be. He blames me for something."

When we arrived in Paris, we checked into Hotel De Rouen not far from Bremen's address, and after a quick meal off we went to Bremen's address on that passport, located at 491-3 Rue Coquilliere 75001. It wasn't far and we walked. It was a rather smallish old-style apartment building of three stories. As someone was exiting the lobby into the street, we entered. We checked the apartment names on a mounted ledger. No Bremen. A young woman exited the small elevator. We asked her if she could speak English, and she said yes. We told her we were looking for a Bremen, but that he wasn't listed. The woman was not aware of the name. I suggested that perhaps he had recently moved away, but she said that she had been living in the building for a number of years. Of course it probably meant that Bremen had not lived there for the past so many years. I didn't want to ask her just how many years she had been living there, so I let it go.

Now what do we do, was the question. As we pondered that, an elderly lady entered the building. We asked her if she understood English. She too answered yes. We then asked her about Bremen, and she immediately answered that, yes, he lived there many years ago, but was only a part-year visitor, because most of the year he lived in America. Tess asked whether she knew where he lived in America and the lady said that she remembered it was a not far from New York City.

"Mr. Bremen would usually arrive in time for Bastille Day and remain here for a month or so each year. He was a very nice man, and we would often talk. He had a definite German accent. He was quite a gentleman. Whenever he arrived, he would bring me a basket of fruit and we would have fruit or cheese and wine and we would have long conversations. He once told me he loved Bastille Day because it commemorated the French Revolution that had resulted in the *Declaration of the Rights of Man*. I've never forgotten that he said that. He was an educated man, Mr. Bremen was. And, gentle and respectful. I remember he also said that he hated that from 1940 all the way through 1944, because of the German occupation, Bastille Day was suspended. Whenever Mr. Bremen mentioned the Germans, he referred to them as Nazis. And, to tell you the truth, I lived through it all and I hate those Germans too. Mr. Bremen and I certainly agreed on that!" She continued, now caught up in her wartime memories. "Oh yes, Mr. Bremen loved Charles de Gaulle and said that someday he wished to be able to emulate de Gaulle's achievements at least in some way. Of course the truth is that I never understood that, with his obvious history from Germany—you know, with that heavy German accent—why he loved the French so much and was critical of the Germans. It always seemed strange to me."

"May I ask you what he looked like?" Tess queried.

"Oh yes, of course. Mr. Bremen was quite a tall man—but of course compared to me all men are tall. He seemed to have a limp or something like that."

Tess continued: "Would you happen to know where he might be now? We're eager to talk to him. I'm sure he's had many interesting experiences. You see we are doing a study in psychology and we were told that Mr. Bremen would know a lot about how people can be anonymous when they travel. It's something that interests us."

"Oh, no. I haven't seen or heard from him in a very long time. If you do find him, please send him my fondest regards."

Walking back to the hotel, Tess and I were talking it over. "He's ostensibly from outside New York City," I said. "If it's true, it puts it much closer to home." But the main point was that we were both shaken when she said he was tall with a limp.

"Let's call the Simon Wiesenthal Center," Tess said. "They're Nazi hunters. Information they initially had ultimately led to the capture of Adolf Eichmann in 1960 in Argentina. They know a lot about a lot. It could be that our friend is affiliated or in some other functional way associated with the Wiesenthal Center. I think it's a good idea. Let's get in touch with them. They might put us back on the track because now we're at a dead end. There's nowhere to go. Also, *how*, and *where*, does this guy get his information about *who* and *where*? That is to say, who are his targets and where are they? It's got to be some sort of Nazi hunter central organization *where* he finds hard facts, then knows *who* he's looking for, knows *where* to find them, and then kills them. The first thing that comes to mind is Simon Wiesenthal."

"Tess, how do you know so much about Jewish things like the Wiesenthal place? You're Irish. Where's this interest coming from?"

"I read Alex, and I'm an Irish national. I like when people have pride in their ethnicity. In that sense, as an Irish ethnic, I'm a citizen of every oppressed people—and that goes especially for Jews. Also Armenians. One of my best girlfriends is Armenian. I don't like what's happened to Jews and I know it all started with church-sponsored hate." Tess then stopped walking and turned to me with a completely different topic on her mind. "By the way, but not at all parenthetically, I'm already thirty-five and I want to have a child—and I want to have it with you, Alex. We can do it as a married couple or just the way we are. I prefer married."

Nonplussed but not at all disappointed, I immediately said: "OK, married it is. We agree the child will be raised in a secular way—all right?" "Absolutely," she answered, "and I think we should raise him—I know I said 'him,'—Jewish. We definitely need more Jews in the world. I feel strongly about it."

"Wow," I said, "that could make me cry. It will be so great because this child will be very bright—you know, Jewish and Irish." But, she continued:

"No, I think we should raise him by giving him a secular bar mitzvah. No rabbi. You, Alex, can be the rabbi-equivalent."

Man oh man, were we flying. It's a boy and he's already thirteen. "When do we inaugurate our plan?" I asked.

"That's easy," Tess answered. "We inaugurate in two stages: first, when we conceive, and, second, when we welcome the child into the world. Agreed?" she asked.

"Absolutely."

*　*　*

"OK, I'll make the Wiesenthal call," I said. "But first I need food. I'm famished." We had food sent up to the room and we ate and talked. As new as our relationship was we were never at a loss for words or, for that matter, for subject matter. But how in the world did this all happen—and so fast? In one moment I'm an odd creature as a single man navigating my early forties, and in the next I'm getting married and having a baby or rather, having a baby and getting married. Either way is OK really, only because it's me and her.

But before we could even contemplate accomplishing that little project of ours, I got the Wiesenthal phone number in L.A. and dialed it. It was answered on the second ring. I asked to speak to the person who handles requests for information and was immediately transferred by the operator to the information desk. I identified myself and asked whether they ever receive phone calls about information particularly focused on knowing the whereabouts of Nazi war criminals. The woman at the other end hesitated, and then told me they receive what feels like a hundred phone calls a day for precisely that kind of information, along with all sorts of tips as to where certain accused Nazi perpetrators are or might be. She added that there was no way to identify any of these callers. I kept it going by asking whether at least did they keep a list of calls, or ever tape these calls, or keep a log-book of visitors who actually visit the center and seek that kind of information? To that she answered they do but were not at liberty to make such information public. "I'm trying to identify a tall man perhaps with a limp," I directly said. "Does that by any chance ring a bell?"

"I'm sorry, Dr. Cole, I have no information to offer you," was the final answer.

And that was that. "Don't look so disappointed, Alex," Tess said. "It's obvious that Paris is not going to tell you what you need to know over the phone. I think we've got to go to L.A. and visit the center in person — and immediately. With my looks and your charm we might be able to get something."

That made me laugh. Then it became obvious that all Tess and I needed to do is be near a bed and the next thing that happens is that we're making love. And so it was. We were having passionate sex and we were kissing. Oh were we kissing!

We made love and awakened together at about 7 am. Showered (no sex), had breakfast, and talked over what Tess referred to as our imminent L.A. visit. Tess wanted to leave Paris immediately and predicted that we would continue to be at a dead-end in Paris if our only objective was to find Bremen.

"Bremen ain't here honey-chile," she said with a southern drawl. "Bremen — gone! Therefore, let's not waste any time and fly to LA now."

Suddenly the phone rang. It startled us because I guess we both were thinking it to be another call with silence at the other end. I lifted the receiver, and Tess and I shared the ear-piece so that we would both be in on the call. Rather than silence, it was the manager of the hotel, who told us with rapid-fire excitement, but in hushed tones, that about ten minutes before, when the elevator door opened on the lobby floor, a man was lying there dead. "He was on his back lying in a pool of blood. A knife had been plunged into his heart.

He said, "This has never happened here. We're asking all guests not to leave their rooms. Please remain in your room. The police will be arriving at any moment. Thank you."

He precipitously hung up.

"OK," I said. "Let's think fast. We know it's him. He did it. And, we know, without absolutely knowing, that the dead man was either a wanted convicted Nazi or possibly one who avoided punishment. And we also know that Bremen, or whoever it is, obviously did it in this hotel because he knew we were here. And I think that the murdered man wasn't staying at the hotel, but he must have accompanied Bremen, or whoever it is, here. Then, in the elevator, Bremen killed him."

"You're right, Alex. You're right. This reminds me of a case that the Baroness had in one of her files. She had diagnosed a man who was having a *Mana Character Personality*. She described it as someone who is so ego-maniacal as to consider himself as having a sense of extraordinary power. I think the word is *megalomaniacal*, like a grandiose paranoid with a world-salvation fever. I think this tall man, Bremen, or whoever it is that's doing it, is such a maniacal person. Perhaps he wants to show you that he's smarter than you, and even better at doing the thing that you either would like to do yourself, or, worry about already having done it.

"That's why he did it right here at this hotel, in Paris, practically in front of you. And I'll bet that no one will be able to identify the killer. But I'll also bet that someone else will be able to say that the killer was tall and had a funny walk. He wants you to know it was him, Alex!"

"We should call Tancredi and bring him up to date," I answered.

"No," Tess instantly said. "Tancredi might make us stay here longer. Let's call him from L.A. That way, we're already on safe ground. When they're through questioning everyone, including us, we'll be on our way. And, by the way, as I'm talking to you I'm also thinking of another point

the Baroness made. She said that these *Mana Character Personality* types
will eventually have what she described as 'a content shift.' She explained it
as the Mana type getting gratification by taunting another person, although
very indirectly, as if by suggestion or some kind of nuance. But then the
gratification is consumed by this indirect approach and this kind of person
then needs a more direct gratification by implementing the taunts, the
insidious behavior more up close—like what's happening now, here. If we
don't get out of here soon, he'll probably kill a forth person right in front
of us."

*   *   *

The interrogation by the Paris police was interminable. After they finally
finished with us, we were free to go, as were all the other hotel guests. But
at first we had to wait about six hours before they got to us. What to do
in those six hours?

I decided to use the time to put it all down in my diary.

"Tess, I haven't spent any time writing in my *Jackal Diary*. It's going
to take me at least a couple of hours to catch up on everything that's happened. The *Diary* doesn't know a thing about Tancredi or you or any of
these crazy events."

I unzipped my briefcase and took out my yellow pads. They were all
blank—untouched. The yellow pad with all of my notes—names, dates,
places, events—was gone! My heart sank. I ran to where my jacket was
hanging and frantically searched the side pockets. No little pad either.
Everything gone. I thought: Jean! When I was sleeping.

"Tess, that woman on the plane, she was a thief. Wait a minute, nothing
else is missing. All the yellow pads are here. Only the one with all my notes
that I had in my briefcase is missing as well as my little notepad located in
my jacket side pocket. Everything else is here."

"You're being followed, Alex," Tess reflexively said.

"My God, all the while I was thinking that I was the teacher and Jean
was the student. Live and learn. I'm really upset about it. All that thinking,
all that writing. Hey, wait a minute. Jean actually asked the stewardess to
change her seat because she wanted the vacant window seat next to mine.
You're right; she was there to shadow me. She did it when I was asleep.
Then when I woke up, she seemed to be asleep—but she was only feign-

ing sleep and probably needed to be alert to me in case I went for my brief-case or note-pad so that in such a moment she would appear to awaken and then of course try to distract me. Wow!"

"Alex, she didn't steal what's in that beautiful brilliant head of yours. Everything is still there. You'll simply spend some time and retrieve all memory of all the events and write it down again."

That relieved me, but I was still unsettled by what seemed to be an obvi-ous conclusion. I was being followed. Then I had another what we might call amusing, yet unsettling thought.

"Tess, since I was asleep, then my observing-ego was also asleep. There-fore, I can't ask my observing-ego to tell me what happened and exactly how she did it."

"The good sign Alex is that you've still got your sense of humor."

I kissed her.

By the time the police questioned us—what I termed our personal inquisition—another hour elapsed. It felt interminable. Over and over, they wanted to know who we were, how we knew each other, where we came from, and on and on.

"No, we never saw the victim before. No, we didn't see the perpetrator because when it happened we were in our room. No, we have no friends or relatives in Paris." Everything was "no," and that's how it all ended. They told everyone the same thing—a hotel full of people—"We may want to speak with you again." And, of course, we were part of "everyone."

We decided to make reservations to Los Angeles the next morning. We never told the police anything about how we were sure that we were indi-rectly involved, although not guilty of anything.

We were expecting to land at LAX at about 8 p.m., L.A. time. Approxi-mately a twelve-hour flight. We checked into the Beverly Wilshire Hotel. It was now 9:30 p.m. and we fell into bed and slept. I woke up at about midnight and sat in a chair and watched Tess sleep. I loved looking at her. As a matter of fact, from the moment I ever laid eyes on her, I've not had a moment when I would look at her and not feel fully gratified and my heart happy.

When we got to the Wiesenthal Center on South Roxbury Drive, we were introduced to the information secretary who ushered us into the office of a vice president. I inquired about Bremen, who, I said, might have been searching for material on Nazi war criminals. Since I, too, was interested in that subject—as I was sure were multitudes of others—I was hoping this vice president, Mr. Nathan Kamen, might recognize Bremen's name and then, as my wish would have it, simply tell me Bremen's address, phone number, and anything else that might strike him as important about Bremen.

We talked a while and I informed Mr. Kamen of my Vienna to Milan to Paris to L.A. trajectory. He told us that it was too bad we hadn't contacted the *Jewish Documentation Center* in Vienna when we were there, because they had voluminous amounts of data on all sorts of wanted Nazi war criminals, as well as on those who disappeared and, what's more, on those who avoided prosecution but are nevertheless openly visible and conducting business in a normal manner—and, he added, "not at all afraid of being arrested or put on trial."

Mr. Kamen was a treasure trove of excellent information and a likeable guy. He was quite knowledgeable about all sorts of things related to the Nazis. He consulted his files, and surprisingly, actually found the name Roland Bremen.

"Yes, here it is. Mr. Roland Bremen is a man who has been here before. He used the reference room and did some research. He collected information on the Nuremburg Trials and apparently comparing it with data he had gotten from, let's see, it says, yes, here it is—obtaining data from the *Freedom of Information Act.* I don't know how he did that, or what he was looking for. The address I have for him is 341 East 81st Street in New York City. His phone number is listed as 212-734-0718.

"Thank you very much, sir," I gratefully said. "We're staying at the Beverly Wilshire. I'll give you a follow-up call sometime to ask whether Mr. Bremen has contacted you again. In the event he does, could you please tell him that I've been trying to reach him and, if you don't mind, could you also phone me at the hotel?"

"Finally," Tess said, as we were bidding Mr. Kamen our good-byes and walking out. "Easy, Tess," I interrupted. "Could be it's a phony address and phone number. This guy's not stupid. He's all planned."

When we returned to the hotel, we called Bremen's alleged phone number and of course I wasn't surprised when an automated voice stated that it was not a working number.

"Man oh man how the hell do we get a fix on this guy?"

The phone rang. A woman asked to speak to Dr. Cole.

"I'm Alex Cole."

"Dr. Cole, you need to visit Harry Houdini's star on the *Walk of Fame* on Hollywood Boulevard. This particular star is located directly across the street from the famous *Grauman's Chinese Theater* at 7001 Hollywood Boulevard. Go there now."

She hung up.

I looked at Tess. "It's a woman. She wants me to go to Houdini's Walk of Fame star on Hollywood Boulevard, but I'm not going. I think it's too dangerous. I can almost see myself lying on Houdini's star in a pool of my own blood with a knife handle as the only visible part of the knife that's fully stuck all the way into me. Nope, I'm definitely not going. This guy is too crazy. How does he know we're at the Beverly Wilshire?

"What should we do?" Tess wondered.

"We wait for another call and tell whoever it is at the other end what it is that we want!"

"Well, OK, Alex, what do we want?"

"Look," I slowly answered while thinking. "He sent me to Harry Houdini because Houdini, who was Jewish by the way, was someone who could outwit any authority and break free from any constraint. This lunatic might be telling me that he's as great as Houdini and can't be traced or tracked and can outwit us all—especially outwit me. I want him to hear me tell him that he's a maniac, a grandiose *Mana Character Personality*—and I'll tell him what that means—describing to him that it means he had decided that in order for him to sustain his mental balance he needs to feel superior to others and especially to me. And then I have to ask him: 'Why me?!'"

"You can't do that, Alex. It's provocative. He could kill you. Let's leave L.A. and head for New York. Call Tancredi and see what he has to say about it?"

That appealed to me. New York City and Tancredi together, made me feel safe.

*   *   *

Tess made the long-distance call to Tancredi and got him at his desk. She described everything that he had not yet known—down to the Houdini appointment I didn't keep as well as to now, our impending trip to New York City.

"I think I need to be there with you," Tancredi immediately said. "I'll call Armand Calle, he's the police chief in Paris. I'll arrange it with him because I know he's personal friends with the police chief, Sanford Garelik, in New York."

Tess practically cut him off. "We'll call you with the latest — if there is a latest. We'll be staying at Alex's apartment on Gramercy Park. His number is, hold it: 'Alex, your apartment phone?'"

"212-982-6607."

With that, Tess and I packed and at the same time were able to arrange the flight to New York. Before we left, we called Kamen again and gave him my phone number in New York.

The long flight to New York was uneventful and by the time we arrived at the apartment we were both exhausted. Sleep ensued and in the morning we decided to make that call to Mr. Kamen. It later dawned on me that we were probably actually expecting the madman to be onto our every move and would possibly check with Kamen regarding any information he would have about us. And we were probably both thinking that this Mana maniac would do this immediately, as soon as we left L.A., as though he was at our side at every moment, but, of course, in an invisible form. It was probably also that we thought he was a so-called sleeper, like a mole: someone maximally surreptitious and, of course, with great ability.

"Yes," Kamen said. "It's amazing. The next day Mr. Bremen called asking about you, and I told him you had informed me you were leaving for New York. I was about to give him your phone number, but he said he already had it. Was that all right?"

"No, no, it's perfectly fine. Thank you so much for taking the time to call me. It was a pleasure meeting you."

I could tell, whether Mr. Kamen knew it or not, that he was feeling the situation with Bremen was strange and that perhaps he was relaying information that he should not have done. In any event, it was obvious that Bremen knew our exact whereabouts — wherever we were and at anytime — now in New York City at my apartment on Gramercy Park.

And Tess said it:

"We'll be getting another phone call, and soon. That's my bet."

"Tess, this is ridiculous. We need police protection and, besides, I need to get you away from all of it. Don't argue. I don't want you even in the remotest proximity to any danger."

"Well, Alex, I feel that way about you, too, and so I'm not leaving you."

"In other words, you feel you're stronger; that *you* need to take care of *me*, to protect *me*."

"That's right. With all your know-how, there's still an innocence about you that reveals you to be an unsullied and unmalicious person. You don't have a malicious bone in your body, and that's probably why this lunatic chose you as someone to emulate and then, yes, perhaps even to destroy! Yes, again, I mean 'destroy.' And he's the opposite—entirely malicious, envious, jealous, and completely sullied, contaminated. He's the quintessential predator. He wants to be you. He can't compete with you, but he's exceedingly competitive. With you, he loses every time and he can't take it. That's right, he simply can't take it, and it's been driving him nuts for who knows how long. Come to think of it, he's probably been on your case for some time, and he needs to always have the very latest information on you that he can get.

"And by the way, this kind of predator is the worst kind. It's like, in order to medicate himself so that he's no longer tortured with this craven envy, he uses grotesque fantasies, all of which probably concerns getting the best of you. If we see it through his eyes, then he wants everything you have and that would in all likelihood include me. But, even more, he wants your intelligence, your talent, your immense productivity. He even wants to eat your guts and drain your blood. 'Everything' means everything. He wants everything you have!" She paused.

"I'm not finished—he's got a confederate, that woman Jean, who took what was important to you. And guess what? Jean is his accomplice."

I was just observing Tess as she continued. She was on it like a pit bull, and decisively so. It got to me. I thought for a few moments:

"The police. We've got to lay it all out."

With that the phone rang. It was a woman. She said: "Dr. Cole, please."

"Yes," I said, this is Alex Cole." I paused. "Hello, Jean."

She was momentarily silent. Then: "Hello, Alex."

"You've got my notes, you know my whereabouts, and now you want what?"

"Don't be rude, Alex, and don't be embarrassed. The message I have for you is a good one. My friend wants you to know that he has nothing against you, but that his mission is to do what he knows you would want to do but perhaps feel you cannot do. He is, in a way, being your surrogate, knowing full well that you—and these are his exact words that I am to deliver to you, 'that you would not have a clear memory of having the will-power, the capacity, the courage, or even a fraction of the planning ability to carry off all of these, shall we say, occurrences.'

"Again, in his words, Alex, he wants me to be sure to tell you that it's not that he's saying he's doing all this himself, but that it may also be that he does some and maybe you do some—or maybe it's really someone else. Yes, he wants you to know that your doubt regarding whether or not you've been actually involved in these occurrences should tell you that you are indeed infused in it all—whether or not in fantasy.

"My own postscript, Alex, is that perhaps rather than me needing to justify my existence, it could be that it is you who is the subject of this, shall we say, existential condition of needing to justify yours!

"Auf Wiedersehen, Alex."

It was a shock. Yes, my bewilderment was a result of all she said, but a greater shock was that she said good-bye in German, literally meaning: "Be seeing you again." I knew it meant just that. They would be seeing me *again*.

I paused and was deep in thought.

"At least I now know one of them," I said to Tess. "How many others, if any, is a mystery. Jean, the tall man, and anyone else? And yes, because she said good-bye in German, does that imply that somehow others who are German are involved, or is it that I'm so paranoid about the whole thing that my mind has lost its ability to discern things, to think?"

What scared me even more was that although I was talking to Tess, she only looked at me. She wasn't saying a word but I could tell she agreed with me. They would be seeing me again, and, moreover there might be others involved. And, these others could be related to something German or something about Germany or, of course, about Nazis?!

Now I wanted to call the police more than before—but I was also afraid to call them. The question was, what to do?

Tess again said: "Call Tancredi and talk it over. We trust him. Tell him everything." My relief at Tess's suggestion told me that that was exactly the thing to do. Tancredi had that special something. I also knew he trusted me and liked me too.

And, of course, he definitely liked Tess.

* * *

"He's going to be in shock," Tess said. "First you're in New York City then you're in Vienna, then Milan, then Paris, then LA., and now back to the beginning, New York. He needs a map with longitude and latitude to follow you around."

"Ha," I mused. "Would you please call him?"

Tess put through the call and left a message for him to call us at my apartment. She left him the phone number.

"OK, let's have lunch," I suggested. But now Tess was deep in thought.

"I don't think so, Alex. I'm actually afraid to leave the apartment. Order in, and when it arrives the delivery man should tell the doorman to announce: 'Lunch for two.' Then we'll know it's OK."

"Tess, you could write mystery stories."

"It's easy, especially when you're living one."

At that point, the phone rang, and we both knew it was Tancredi. It was. We filled him in A to Z. He told us to sit tight because he was going to call his contact at Interpol and arrange a meeting between their agents, us, and Tancredi himself. We would need to wait to hear where this meeting was to take place. My hunch said Paris, which meant another trip across continents, oceans. My outside hope was that we would all congregate in New York City so that I would finally be home where I wanted to stay and where I was definitely yearning to see Dr. Martin again. Man oh man, did I have a story for him!

Tancredi made it clear that this seemed to be much bigger than even we thought. After all, it involved a variety of murders in a variety of countries. Some in various places in Europe, some in South America, and who knows how many in the United States.

So we sent for food and hoped that when the delivery person arrived, the doorman would then utter the words "Lunch for two." We sat and talked for about a half hour when the doorman called up. "Dr. Cole, 'lunch for two' is what I'm instructed to say."

"Lunch for two it is. Send him up."

The doorbell rang and Tess jumped up and went to the door. It was all on the up and up. She thanked him, tipped him, and we were grateful to have something nice to eat. The next several hours were a bit tense because I was trying to rewrite as much of my notes as possible, continuing from what I had written in our Paris hotel waiting to be interviewed by the Paris police. I was writing it down as fast as I could, and doing it while narrating the events to Tess. At about three hours into this maddening project, the phone rang. Tess and I looked at one another. We both knew what the immediate possibilities were. We probably both considered that it was either Jean or maybe the tall guy, or whoever it is that hangs up and leaves us talking into a dead phone. Or, hopefully, Chief Tancredi.

"Hello," I said, holding my breath.

"Dr. Cole, it's Aldo Tancredi. It's all arranged. We'll meet in New York City. I'll be there, as will Carl Persson. Persson's the president of Interpol, the International Criminal Police Organization. He's from Sweden and has held the position of president of Interpol for the past three years, since 1976. He's a friend. We've had two personal meetings in the past three years and about a dozen or so phone conversations. I've already filled him in on as much as I know of the situation. We'll also be joined by Chief Sanford Garelik, who, by the way, is the first Jewish chief inspector of the New York City Police Department. I've now also filled him in—although more briefly. He was eager to join us because I indicated that some of this assassination business may have occurred in the United States—and I repeated that to him by adding—perhaps even more than once."

We talked a bit more and Chief Tancredi bid us farewell. The date to meet was set for the following Tuesday, in four days, at Chief Garelik's office. As I was taking down Garelik's address, Tancredi mentioned that we also would be joined by a third person, Inspector Jacques Grimand, who Tancredi wanted me to know was a French Jew of Italian descent and who was known by Interpol to have been working on the list of assassinations or killings of former Nazis. Apparently, Grimand had been investigating these killings for several years. Tancredi said that Grimand could be extremely helpful.

"By the way," Tancredi said almost boastfully: "It's Inspector Jacques Grimand of the French Secret Service. And he agrees that this meeting could be very important. The theory he and Persson have talked over for several years now is that the killings are specifically a plot by a Jewish gang hell-bent on vengeance and therefore will keep up the assassinations of these Nazis, or alleged Nazis, until these Nazi fugitives are successfully eliminated by serious gunfire, or whatever else, and/or these Nazis eventually die of stage 4 senescence."

I gave Tess a word-for-word repeat of what Tancredi had told me. We now had four days to meet at Garelik's office.

Tess and I planned we would continue to live like a married couple in my apartment on Gramercy Park, a completely protected apartment building fully staffed with twenty-four-hour doormen, porters, handymen, and a live-in superintendant.

·6·

ROSTMANN AND BREMEN

Marcus Rostmann was a man who looked to be in his mid seventies, who spoke English rather well, although with a discernible German accent. At one point he was apprehended in Paris by the French police because he had been in a crowd of people who witnessed and/or heard the sound of what seemed like a shooting. Several people in the crowd agreed on what they heard. It was like four pop pop pop pop sounds that could have been made by a silencer. All who were questioned were absolutely sure it was four pops they heard. Since Rostmann was identified by others as the person physically closest to the victim, he became the focus of what was considered to be a rather extensive police interrogation.

The victim was identified as Klaus Gruber. It was later ascertained that Gruber was an escaped Nazi war criminal. The fact was that he had been on the run for the past thirty-four years, since 1945, about when he was in his late forties. It was figured that he was now in his mid to late seventies or perhaps even early eighties. The person called in to lead the investigation was none other than Inspector Jacques Grimand, the same Inspector Grimand that I was to meet in New York City in the coming days, and the same Grimand — the one Tancredi told us was a French Jew of Italian descent — who was also the chief investigator on crimes involving former Nazis. He and Persson called these alleged Nazis "persons of interest."

Mr. Rostmann told a strange story. He identified himself to the police as Roland Bremen, a retiree and the former registrar of the local college in his town of New Paltz, New York. He said he was in Paris on vacation and happened to be at the scene of the crime because the theater he'd attended had let out and he, along with the crowd of others, began streaming out into the street. It was then that they heard the four pops. Rostmann was required to produce the theater ticket stub and to describe the performance. He did just that. Rostmann seemed as normal as the rest. He was first asked to produce his identification card, his passport, and his driver's license. In each case, his name was Roland Bremen, but his picture, unbeknownst to the police, was that of Marcus Rostmann. On the second day of questioning, as Rostmann had described it the day before, he again reported that when he saw the victim lying dead in the street he became a touch queasy. He swore that he had absolutely nothing to do with any shooting nor did he see anyone else who might have been responsible for it.

Rostmann was believable. But the story was an instance of extemporaneous fiction. An out and out lie! The fact is that Rostmann really knew that the victim was Klaus Gruber—who was close friends with at least two other Nazi escapees—and he knew the identities of the others as well, all of whom had been at large—loose in the society and successfully evading justice—not only for years, but for decades.

None of the individuals who were coincidentally part of the crowd that happened to be there during the shooting of Klaus Gruber—including Marcus Rostmann himself—could be held or incarcerated on suspicion of murder because there was not a scintilla of evidence against any of them.

For the time being it was good-bye to Marcus Rostmann, aka. Roland Bremen. However, the entire incident was carefully written up and in the possession of Inspector Jacques Grimand of the French police.

*   *   *

By the time Tess and I and the others had convened in Garelik's New York office and were introduced to one another, Grimand gave us a rundown of the Klaus Gruber case. When Roland Bremen's name was mentioned, I practically jumped out of my chair.

"That's it," I shouted. "That's the name on the passport I found in my safe deposit box even though I personally never put it there."

Yes, Roland Bremen was the one being questioned and suspected, but Grimand, Tancredi as well as Garelik all snickered. I was still standing there aghast at the name Roland Bremen, and Tess and I wondered why the three of them were amused. Garelik took the lead and told us that the police had nothing on Bremen. "However," Garelik continued, "during the war, Gruber had a top secret assignment to be part of a contingent that was guarding a bank in the north of Germany. Inspector Grimand has had this information about Gruber in his files for a long time."

Grimand, who spoke a king's English from his education growing up in London, picked it up and, looking at me, said: "Dr. Cole, the very fact that you found a passport in your possession with the name Roland Bremen on it confirms my own suspicions about this Bremen. We now have a watch on him. We'll get into that later."

But that was ridiculous because, before you knew it, Bremen/Rostmann was gone. The watch on him lasted less than a day. He must have expected it and, with hardly any effort, he gave it the proverbial slip. But Grimand continued.

"At the moment, I should say that I learned about this group that was guarding the bank from one of the other squad members, who, it turned out was also shot and killed. His name was Heinrich Jaeger. He was shot more than a decade ago while living in Holland. Before he died, he said something about the squad guarding the bank, and then something about that everyone in the squad needed to be a senior career officer of at least 40 years of age. His last word was *north*. We took that to mean north in Germany, but, of course, regarding what "north" meant, was just an educated guess."

Grimand again continued along the track that no one could find the weapon that killed Gruber and no one could identify Bremen as the shooter. Therefore it was understood that Bremen, along with all the others, would be released. He couldn't even be remanded because he was not accused of anything, nor had he been formally arrested, and they knew that he had never been incarcerated. Grimand told us that his police personnel did a cursory check on Bremen, and there was nothing there. Thus all they could do with Bremen was what they did with the others—question him and release him, especially since others attested to his presence among them when the shots were fired.

Then Grimand returned to the story of the wartime Gruber assignment, presumably in the north of Germany. Grimand went on:

"It all alludes to the possibility that these seemingly random murdered Nazis were not a random collection at all, but rather perhaps part of some identifiable collective thing, like a group of mature officers who did something, and that something needed to be protected and covered up or they would all swing. I've theorized about it for many years. It couldn't be young soldiers because they could be easily tempted. Tempted about what, I asked myself? It's got to be money—and lots of it. Therefore, the killings were not, and are not, random. Of that I'm sure. So what we know is that during the war Klaus Gruber was part of a contingent of senior soldiers in their forties, assigned to guard a bank perhaps in the north of Germany. And we know that Hans Milch had also been given an assignment in the north of Germany. No, no, my friends, we're dealing here with links between all these assassinated individuals. And it's clear to me that these killings were assassinations and probably, as Chief Garelik correctly surmises, by one of the band. It's brought me to the conclusion that my initial hunch that a either a gang of revenge-seeking Jews, or perhaps a sole Jewish Nazi hunter, was at the bottom of it was wrong. Now I believe the killer—singular—was one of the band that was guarding that bank—again, perhaps in the north of Germany."

We were excited about the possibility that all of it might be tied together. But Grimand wasn't finished.

"It's possible," Grimand continued, "that the witness, Bremen, could be a vital source of what could turn out to be crucial information." Grimand further told us that, among others, Bremen was commanded to remain in Paris, at least for two more days, until he, Grimand might want to talk to him again. Grimand then added that an around-the-clock surveillance of Bremen's whereabouts had been established.

Grimand finally told us why he became suspicious of Bremen. Apparently, Bremen appeared to like the idea of being consulted and being part of this process of police work. It seemed to be an exciting and welcome contrast to him: this positive police work going up against some negative Nazi group. When Grimand, quoting Bremen, said "negative Nazi," my first thought was: *redundancy*.

Then Grimand dropped a bomb. He stated that before Bremen excused himself and was about to take his leave, he turned to Grimand and said: "Chief Grimand, you're not the only expert on this case of serial killing of ex-Nazis. I've been following these cases now for years. I've known all about your work and have followed your investigations of these murders. I've been trying to tie them together because I believe there *is* in fact a tie-in (he emphasized the "is"), and I think I intuit one or two more things that could be a further tie-in."

In response, Grimand said: "Mr. Bremen, we need to protect you because there was uniform confirmation from each and every person we questioned. They all agreed to have heard four pops, four shots. You've also reported hearing the four pops. Two of the bullets hit Gruber, but the other two have not been found and no one else was hit. Could it be that you yourself or some other person in the crowd was a possible second target?"

Rostmann seemed to disregard the suggestion as though it was completely irrelevant.

Grimand said that Bremen's intrigue regarding the killings of these Nazis usually reflected a suspect's obsessive focus on such an issue and, similarly, reveals the suspect's actual connection to the crime. Thus Grimand was almost sure that Bremen needed to be investigated.

At this point I couldn't help but intervene. "By the way, Inspector Grimand, what you say about Bremen's interest in such cases and his leaning into it might by some be considered what in psychoanalytic language is called counterphobic behavior; that is, moving into a situation about which, underneath it all, you're basically fearful and, in fact, would rather be away from. It's a way of denying one's fear. However, even more relevant regarding Bremen's behavior is that it has the diagnostic feel of psychopathic bluster. I, myself, would not assess his leaning into you, or it, as a counterphobic reaction. There's no doubt in my mind that such behavior, putting himself in the limelight, is strictly psychopathic and, on second thought, not at all counterphobic."

I was reminded that immediately before Garelik took the baton to start the meeting, Grimand said: "Bremen is a prime suspect." And to that I asked: "Is Bremen short or tall?"

Grimand answered: "He's kind of tall but has an awkward gait."

"That's it," I quickly said, excitedly. "That's it. In at least a few of the killings, a tallish man with an awkward gait was seen on the scene. Now, that's something!"

"Yes, said Grimand. "For me, that says it all." Looking at Garelik, Grimand asked him to finally again introduce us all to one another and suggested that perhaps we should say what we do as professionals, specifically. Garelik did just that. There were eight attending: Garelik, Grimand, Tancredi, Persson of Interpol, Tess and I, and two other officers, Detective Dave Stein and Detective Jack McBride. We were told that Stein and McBride were best friends and had worked together for many years. Among other talents, they were noted specialists in tracing and tracking. Garelik made a point of letting us know that he specifically wanted Stein and McBride to be part of our joint efforts. We all said a word or two about our specialties.

Of the eight of us, Garelik, Grimand, Stein, and I were Jewish — half. I was surprised by this little metric because of the stereotype and incidence of both the ethnicities of police, on the one hand, and people that get into trouble, on the other. This kind of demographic stereotype is usually not related to anything or anyone Jewish. Of course, it happens, but not usually. For example, here in America the proportion of Jews that commit violent crimes is significantly lower than that of the mainstream Christian population, and the proportion of Jews working in law enforcement (not counting lawyers or judges) is also significantly lower. I was guessing this Nazi thing as it relates to Jews got my nerve endings to vibrate right down to every fiber and organ of my body.

Grimand was a tall robust man. He spoke great English, with a touch of a French accent, and, despite his Italian heritage, there was no trace of an Italian accent. He was very natural and respectful, and it was evident to everyone present that he was quite competent. Tancredi told us later that from the moment he met Grimand, several years before, he liked him immediately, and, it seemed, for the same reason we all did.

Garelik was all business. He spoke in a kind of monotone, but it was obvious that he quickly became absorbed in the problem at hand. He seemed to be the perfect example of someone who valued group think. Stein and McBride didn't say much — actually nothing at all. They just took it all in. Tancredi and Grimand did most of the talking, while Persson was listening intently, also taking it all in.

One of the things Tancredi mentioned concerned the peculiar find in my safe deposit box that I had told him about, and about which I had earlier felt shocked and, as a result, jumped out of my seat when I heard the name Bremen.

Addressing Tancredi, I immediately said: "No photo there, only the passport." I then added that I had no idea how that passport got into my safe deposit box.

After we talked about the Bremen passport we seemed to agree that a definite link existed between those that over the years were murdered, and now the Bremen passport in my bank safe deposit box. Further, Garelik seconded Grimand's theory that I also originally thought of as born of an edgy far-out idea — actually a radical one — that one of a certain group might be trying to eliminate all the others of that group as a way of protecting himself from prosecution or for some other reason. Garelik also admitted that the theory was, as he put it, "a speculative presumption." At the same time, he didn't dismiss it. He added: "In addition, and in my experience, whenever there's something this complicated — either a big case like this or even some other less complicated one – nevertheless it's usually a good guess that somehow money is involved."

Grimond picked it up. "I think the theory is growing. It would mean that, of these Nazis that we know were murdered, they could have been part of a group, and it was this particular group that did something so bad that, at all costs, the revelation of this deed, whatever the deed was — was possibly, according to one member of the group, needing to be forever in a state of the most inert condition of silence." He continued: "And that would mean: Kill them all!"

"I believe," Grimand proceeded, "that one of the group can be imagined as the one whose sentiment is to 'kill them all.' For me, the iota of, let's say, 'almost-evidence' of this theory is that a single operator is doing it all and that this operator, acting perhaps alone, is solely at the bottom of it. Of course, the whys and wherefores remain to be determined."

It was obviously and finally agreed that Bremen was our only lead.

* * *

Garelik was as always, all business. He insisted that Tess and I pack up and move into a suite at the Waldorf, all payment taken care of. He said: "No arguments!" So back to my apartment on Gramercy Park, packed up again, and headed to the Waldorf, accompanied by two detectives. One of them escorted us to our two-room suite. We were in our room, and he entered his. The other detective stationed himself in the lobby, located so that he would have a view of who was walking toward the bank of elevators as well as of the concierge's desk. The desk people were informed that any phone calls to Dr. Cole's room should immediately be signaled to the detective sitting nearby, the one monitoring the path to the elevators and near the concierge desk.

We weren't in the room ten minutes when the phone rang. It was Detective Stein. He and McBride wanted us to know that they would be in constant touch with us in order to give us a running commentary of their plans and their progress. McBride wanted me to know that he believed in intuitive spontaneous associations to things—especially those things that in some way might relate to the case. Therefore, he said that since I was the one involved from the beginning, he wanted me to be free to tell him any thought, no matter how wild I might have about anything even remotely related to the case or anything else I might decide not to say because I thought it to be entirely ridiculous even to mention. He assured me that it was those kinds of thoughts that interested him. I promised him I wouldn't hold anything back, no matter how ridiculous it might feel to me. I also mentioned that it's that exact kind of faith in free association and in someone's stream of consciousness that qualifies as my bread and butter in the work I do—both in the classroom and then again especially in the psychotherapy room.

McBride ended our conversation on a high note by telling me that although he had never been in psychotherapy, nevertheless he believed in it and, in addition, felt that he might have been good as a therapist. He told me he had often contemplated how he would be with patients in such situations. My response was positive, and I told him I agreed, that I thought he would be very good. I meant it.

Stein got on the phone and told me that they were planning a major sweep of all the various documentation centers housing archives of the Second World War. They were also going to see if they could get a fix on the town of Bremen, in Germany—in the north of Germany. They decided it was that town that attracted this squad of Nazis to do whatever it was they did. Apparently, in their search of towns named Bremen in the north of Germany, they found that one. They quoted Garelik, who once said to them: something "interstitial," a "bridge," to the name Roland Bremen is what was needed.

About ten days had passed, and we were still nestled at the Waldorf—the three of us. Tess was told by Tancredi that he would make it

OK at her institute, meaning that her absence would not be seen as a mutational event as though it were an abandonment. In turn I also called the dean at the university, expressed my apologies, and explained that I was taking an emergency leave that might last for some time, which I would explain upon my return.

Tess and I stayed mostly at the hotel. We took occasional walks, and in these instances we were accompanied by our two detective-shadows.

Then, when we were beginning to go stir-crazy, Dave Stein called to say that, in fact, the first thing they did was to research the Bremen town in Germany. They were excited that a major attraction in the town was a large statue. Then he said:

"Are you ready for this? The statue is none other than someone named Roland Bremen." Apparently, Roland Bremen was referred to as Knight Bremen and was considered mythically to be the city of Bremen's forever protector. Roland, the Knight Bremen, was known as Charlemagne's knight. Charlemagne was then known as Charles the Great or, in German, Karl der Grosse. Sometime about the ninth century Charlemagne was known as the so-called father of Europe. Stein also reported that their research revealed that Roland Bremen's fame, his notoriety, only crystallized in the earliest part of the fifteenth century, about six-hundred or so years ago, and he was eventually immortalized by that huge town statue on the main square, symbolically standing guard opposite the cathedral, for any visitors and for all people of the town to see.

They got all of this information while they were paying a visit to Bremen, where they perused the town and then spent a great deal of time scouring records kept at Bremen's Town Hall. The most important thing they hit upon was that during the Second World War, on October 8, 1943, Bremen was unmercifully bombed by allied forces. Much of the bombing was done at night, and the target was the Bremen shipyards, which were successfully destroyed. These were the shipyards that were largely responsible for building Hitler's Navy. They included Atlas Werke Shipbuilding Co., Bremer Vulcan Shipyard, DeSchiMAG (A. G. Wesser) Shipyard, and Valentin Submarine Pens for the shelter of U-boats. Feller Industries owned the land, so that Feller was, in essence, the umbrella covering it all.

The history of the bombing raid was described meticulously by a variety of elderly townspeople. Through the interviews, information was pieced together about the bombing. Apparently, during the air raid the town was under a blackout order that was strictly enforced. No lights anywhere! Stein said that then it became interesting because he and McBride double-checked this story with the British Secret Service (known as the Secret Intelligence Service [SIS] or as the Military Intelligence, Section 6 [MI 6]), which quickly located the log of one of the pilots of the raid, who, in his sworn testimony, stated that the town was initially completely blacked out so that there was no way to see where or what to bomb. But suddenly, he saw a powerful headlight or some other kind of spotlight that seemed to be shining directly at his plane. This powerful light was also spotted by the other pilots and so the bombardiers in all the planes were ordered to drop their bombs. The town was devastated, the main target, the Bremen shipyards, were essentially wiped out — rendered useless.

Stein also related that the pilot who reported it could swear that the light that shone so brightly was deliberately turned on to call attention to the target. The other fascinating finding was lifted out of one of the narratives given by a parishioner of the town's cathedral. He said that there was a contingent of soldiers, actually a squad of about ten or twelve soldiers whose duty it was to guard the town bank. Apparently, the bank contained most of the treasure of the town, plus a phenomenal amount of money that was going to be paid to the Bremen shipbuilding companies.

"We also traced records of these shipbuilding companies that were recorded in the Feller books. The records showed that payment to these companies held in the Bremen bank amounted to one hundred million dollars. And, remember, Stein iterated, that this was the early 1940s and that kind of money was a once in a lifetime fortune. The interview with one of the survivors of the bombing, a Herr Hoepker, who worked as an administrator at Feller's, said that to the best of his memory the shipyards were contracted to build three destroyers, a number of smaller craft, and submarines, and that the numbers of submarines had not yet been specified in the contract, but it was the number of submarines that was most important, despite the fact that an aircraft carrier was also ordered.

"He said the issue was that disbursement to these shipyard companies was not to be finalized until the number of submarines — U-boats — was decided upon. Herr Hoepker vividly remembered the controversy about the payment. It was finally specified that the General Staff wanted six more submarines. The problem was that Feller couldn't yet estimate whether or not the combined shipyards could provide another six submarines, no less an aircraft carrier. Feller figured that the best estimate was four submarines—two-thirds of the total required. The worry was that work at hand in their four shipyards—linked one to the other and spanning a distance of about one-half mile—was all at full capacity already, and so to produce all that was ordered would probably not be possible. Four subs perhaps, but not six. Yet Berlin insisted, so that's what the deal was with the contract, thus keeping the leviathan payment securely held in the bank.

"These shipyards comprised a major employment industry; employing more than three thousand workers. It was the largest industry of the entire Bavarian region. When the ships and submarines were finally ready for sea, they were launched from a major port on the River Weser in Bremen. The shipyards abutted the river, and the launches, whenever they occurred—and they indeed occurred on a regular basis—were always accompanied by a big gala send-off.

"Now comes the important stuff," Stein added. "The money, that humongous amount, was never recovered, and the ten or so soldiers never heard from. The conclusion of an investigation claimed that everything was destroyed by the devastating carpet bombing, and that ended all discussions."

Then Stein warned us: "Are you ready for this? We contacted the tactical command in Berlin and asked them for the names of the ten or twelve soldiers that comprised the squad ordered to guard that bank in Bremen, during the allied bombing raid occurring on the night of October 8, 1943. They assured us that they have the information and we would receive it in a day or so. We've called Garelik, and he's called a meeting three days hence for us all to attend. Notification is going out as we speak."

I told Tess what I had just heard and we both felt that in our usual unheralded day-to-day work we were now starring in a major undertaking. Yet we dreaded waiting three more days, but at the Waldorf, in New York City, at least we would have no need to take a transatlantic flight or a flight across the country in order to get to Garelik's office three days hence.

PART 4

ROWDY

·7·

ROWDY

We all convened at Garelik's. No one was late. Only the principals attended, Tancredi from Milan and Grimand from Paris. Persson from Sweden also attended. Tess from the USA but was situated in Milan. Dave Stein, Jack McBride, Garelik, and of course me, all from New York. Garelik greeted us and started out with a bang.

"Dave and Jack our expert tracers and trackers did their jobs very well. Congratulations, guys." We all nodded and were excited about what was coming.

"OK, here it is," Stein said.

" OK. Jack and I have been to Germany and talked to various people at their BND—that's their secret service. We've also contacted the British Secret Service and checked the various Jewish documentation services worldwide. Here it is." Then, as a surprise, he announced, "Bremen, the guy named Bremen who was questioned in the Gruber killing, and the statue named Bremen, and the passport Dr. Cole found in his bank box is also the town in Germany named Bremen. And we tracked how that allied bombardment destroyed the town and shipyards, killing a few hundred people in the raid. Jack, you tell it."

Jack jumped right into it. "Okay, the bank was being guarded by a contingent of exactly ten soldiers. This squad was guarding what was in the bank—a hundred million dollars as payment to the shipyard companies for the construction of an armada of ships. Here's something fascinating. We believe that this squad deliberately made it possible for the bombers to pinpoint the town for destruction. Dave and I think it was the perfect way to cover their tracks because it was obvious that they had already transferred the money. By the way, can you believe this? It was cold U.S. cash. They must have transported the money in trucks, as quietly as possible in the dead of night while the town was asleep. Then we believe they decided to destroy the whole town and as many people as possible. If this is true, these ten men are responsible for the deaths of all those people. We're in the process of getting that information but we don't have it yet. To this day, as far as we can tell, no one knows where the money went or who has it.

"And here's the count of the ten sent to us by the German Secret Service in Berlin."

Jack nodded to Dave and Dave started listing.

> "Klaus Gruber, the guy just recently shot dead.
> Gerhardt Eisler, killed with a shotgun fifteen years ago.
> Hans Milch, recently stabbed to death.
> Horst Kabkow, also recently stabbed to death.

"This information came from our friend here, Jacques Grimand, who knew of three others who were gunned down." Dave gestured to Grimand who took the floor.

"There's Alois Amsel, Heinrich Jaeger, and, Franz Hoch—all gunned down."

Jack added, " these are also the names the Secret Service in Berlin sent us as part of the ten. So now we're up to seven. The remaining three haven't been located. Their names are:

> Wofgang Kluge,
> Walther Koertig and
> Marcus Rostmann."

"My God," I practically shouted. "That's Rowdy's middle name: Rostmann."

Then it hit me. "Wait a minute," I said. "I have a friend by the name of Rowan Quinn. His full name is Charles Rostmann Quinn. He calls himself Rowdy. Once when we were adolescents and were becoming friends, he mentioned his middle name was Rostmann. We never talked about it again. There's a weird Rostmann connection here. Also, wait a minute, Rowdy's tall and bony, very thin. He has some disease, the diagnostic name of which I can't quite remember. But he can't gain weight, and because of this bone thing he walks in a peculiar, kind of semistooped manner. He calls himself Rowdy—as a nickname—but when he wants to be formal he changes his given name, Charles, to Rowan, but prefers his nickname Rowdy.

"He's my friend, but quite frankly he's sometimes difficult to be with for any stretch of time because he's never relaxed. He's a guy who is highly competitive with a gigantic inferiority complex. To tell you the truth, I've always felt he's competitive with me but he feels he can't really win the competition. If he ever saw Tess here, he would drop dead on the spot.

"I'm not sure how or if it ties in, but I can't help seeing the Rostmann coincidence. Rowdy's my age. This one is difficult for me."

Before I could continue, Persson, for the first time, said, "It's interesting," and, almost at the same time, McBride chimed in and simply accented Persson: "Yeah." Tancredi was shaking his head in agreement, and Grimand was looking at Tancredi, also nodding yes. Garelik was taking it all in, and Tess and I were looking at each other in wonder, but I was also feeling concerned—about Rowdy.

Garelik assigned Stein and McBride the task of getting a full dossier on Rowdy. He wanted anything and everything on Rowdy and any family members. Names, dates, places. He wanted a thorough examination of it all, and he wanted it done by his tracing and tracking experts. He told them to be in constant touch with Grimand because, whatever data might be uncovered here in America, he wanted Grimand to follow through with it in Europe.

He then told Tancredi, who would be doing his own checking out of his office in Milan, to be in constant touch with Grimand in Paris. He asked Grimand and Persson to also follow through interstitial leads that might be connected to anything else or on other individuals they might have in their files that in any way related to the name Rostmann or, for that matter, to the name Bremen—Roland Bremen. He also again explained that *interstitial* means like something that forms a bridge between one thing or another—and, in this case, between the name Rostmann and/or Bremen and/or any other person.

Looking at me and at Tess, Garelik said that for the purpose of protecting us, he was going to maintain his twenty-four hour surveillance. He also wanted us to keep a tally, a log of where and why we went wherever we went. And with that, he told us all that at some point he would schedule another meeting.

We all lingered a bit and talked. But it wasn't random talk. We talked only about the pressing issue. And the pressing issue was to try to figure out this Rostmann thing. However, if Rostmann was the culprit, then he's the Nazi worm, who was protecting himself by killing other Nazi worms. It was a lair of Nazi conspirators who, Detective Stein impulsively said, had made themselves very rich by murdering and stealing. McBride chimed in to say that whatever they took must have included something extremely important. Otherwise why all these assassinations? We all agreed it had to be about money.

It suddenly got very quiet.

"Wait a minute," I said. Wait a min-ute." There's no doubt. Rostmann is the one doing the killings. He's in back of it. If he kills who is it," I hesitated. Dave volunteered: "Wolfgang Kluge and Walther Koertig."

"Right," I said. "If he kills them, then he's got whatever loot is left and I'll bet it's still an enormous amount. It accomplishes two things — he then would be free of any accusation as a traitor and murderer and also, he would no longer worry that one of the others might get *him*. Obviously, at the moment they're all afraid of each other and are in hiding. At least the two, Kluge and,"

"Koertig," Dave chimed in.

"Right, Koertig."

Tancredi took the floor and said: "Alex, we've got to get to your friend with the Rostmann middle name — Rowdy. You're going to need to start a dialogue with him, and we all need to hear it. With all of us present he won't be able to conceal anything. We'll get it out of him with relative ease."

"Nope, Chief," I said. "Rowdy would never go for that kind of audience. He's a bit closed off. With strangers he would play it close to the vest. He'd be tongue-tied in such company. I've known him for a long time and I've seen him in a variety of situations. I'm sure I'm right about this. I'm going to have to have that conversation with him in private because he'll insist on it.

"In that case," Garelik interrupted, "should you know the meeting place, we'll get there first and set up to record it all."

"Rowdy's too smart for that. He'll probably tell me at the very last minute where to meet. I'd bet on it. And if you're thinking of wiring me up, that could be dangerous, because he's definitely going to guess that I might be wearing a wire and he'll want to check it. Even though we've been friends forever, I'm now feeling a bit worried about meeting him in private because of this Rostmann thing. I have an image of Rowdy either as an accomplice to these goings-on, even though that's also very hard for me to believe, or as the killer himself, and that's even harder for me to believe. And my so-called paranoid concern is anchored in the reality of the situation. Murders have been committed!"

Then I thought that for me the most interesting psychological thing of all is that my unconscious dream-ghost was telling me: "Be careful of Rowdy." Now I'm thinking—"or something connected to Rowdy." Of course, now I think I understood why I didn't permit my ghost in my dream, my observing-ego, to tell me it was Rowdy. I didn't want to know, to find out that Rowdy, my friend, may have been involved in it all.

* * *

Nevertheless, I dialed Rowdy's number from Garelik's office phone. Garelik said the phone was safe in that it doesn't permit tracing. I got Rowdy's voice mail and asked him to call me. I told him I wanted to talk something over that he might be helpful with.

Now, I thought, we wait.

I looked around the room, and everyone was looking around as well. Sitting at his desk, Garelik was leafing through a thick file of all of the notes and verbatim transcripts taken down by his tracing and tracking experts as well as by other detectives who had questioned witnesses at a number of the other killings.

"How about this one?" he announced. "Here's a lady, name, Gina Herrera, forty-four, who was questioned about the stabbing on the street in Milan." Looking at Tancredi, he said: "Aldo, this was your case."

"Yes," Tancredi answered. "I remember her clearly. She was quite attractive and was the only one who had a different description of the guy who she said was walking nearest the victim. What was his name? Here it is.

He's the one we discovered was Hans Milch, the same Hans Milch on McBride's listing of one of the Nazi ten, who in 1943 was apparently 40 years old when he was on the squad.

"Anyway," Garelik continued, "she said the killer might have been this guy who was in the street closest to Milch. She figured he might very well have been the killer. The note quotes her: 'You couldn't miss that he was short and stout.' She called him 'burly.' It says here she estimated his height to be about five-five, or five-six, calling him 'kind of short but sturdy.' She added: 'He was 'thick-bodied.'"

"Oops," I jumped in. "That's out of line with every other description of the possible killer, and not only with respect to the Milch killing but to every description we have of the other assassinations. It's the exact opposite. All these other descriptions of the man walking away from the murders described his height as being tall or tallish—not five-five or five-six—further, this lady called him sturdy and thick-bodied. Our guy was always identified as not so sturdy—some people said he had a limp—and that he seemed, let's say, a bit fragile, but definitely not thick-bodied."

That sounded right to the others, and just about everyone sitting around was nodding yes. Dave Stein volunteered: "I think we should check on what's her name: Gina something."

"Herrera," Garelik instantly answered.

"That's right, Gina Herrera," Dave confirmed.

"Let's do it right now," Garelik ordered. "Jack, look up this mid-forties gal. Let's see what comes up."

"It's a huge contrast, Dr. Cole," Garelik said. Of course we all agree with you that everyone describes the guy the same way except this lady who then goes ahead and describes him—or someone—in exactly the opposite way, and on all counts."

Carl Persson of Interpol, who was usually pensive and thoughtful, with the manners of a saint, couldn't resist querying me:

"Dr. Cole, what do you mean? What are you suggesting?"

"I'm not sure, but I confess that I'm a bit paranoid about this whole case. And, I've also been having some psychological symptom of my own. Chief Tancredi and Tess here know about it. I've started to see a shrink about it. It concerns—and I hate to say this—my nagging feeling that I've done something wrong, like maybe shooting someone. It's technically, in shrink-talk, called an enosiophobia. That means I'm convicting myself of something that I really had nothing to do with. I can sense it or something like it, but not always. It's when I awaken from a dream sometimes. As a matter of fact, in one or two dreams I've had this same feeling. These were dreams in which my friend Rowdy also played a part. One dream had to do with finding a bag of money in a canvas bag that belonged to a bank and Rowdy and I took it and kept it. And, no, I've never killed anyone and never robbed a bank. I know that, but I've reminded myself on more than one occasion that what one knows is never as compelling as what one feels. So there you have it. My knowing I'm in the clear is not really sufficient for me to feel free of guilt. That other stuff lingers."

They were all looking at me—I broke the silence.

"I can honestly say that everything that's happened, especially the killings, where I was there, as I might say, as a witness, for me, the comforting thought was that I was never anywhere near those assassinations. This was confirmed by several people, including Chief Tancredi here, and Dr. McFarland—Tess. This empirical stuff, I think, has liberated me from the din, from my own obsession. I might be free of it." I paused. "Maybe."

At that moment, the door opened, and McBride, who Garelik sent out to get some data on the Herrera woman, rushed in. "There's no such person as Gina Herrera at the address she provided. I also checked our data bank. Nothing. No Gina Herrera."

"Jean!" I shouted. It hit me. "It's Jean, the woman I met on the plane and the one who called me on the phone at the hotel." I looked at Tess. "Tess, it was the same woman. I'll bet she's Gina Herrera and that she deliberately gave a contrary description of the killer over and against the description offered by everyone else."

Dave Stein piped in: "Gina or Jean: It's the same name."

"OK everyone, here's a thumbnail sketch of my contact with this Gina, or the name she gave me, which was Jean. Pretty close, Dave's right. First, I met her on a flight to Vienna. She was someone I would usually try to avoid, because she was a true manic talker. Talked a blue streak. Then in Paris I discovered she lifted some papers I had that actually were loaded with notes on my concern that I just mentioned here related to my enosiophobic condition. She lifted those papers while I slept on the plane in the seat right next to hers.

"Then Tess and I almost simultaneously predicted that Jean or Gina was a confederate of the killer or had some connection to the killer. Later she called me at my apartment in New York. I confronted her and she didn't blink. She just told me she was instructed to give me a message. The message was actually a taunt that the other person, maybe the assassin, wanted me to consider. The taunt was essentially telling me that I would never be sure that the killings weren't my doing, that my guilt may be justified, and that he himself may, or perhaps may not, be involved. Clearly, the taunt was designed to confuse me, to sustain my enosiophobic tension about the whole thing.

"The truth is that after the phone call, and especially if Tess had not been there, I might have gone a bit bananas with anxiety, although I'm sure I wouldn't have gone off the edge. It was because the taunt worked. It elevated my sense that the enosiophobia might not be a psychological symptom but a reality—not that maybe I might have done something wrong somewhere, sometime, to someone or someones, but that I did, in fact, do whatever it is that I thought was wrong to do. In this case it was assassinations—plural. Tess rescued me from all of it by pointing out that his whole message to me was too dramatic and an obvious attempt to bait me. At this point I'm no longer obsessed—I think—at least in that way."

"You've got my vote," Tancredi said. "Me too, Grimand chimed in." McBride and Stein were nodding yes, as was Persson—and Garelik was just taking it all in. He wasn't saying a thing. Nothing. But then he broke his own mood.

"OK," he said, "the plot just thickened. We've got a cast of characters: the assassin or assassins, this Gina or Jean, and the seven dead Nazi soldiers along with the three others, one of whom might be the star. The question is can everyone in this room, as our contingent, our squad, be good enough to triumph over their squad?" And, for whatever reason, maybe to be cute, he added: "When I say everyone in this room, I mean you, too, Dr. McFarland."

Garelik had charm.

*   *   *

Several days later this entire squad, our contingent, was notified by Garelik that one of the remaining three Nazi fugitives, Walther Koertig was confirmed by a relative as having died of natural causes at the age of eighty-eight in a small village in Germany. Garelik's note was communicated to every member of our unit. Apparently, after this relative found Koertig dead in bed, he called the police. Cause of death was listed as heart failure. The police discovered that he was a disappeared person who remained on their list of suspected Nazi criminals. The notification by Garelik also stated that McBride and Stein were immediately dispatched to Germany in order to see what they could uncover about this Walther Koertig, whom we, not so coincidentally, also had on our list of the squad of ten.

Garelik's note added: "Here's what our guys sent."

> We're in Bavaria, in town of Dinkelsbuhl. Tiny town. Not tourist attraction. Koertig living with relative more than two decades. Relative, close cousin. Cousin said Koertig rarely left house. No vacations, no visits. Every few years would take leave for one to two weeks, but cousin never told where or why. Cousin sure not for purpose of vacation. Only people Koertig spoke to or saw was cousin, also delivery people in town. Cousin said subject was avid reader, loved puzzles, all kinds, even jigsaw. Dinkelsbuhl not touched by allied bombing. Town always intact. In 1961 Hollywood company MGM filmed *The Wonderful World of the Brothers Grimm* in Dinkelsbuhl. Town flooded with film people. Cousin stated Koertig private person, but relationship with cousin good. World War II—Koertig soldier in army, assigned to battalion in Germany—north. No further information on this yet. Cousin stated Koertig paid all bills. Cousin forever grateful. Never had to work. Koertig paid for everything. Koertig never spoke about money. Cousin never asked. Only thing cousin knew was strange was every few years Koertig would leave for a week to ten days, but then always returned without ever mentioning where he went, but carried with him two or three heavy suitcases. Cousin never knew what was in the suitcases. Also, cousin knew Koertig would keep money in his bedroom. Cousin said understanding between them was no questions. Still gathering info.

Garelik then ended the note by reminding everyone that the only other two survivors of the squad on the list were Wolfgang Kluge and Marcus Rostmann. He didn't neglect to again refer to McBride and Stein as having a kind of collective genius in tracing and tracking. He was obviously proud of them; anyone could see how much Garelik appreciated their participation on the case.

*   *   *

Tess immediately re-read Garelik's note, looked at me and said: "If he gets Kluge, he'll have the entire remaining treasure—and I'll bet it's a lot, maybe most of what they took—and no one will ever hear from him again. There will be no one else to kill. He'll be entirely hidden in personal disguise, and geographical disguise. The only chance to get on to him is going to be your hopeful conversation with Rowdy."

She was right. Rowdy was the only solution here. He either knew about it all, or at least about some of it, or he's actually in on it, or we're barking up the wrong tree. There's also a chance that Rowdy knows nothing about anything, but is acting-out some craziness about himself in relation to me. Quite frankly, I didn't have much faith in this last probability. My hunch was that it was rather one of the two. Either he knew about it all, but never revealed anything for fear of compromising a relative—perhaps a very close relative, or, he was an accomplice to serial assassinations. There's another possibility. Maybe Rowdy is acting-out some perverse competitiveness with me, and successfully aggravating my enosiophobic torture—whether willful on his part or not.

I had a final thought. Tess said he would have no one else to kill. That shook me for a second because, well, I didn't immediately know what the "because" was. Then, of course, it hit me like a Mack truck. The one other person he might have reason to kill is me. He might think that because of my relationship with Rowdy I might know sensitive information, which, of course, I don't. But, given the stakes here, I really don't think he would take a chance on just letting it go.

No, I thought, I could be on his list.

Then I looked at Tess and she was startled.

"Tess, think of this. What if Kluge, the remaining one, other than Rostmann, is also a killer, also an assassin, and that he, too, was responsible for some of the assassinations. Rostmann and Kluge might be suspecting each other as having a race to be the last man standing, or could it be that they were in cahoots?"

"Oh my, Alex, you can't resist complexity."

"Maybe the world is complex, Tess. How about that? I'm calling Garelik.

* * *

The Waldorf was getting more and more comfortable. Food was always available, laundry taken care of, our shadows invariably shadowing, Garelik kept in constant touch, and so we languished in luxury. Then the phone rang.

"Al, it's Rowdy."

My heart was racing. "Yeah, Rowd, you actually called."

"Yeah, of course. What's up?"

"I've got to talk to you about something important, but I want to see you in person. Can we get together and talk about it. OK?"

"Not OK, Al. Something funny's going on. Why can't we talk on the phone?"

"It's not that. It's about my enosiophobic condition. It gets worse, it gets better. But mostly worse. I think it's related to a couple of dreams I had about both of us finding things and then I would wake up thinking I did something wrong. I want to tell you the dreams in detail and talk about what I think they might mean."

"I'll tell you what, Al, let me check my schedule, and I'll call you back with a place to meet. That's the way it would be best for me."

And that's the way this brief but intense few-sentence conversation ended. Rowdy promised to call. My first thought when I hung up was really an image. In my head this image was of both of us sitting together somewhere and me saying to him: "How's Jean, Rowdy?" When I had that image I felt both exhilarated and a bit as though I had just jumped off a cliff. I felt happy but also tense—relieved to finally get it off my chest. I turned to Tess.

"Tess, it's starting. Let's see when or if he calls back. I'm calling Garelik. I'll tell him about Rowdy's call. At the moment I don't know if I'm tense or just excited or maybe even happy. I think it's all three rolled into one."

Like me, Garelik was excited by the news of Rowdy's call. He told us he had a trace on the phone in our room and that Rowdy had called from a public phone, so obviously there was no time to place a location on him. He said he expected Rowdy to call again and from another public phone, and then give me instructions about where to go next to pick up his second phone call. Then in that second phone call he would settle on the place to meet.

"In addition," Garelik said, "when you arrive at the place of the second phone call, Rowdy himself, or someone else in his place, would be spying on you from who knows where. Rowdy'll want to make sure police are not tailing you or in any other way monitoring your movements."

"Or," I answered, maybe it's nothing like that. Maybe he's entirely in the clear."

"Not a chance," Garelik answered. "Not a chance." It's all leading to Rowdy. He's very involved and he knows you know and he knows we know. He knows for sure that you've been talking to the police. I think it's him, and I think he or someone he's working with was tailing you in Vienna, in Milan, in Paris, in L.A., and now in New York City. So it's probably him and maybe the older Rostmann and maybe the woman Gina/Jean. This guy, your erstwhile friend Rowdy, is plainly nuts. You're dealing here with what's knows as a nut-job, an obsessed killer — or, if not a killer, than some sort of accomplice — but a crazy one.

"I've asked Dave to generate a dossier on Rowdy. I have it here, and there's nothing to it. It gives his name and his age — same as you, Alex, forty-one. His school record is actually mediocre, and he only had one semester of college and dropped out. No job experience whatsoever. Never married. But he has a travel record. Many trips to Europe."

"Just like my trips," I interjected. "I'll bet he was in Europe every time I was. That's it! Of course! Whenever I went to Europe I gave Rowdy my itinerary. He always knew where I was."

"Alex, we need that information," Garelik interjected. "I need you to compile a list of European trips you made — all of them. We need to know where you went, for what reason, and when you returned. Then we'll try to cross-check it with whatever we can put together regarding trips to Europe that Rowdy took.

"By the way, Alex, how did you and Rowdy originally hook up? I know this is a long phone call, but let's get it all worked out."

"OK then, here's my history in a nutshell. When I got to the states,

I was going on thirteen and I guess I learned English during that year because when I was fourteen I was placed in the first year of high school, and that's where we met. We've been friends ever since—now for more than twenty-five years. I never married, and neither did he. We were both only children. He lived with his father, whose name was Michael Quinn. His mother had died—I'm not sure how old Rowdy was when she died, but I think he was probably about twelve. She died sometime before we met. I lived with my cousins and, for whatever reason, I always noticed that Rowdy would visit me in my apartment much more than I came to his. I also always liked it that we were not in the same professional field—actually he wasn't in any field.

"In any event we always had things to talk about, but never really about psychology stuff, and for whatever reason on my part, like I said, I liked it that way. That's about all that comes to mind now. And, by the way, Rowdy's very smart. Oh, yeah, wait a minute," I almost exploded. "Now I got it! I once needed help—maybe about five years ago. I was calculating my expenses and needed to read them off to someone who would then jot them down on a sheet of paper. It was a lot, especially because of my European trips. Rowdy was the logical person to assist me with it. I knew he always liked getting together, and he actually loved when we did things together. You know, his life was pretty empty.

"In this case we were in my office at the university. I was sitting at my desk and Rowdy was at a little table near the desk. I was reading numbers to him and he was taking them down. My desk and his table were full of my financial material. It took about a half-hour or so to finish. I'm sure that must be when he slipped the Roland Bremen passport in along with a stack of papers. It's gotta be. Wow. But why in the world did he do it? What does it mean that he wanted that passport in my possession, knowing full well that someday I would find it there? And that's really the issue. He knew I would find it there! What does that mean?

"That's an important insight," Garelik said. "And," he added, "of course an important question. Why? Could it be that Rowdy knows all about everything and that he can't hold it in—that he must be rid of it or let someone know about it, even in this chopped-up and incomplete way? What that tells me is that he did not do the killings, but knew about them, and knew who did them. And it suggests to me that he got the passport into your safe deposit box because it was his way of confessing. In reality, it's a nonconfessional confession. So I think I was initially wrong. Rowdy's probably not the killer. Maybe an accomplice, but not the killer."

I was greatly relieved that the situation with Rowdy might be redeemable. Garelik reminded me that the next meeting was at his office at 2 pm the following day.

When we met at Garelik's office, Carl Persson of Interpol could no longer maintain his composure.

"Great supposition, chief. Just great. I agree 100 percent," he exclaimed. It was his enthusiasm regarding Garelik's inference that Rowdy was probably not the killer.

We were all there at the meeting and I noticed that we were all sitting in exactly the same seats as they had been arranged in Garelik's office and around his desk. It was as if we had been assigned the seats. I knew from my group process research that, using Garelik's position behind his desk as the main position in the room, the center point, then wherever anyone else sat would be a pretty good estimation of how they felt in relation to the leader.

The first thing I noticed was that Tess sat opposite Garelik. I knew from my studies that opposite means just that: oppositional. Then I thought: Is that a harbinger of something regarding how Tess would be eventually in a marriage—oppositional? I canceled that thought because I also realized that there I went again, finding a reason for the two of us not to work. Nevertheless, against my conscious wishes, the thought, still in all, squeezed itself into the position directly next to the one in my heart that indicated not only that I loved her, but was crazy in love with her.

The consistent seat I took was the one directly to the right of Garelik. I also knew that that particular position meant that I was insecure and needed Garelik's protection. Luckily, Tancredi sat next to me. I say luckily because being sandwiched by Garelik and Tancredi was, for me, a very safe place to be. I also knew that Tancredi and I had quickly become allies, friends, so that when he initially saw me sitting there, he naturally took the seat next to mine.

To a person, everyone was nodding in agreement with Garelik's inference or perhaps even his conclusion that Rowdy was not the killer—not the killer of anyone.

OK, Rowdy's not a killer, I thought. But it's probable that he knows something about it and because of that he could still be quite dangerous, even as an unwilling accomplice.

Garelik summed it up again. "Now we wait for the phone call. The question is: are you up to it, Dr. Cole? Do you want to meet with him? We can't put a wire on you because he'll find it in a second. We can't give you a weapon because a) he'll take it away, and b) you wouldn't know how to use it anyway. Therefore, it will be you and him — mano a mano. Are you ready for this?"

I later talked it over with Tess, point by Garelik point. Tess was upset.

"Don't do it. It's too risky. When that kind of loot is involved, no one will be fooling around. With that kind of money, and it must be a lot, no one takes chances. If they feel you're chancy, they will do their best to finish you. And we know for sure that their best is very good."

I knew she was right but in my unconscious mind I had decided to go. Consciously however, I was confused and even ambivalent. And I knew from my reading the social psychological literature that no one likes to live with ambiguity. I was in a bit of turmoil. It was of my own making, because my unconscious mind said go, but consciously I think I was saying don't go. It was not only ambiguity that was confusing me, it was also ambivalence. And ambivalence means that two things are pulling in opposite directions.

* * *

In the town of Hempstead, on Long Island, perhaps about thirty miles or so east of New York City in Long Islands' Nassau County, in a private house on a suburban street of private houses, Marcus Rostmann was dressing and packing a bag. He was the same elderly gent, perhaps in his mid to late seventies, or even early eighties, and going by the name of Roland Bremen, who was questioned on the Klaus Gruber killing in Paris, by none other than our illustrious Jacques Grimand.

Rostmann placed a revolver in a holster on his hip, finished dressing and packing, looked around, and walked out of the house. He drove to the railroad station and boarded a train on the Long Island Railroad to New York City. At Penn Station he hailed a cab and told the driver to take him to the Waldorf Astoria Hotel on Park Avenue.

At Park Avenue, he got out of the car and, rather than entering the Waldorf, he walked across the street, and waited. It was about 8 a.m. when he got there. He was still there at noon. Also still there at 2 p.m. Shortly after 2 p.m. he grew instantly attentive when he spotted Alex Cole exiting the Waldorf accompanied by the woman whom he identified as Tess — along with another man. No doubt, he thought, a detective.

At this time in the afternoon the street was crowded. It was a bright balmy day in May. He took his raincoat off and draped it over his arm. He then reached for his revolver and with his finger in a tight embrace on the trigger of the gun he began to maneuver himself a bit here, a bit there, in order to get the perfect shot. But it was not to happen. He changed his plan and kept walking along Park Avenue in a southerly direction, downtown. There was no doubt that he had been gunning for Cole — perhaps even for Tess. He realized his plan, to at least shoot Alex, was off the wall — especially also because Park Avenue was too wide to get a good shot.

He made a phone call on one of the street corner phone-booths.

"Jean, tell Rowan to set up the meeting with Cole. I'll take care of everything when they meet."

With that, this distinguished-looking gentleman, Marcus Rostmann, hailed a cab — first destination, Penn Station, second destination, Long Island Railroad. He was Hempstead bound. Again, he knew his plan to kill Cole and maybe Tess, too, was a terrible one — without credibility. He hadn't understood the nature of how crowded a street gets, especially on the Waldorf side on a sunny weekday afternoon. It was clear however, that he had intended to gun down Cole in broad daylight. He knew it was brazen to an extreme and, of course, unthinking and foolhardy — again, especially when he saw how wide the street was.

It was clear that Rostmann obviously could get frenzied. The question was why? Why was he so stampeded? He knew why. He needed to eliminate Alex Cole, Tess, and finally, of course, Wolfgang Kluge, the last remaining witness — if Kluge could ever be found. Then, of course, Rostmann's twisted runaway fantasies of ultimately being apprehended and then incarcerated for the rest of his life, would, in that correspondingly twisted mind of his, be inexorably leading him to the conclusion that Rowdy himself needed to go, then Jean, and even the caretaker of the cathedral in Bremen, as well as Konrad, the minister of the cathedral. Oh that cathedral!

Yes, this would-be assassin, Marcus Rostmann, was the squad leader of the 10 Nazi thieving murderers in Bremen. He was, no doubt, Rowdy's relative, maybe even his grandfather. If Rowdy was a sick competitive type, then Marcus Rostmann was a man psychologically twisted and eaten up with a me-first or even a me-only sensibility. Greedy Rostmann, with a bone disease, passed it on with it skipping a generation, appearing then in a thematic variation in his relative, probably the grandson. Thus Rowdy appeared in all of his compensatory behavior—also with a bone disease. Like grandfather, like grandson?

Now it seems that, according to Rostmann's instructions to Jean, it would be Rowdy's turn to call Alex and make the arrangement to meet. Of course, Rowdy would need to get back to this probable grandfather in order to finally coordinate it all.

In the meantime, Alex and Tess had the rest of the day out—out of the hotel room and into the world. They had a late lunch. They returned to the Waldorf, all the while being shadowed by Garelik's man. In their room Tess had a brainstorm.

*   *   *

"Alex, know what I think? I think that Rowdy's been subsidized with the monies squirreled away by Rostmann—as you believe, his probable grandfather. And the subsidy's been financing him all his growing-up years—just about all of his life. Because of it, Rowdy never needed to go to school, or work at a job or do anything. He would simply count on Rostmann for whatever he needed and, without any commotion, he would get it. Please, Alex, keep this in mind when you speak to Rowdy—if you speak to Rowdy."

"Listen, Tess."

"No, wait—something else. Has it occurred to you that if Garelik doesn't ever get to Rostmann and end this nightmare, we're destined to spend the rest of our lives living in the Waldorf and grow old with this watchdog up here with us doing his job by time to time spying on us from the adjoining room. Wait, I'm not finished yet. I'm also including the other one downstairs monitoring the elevators and checking constantly with the concierge. Is that what's going on here? Is it that we're destined to raise our children in this room?"

"Listen, Tess."

"No no, wait—I'm still not finished. I might never be finished. The truth is I need to get back to the institute and complete my year in Milan. Then I can begin my life with you—in this room?!"

"Ha, ha. Very funny. Well it's not funny at all. Rostmann absolutely must be apprehended. You're right. And the situation with Rowdy also needs to be resolved. I'm not going to feel normal until the Rowdy thing is settled. And I have a burning desire to see Jean again to have closure about the whole mess. This Jean thing's got my goat. I thought I was on my high horse when we talked on the plane while during the entire trip she was essentially laughing at me. She was doing me."

"That clears it up for me. I'm definitely going to meet with Rowdy because in all likelihood it's the only way to get to Rostmann."

"Right, I understand the logic of it, Alex, but I also know that both the grandson and the so-called grandfather know that as well, and they will be hell-bent on stopping you. And whether you know what I mean or not, I know what I mean!"

With that little typical Tess roll, I realized that the introduction to my meeting with Rowdy was now established—at least in *my* mind. Therefore, I *am* going to meet with him.

* * *

The phone rang.

"OK, Al," Rowdy said. "Let's meet. Just you and me. I'm not stupid, as you know."

"Rowd, I know you feel you're in a little bit of trouble. Am I right?"

"We'll talk about everything. Nothing gets left out," he answered.

"Rowdy, I hope what you're saying is true and, just as important, that what you say is coming strictly from you and no one else. As far as our lifelong brotherhood is concerned, that's what I'm banking on. You'll tell me things, and I'm sure you'll want me to tell you things."

"And," Rowdy said, "this is what you meant on our last phone call, that I could be helpful to you. Right?

"Yup, that's it. So where or how do we meet? And, to tell you the truth, at this point, for us to talk in these mysterious ways to one another is very uncomfortable for me. Does it bother you, Rowd?"

"Yeah, it does. I'm upset about it."

"In a way I'm glad you're upset. Know what I mean? I think we both know it means that together we have the kind of bond that's first among any other bonds each of us might have. As I'm sure you know, Rowd, my new best pal is Tess. But my bond with you goes back just about all of our lives, and that means something—especially also because, when a person gets older, making best pals becomes almost impossible to match how best pals are made when you're a kid. Right?"

There was silence.

"C'mon, Rowd, right?"

"Yeah, it's right."

"OK, where do we meet?"

"I have to tell you where to meet, but I can't say it. I just can't say it. You know what I mean?"

"I think so. I think so."

"OK then, you tell *me* where we should meet," he said.

I thought quickly because I could tell that Rowdy had probably had enough—that he had probably never killed anyone, but that now, probably knowing that Rostmann was planning my demise with Rowdy as the set-up man—Rowdy couldn't do it.

"Come to my hotel suite at the Waldorf. I'll do everything in my power to get you off completely, or, if I can't do that, depending on what your whole thing is about I'm sure I can make it as easy as possible.

"I also want to introduce you to Tess. She'll like you. She's heard all about our history. Whatever you were into, I'm sure you were a bystander—I hope you were. Of course that doesn't mean you didn't know anything. And, by the way, I found the passport in the safe deposit box and I know it refers to Bremen, Germany. When we meet, you'll tell me everything and I'll tell you everything.

"However I arrange the meeting, you've gotta trust me. OK? Come to the hotel tomorrow at noon."

"I'm not really hesitating about coming to see you," he said. "My only hesitation is in wanting to know who else will be there."

"OK. I think about eight or nine people or maybe even one or two more. These are the people who've been on the case."

"Will they be with us in the room?"

"I don't know, but they might be. I think we both would like it so that we're alone. Right? But, if I can arrange it that way, I'm also pretty sure they'd want to tape it. I wouldn't object to having it all taped, would you?"

Without any hesitation, Rowdy said: "No, no objection to any taping. I don't care anymore. OK, I'll come to you tomorrow at noon."

"Rowd, one more thing. It's your grandfather, right?"

* * *

"Tess, it *is* his grandfather, and Rowd's coming here. He agreed. He knows we'll have others here as well. He's ready to spill it all, and, provided he's never hurt anyone, I'm going to get him a deal — if possible, no booking, no accusation, no trial, no jail. If Garelik catches Rost-mann, then the terrible decision needs to be made as to how Rowdy will need to testify against him. I don't think he'll be able to do it. How's he going to testify against his grandfather? Rostmann continued to subsidize him for just about his entire life. But whatever the reason, Rostmann is the type that only does something that's in his own inter-est and not at all in the interest of the other person, even if it looks like it might be. Rowdy's appreciation though of his grandfather's largesse could put a little wrinkle in the deal, but we'll get to that. We'll need to iron it out — somehow.

"I'm calling Garelik."

I made the call to Garelik and filled him in. Tomorrow at noon it would be. He told me that Tancredi, Grimand, and Persson were planning to leave for Europe, but that time was on our side because they were still here. I mentioned to Garelik that I thought all eight of us should be at the meeting, and he agreed. That meant me, Tess, Garelik himself, Tancredi, Grimand, Persson, Stein, and McBride. With Rowdy there, I said, it would make nine, but then, thinking about it, I realized that Garelik's two detec-tives shadowing Tess and me would make it eleven.

"Chief Garelik," I said, "how are we going to fit all those people in the room?"

"No, it's good that way — crowded. It's like I said, the more crowded and intimate and even claustrophobic it all is, the greater the probability that whoever is being questioned will automatically spill. And Rowdy's the one being questioned. We've had a lot of experience with this. The only time that kind of throng doesn't work is when you're dealing with a true paranoid narcissistic killer who takes great pleasure in holding the stage and fooling everyone with his act. In this case, I hope we don't have that."

"No," I said. "Definitely not! Look, I believe he is going to open up and I told him perhaps the conversation would be taped. Everyone could be in another room and listen to what's being said in real actual time. It sounded to me that Rowdy is sick and tired of being—I guess the word is being so *duplicitous*. He's sick of it and can't be part of it anymore. But I still think mobbing him is not the thing to do. Mobbing is not for Rowdy."

Garelik thought a moment and said: "OK, we'll tape it, but we'll all definitely be close by. We'll set ourselves up in another room. But he'll be frisked the moment he shows up."

"I'm sure he'll be expecting that and he'll have no objection," I said. "I'm so stirred up by this I don't think I'll be able to sleep tonight."

But I did sleep, and at 10 a.m. the next morning we all congregated in the suite reserved for everyone else except Rowdy and me. Chairs were brought in, and I had images of it being a tight fit. On the contrary, the suite was quite large, so it wasn't a sardine case, although the room was in fact, very full.

It was agreed that the most important thing was to let Rowdy talk. Garelik indicated that he didn't want anything to interfere with the material we all thought was about to flow. I said that I thought I would start it off, and Garelik said: "Good, that's good. But, Alex, I repeat, we're frisking Rowdy before he gets anywhere near this room. We can't be sure he'll be clean, meaning without any weapon. Also keep in mind that some of these men were knifed to death while others were shot."

With that, McBride took over and went through the points that needed to be discussed. There were many.

"We need to know everything about Marcus Rostmann: where he lives; how he travels; his relation to Rowdy; the whole thing about where the loot is, how much there is, and is it hidden in the Bremen cathedral?; Who's the caretaker of the cathedral, who's the minister, and do either one of them know anything about the stolen money?; The story about Rostmann's squad of Nazi soldiers; the story about the bombing raid and whether Rostmann was the spotlight instigator; who was it that killed the others, like, for example, who stabbed Milch and who stabbed Kabkow, and who killed the other few earlier on?; Was there more than one killer?; Who is Jean or Gina?; and, What's Jean's relation to Rostmann?

McBride stopped, and Garelik ended it by adding, "And we need to hear specifically how the whole thing ties together—with all the pieces. But, of course, according to Rowdy and from what Dave and Jack have told us we need to put a noose around that cathedral in Bremen and pull it tight."

· 8 ·

ROWDY AND ALEX

At five minutes to noon, Rowdy was at the Waldorf entrance. He walked up those iconic stairs into the grand Waldorf lobby, made a beeline to the concierge desk and asked for Dr. Alex Cole's room. The man glanced toward the detective stationed in the lobby. The detective picked up the glance and walked over to Rowdy and asked him to put his hands on the desk. Then in full view of everyone, he frisked Rowdy. Within seconds they were joined by another detective who was near the lobby elevators. They both escorted Rowdy into the elevator but wouldn't permit anyone else to enter. They exited on the twelfth floor and the three of them took the stairs to the thirteenth.

As the three of them approached the room occupied by Dr. Alex Cole, our two detectives were in the corridor—covering both ends of the floor. Both detectives converged at the door, and now Rowdy was escorted into the room by four police officers.

* * *

As he entered, Rowdy quickly took it all in and spotted me. He was instructed by one of the detectives to stand between Garelik, and next to Grimand—both of whom were standing opposite me. Rowdy, uneasy, was obviously relieved that I was there.

I started. I told him I was very happy he consented to be there. Garelik took it from there. He told Rowdy that they were all police personnel directly involved in the circumstance that Rowd and I would be talking about. He said they were all going to leave, and he and I would be alone to talk. Garelik added that he knew Rowdy was OK with the taping of our conversation. Rowdy nodded. Then Garelik motioned everyone to leave the room. He also asked the four detectives to join the people who were filing out. The whole thing took about twenty seconds. In the meantime I asked Tess to wait. Then I introduced them.

"Rowd, this is Tess. She's with me—looks like permanently. Know what I mean?"

"Sure, hi Tess."

"Rowdy, I've heard so much about you, and about you and Alex. I'm very glad to meet you."

Rowdy just looked at her and thanked her. I know he was sincere. Then Tess left the room and it was just Rowdy and me. I immediately started.

"Rowd, as you know we need to get down to it all. I know you're with me."

Rowdy said a wobbly "yes" and then, with his head down, he began to whimper, to cry—actually sob.

"I never killed anyone. I know you may think I might have, but the truth is I never have and never will. But I do know who did and it's very hard for me to say it."

Without any prompting, he continued. He looked up at me and said:

"My grandfather, my mother's father, is alive. He's at the bottom of it all. I hate saying that because he's been extremely good to me my whole grown-up life. He's supported me to the point where I never had to work. I do love him—I think—and," he paused, "I hate him too. I think I'm afraid of him because I know he's capable of doing anything at all, and I mean *anything*, to keep his money safe and not get caught. All these years I let it go because I made myself believe that he was doing a good thing by killing Nazis. When I got a little older, I realized I knew that he was also a killer and a Nazi himself—no, I fudged that. He *is* a Nazi—and he escaped."

He paused, looked at me, and continued: "He's the killer the police have been looking for. I've had to keep it from you, Al—all these years." And then the words rushed out of him. "He tells me all of it. He *wants* to tell it to me. It's like he needs to get it off his chest. Or maybe he needs to review his skill at it. Yeah, I think that's more it. He needs to repeat exactly what happened, replay it, and see—again and again—how he did it. He thinks he's a genius. He *is* a genius."

Rowdy stopped. He looked directly at me and said: "Alex, ask me something, anything."

"OK, Rowd. I can't help thinking your grandfather may have even told you about all of it, including his 'skill,' as you say, even when you were young like when we became friends in our first year in high school. Did you know about it then?"

"Yes, I knew about it even before that. Maybe about a year before we met. He came to live at the house. My mother was gone. She had died, so he came and stayed with us. Eventually, he bought the house from my father and lived there when we moved into the city. That's why you never met him. He's an isolationist. That's what I would call him. He stays completely to himself. But he's very rich, and I know about that too."

I knew that Garelik, and all of us, needed to have Rostmann's address, so I interrupted Rowdy and asked him for his grandfather's address.

"He lives in Hempstead, Long Island, right near Hofstra University, at 25 Hope Street. He bought that house some years after he bought our house. The house is adjacent to the campus.

"Yeah," I said. "Remember my friend Arty? Well he attended Hofstra. Actually, he recently told me that the school is in the process of engulfing the whole neighborhood with how it keeps expanding. I'm surprised your grandfather's house is still standing."

"Oh, it's standing all right. And believe it or not, it's probably being held up by tons of money tucked inside the plaster boards of the walls. That's a joke Al, but maybe it's not a joke."

"Lots of money, huh?" My comment was simply to confirm what Rowdy was referring to but at that moment I decided not to take it further. I immediately realized, and Garelik confirmed it with me later, that the moment Rowdy stated Rostmann's address all our other operational personnel in the room with Garelik were vibrating with the information. What happened was that Garelik looked at the two detectives who had escorted Rowdy into the room. He nodded and both detectives left immediately. Obviously, Marcus Rostmann was about to have his house surrounded.

Without any interruption in his mood, Rowdy continued.

"More than twenty years ago, when he was in his sixties he met a twenty-five-year-old beautiful girl who worked at the college. The story he told me is that as she drove out of the parking lot that was close to his street, she pulled over with a flat tire. He happened to be there and offered to change the tire for her. He invited her into the house for refreshments and they've been together ever since, even though he's more than thirty years older than her. She actually joined him in the things he does. She's completely taken care of by him. He gives her whatever she wants. He's always been generous with money for her—and for me."

Rowdy paused. "There's something not so normal about her. My grandfather told me that he could tell she probably wouldn't have wanted to come back for a second visit because she was either shy or afraid. But he told me he worked on her. That's right. Like he kept on telling her that he realized he was very lucky to know her because he could never meet someone so much younger and beautiful. He kept telling her that he would do anything for her and that she should never be afraid of him or even shy around him. He knew he was giving her the feeling that she would be boss and he would do anything she wanted. I guess she had nothing in life so she began coming back, and every time she came back he kept asking her if there was anything she wanted him to do—either for her or around the house, like chores or something. She slowly changed and she broke loose and soon started acting like the boss. She wasn't shy anymore. He told me that from that time on they had sex. But she's crazy. She used to tease me, like sexual things. Sometimes when he wasn't there she'd walk around in a bra and slip."

"Rowd, did you feel like frustrated about it, the sexual stuff?"

"Yeah, I did. A lot. But nothing happened. But I thought about it all the time. I know you want her name, Al, and I know you're already guessing what it is. So you're right. It's the same Jean that you met on the plane to Vienna. Gina was Jean, the same woman who gave the police in Milan a false identification for the man who killed Hans Milch. You know, Alex, my bone disease that makes me stoop is inherited from my grandfather. It skipped a generation, because my mother never had it, but it got me. We're both about the same height, 6'2," and we both stoop. But he has a limp that I don't have. It's because one of his legs is shorter. My legs are equal.

"I feel bad, Al, that I couldn't tell you this before, but I couldn't. It was my grandfather. Understand? And I couldn't tell you about how I felt sexed-up for her. I was about sixteen."

"We'll talk it all over, Rowd. Right now, keep going about him, like where he lives."

"Well, the house is a nice little house on a quiet suburban street where all the houses have manicured lawns. You can hear a pin drop in the street wherever you walk. It's a perfect place for him. He keeps to himself, and, even though he's been living there for many years, he doesn't really know his neighbors except to nod if he happens to pass one who's on the street.

"I know that whenever he needs money — but it's not often — he goes to Europe, to a little town in the north of Germany called Bremen. I slipped his passport without his picture into your papers when we were figuring out your tax stuff. It was the only thing I could do in the way of letting you know. On his passport he names himself Roland Bremen. He told me that the townspeople of Bremen consider the real Roland Bremen to be a hero. So my grandfather took Bremen's name. He also told me that the money is hidden in the town's cathedral and it's protected by some care-taker there. He trusts the caretaker, Torsten Koppel is his name, because the caretaker was a favorite of Bishop Hudal, and that Hudal and Koppel were big shots in the bishop's Odessa underground railroad that took Nazis to other countries for their protection. Can you believe that — an under-ground railroad?

"My grandfather kept repeating these stories to me every few years. I'm sure that if he knew I was here telling you everything he wouldn't hesitate to kill me. If someone crosses him, he would kill them in a minute. I know that nothing is more important to him than his own safety. I think that even Jean wouldn't be safe, if it meant that, because of her, he was going to get caught. This, is in spite of the fact that she's loyal to him and feels attached to him.

"You know, Al, in my heart the same would be true of me. If he knew that I could get him into any kind of trouble, I don't think I would be safe either. He's not normal.

"And Mr. Koppel wouldn't be safe either if it meant that my grandfather could be in any danger because of him. He says there's so much money there that it can't all be carried away. He's also told me he worries about what would happen to it all, when him and Mr. Koppel die. He said if all goes well and he's safe, then all the money should go to me and to Jean. I think he said that Mr. Koppel keeps track of the total amount, and that it took Mr. Koppel almost a year to count it all because if he thought he made a mistake he would do it over. Then he would stack it all in smaller piles so that when someone came for more money they could carry it away easier."

With that, there was a knock on the door. I opened it and was handed a note. The note was from Garelik who wanted me to engage Rowdy in a discussion about the squad of men who originally stole the money. Garelik wanted me to read his message to Rowdy. Instead, I gave the note to Rowdy and asked him to read it aloud:

> "Mr. Quinn, could you tell us more about the squad of men that your grandfather commanded. Do you know about that?"

"Yes, I do. I know about it," Rowdy said, raising his voice as though to speak into the tape recorder.

I interrupted: "Rowd, the note is from Chief Garelik. He's in charge of the police in the city."

"OK. Yes, I know about the squad. They were Nazi soldiers who transferred the money from the bank to the basement of the church, uh, the cathedral, even before the allies bombed the city. So even though the bank was destroyed, and the cathedral was also hit by a bomb and badly damaged, the money was safe in the basement of the cathedral."

Picking up on Garelik's interest, I continued our dialogue by asking: "How was the money transferred?"

"Somehow I think with trucks, but I'm not sure why I'm saying that. I don't have a memory of my grandfather telling me anything about trucks. But he must have because I must have gotten that from him. I do know that my grandfather told me that Mr. Koppel could take whatever amount he needed for his own life. So far my grandfather estimates that about fifty million dollars was distributed to men of the squad. And this is over about a thirty-five-year period or so. Of course some of the men only collected for a few years because they were being killed. He says that more than half of what was there originally is still there. Grandfather says that millions were taken by the men each year, and grandfather has been accumulating his share all these years too. I've seen it. He keeps it in the walls of the house—that's right, in the walls, especially in the basement walls. He's an excellent carpenter so it's really impossible to see that the walls have been tampered with. Some people use asbestos as an insulator for houses but my grandfather uses stacks of hundred dollar bills. That's the truth.

"The house was built in 1940 so it's pretty old. In one of his stories, grandfather also told me that Mr. Koppel would not talk to the members of the squad, although he knew each one. When one of them would arrive, Mr. Koppel would tally out the money and then the squad member would leave with millions—usually in truckloads—oh yeah, that's where I got the idea of the trucks. Anyway, the trucks would always arrive at a nearby private airport. The packages of money would be transferred to a plane, and off they'd go.

"When news got out that one of them was murdered, grandfather said that the others, wherever they were, would have certainly gotten scared. And, even though they might have suspected one of them to be the assassin, they never knew which one it was. Until now, of course—Kluge and grandfather are the only two left. Grandfather knows that Kluge now knows that Marcus Rostmann, my grandfather, the captain of the squad, is the true assassin."

"Rowdy, that's absolutely fascinating. I'm really glad you had nothing to do with it. I know it would be almost impossible for a grandson to implicate his grandfather in any wrong-doing so I understand why you couldn't talk to me or anyone else about it. Do you know anything more about the bombing raid? Did your grandfather ever tell you any more details about it?"

"Yes, I know a lot about it. Grandfather was the one who hatched the plan, and they all went along with it. That's what I was told. They wanted to cover their tracks so that destroying the town would be their cover. Grandfather had one of the others direct a spotlight up to the sky so that the bombers would be sure to see the town. I wouldn't be a bit surprised if the allies used that destruction of the town of Bremen as a model, later on in the war when they later flattened the city of Dresden."

"Rowdy, did you ever talk to your grandfather about me?"

With no hesitation Rowdy went into it.

"Yes. I told him and Jean all about you. I told them you were my best friend, but I also told them about your *enso* thing and about how you were so successful and how I wasn't."

As Rowdy went on I was sure that all of the people in the other room were fascinated with the story, especially that Rowdy told Rostmann and Jean about me. Rowdy described how he always kept Rostmann apprised

of my situation in life. That disturbed me, but it was confirmation that
Rostmann used the information to psychologically taunt me—sadistically
torturing me.

But now it was time for Rowdy and me to have our personal talk. His
information seemed to cover all bases. Now, we needed to iron out the
wrinkles in our almost lifelong personal relationship. What was clear to
me was that Rowdy was a terribly contaminated person and that needing
to keep it all to himself all his adolescent and adult life must have surely
twisted him. Yet he was naturally intelligent. I was aware of that all of our
years knowing each other.

"Rowd," I said, "it's time we talked about us. We need to be honest with
each other. OK?"

He nodded. "You start."

*   *   *

"OK, here goes. We were friends right off the bat. When I first walked
into class not knowing a soul, you came over to me and introduced yourself. It made me feel very welcome and I never forgot it. And we've been
through a lot together. The difference is that I kept going to school, but you
didn't. I told Tess all about our history. I told her that you always had enough
money in your pocket and would even treat me to things when I didn't have
any money. She guessed that, because you had money you didn't think you
needed to put the effort into any of the school requirements. She got that
idea because I also told her you never did homework and never had a job,
but you always had money. Now, of course, we know why."

I continued. "I became a professional psychologist teaching at a university, seeing patients privately, and writing books. I want to know how you
felt about my doing all those things because if I'm doing all that and you're
not doing much in terms of advancing yourself, in terms of making some
kind of a contribution somewhere, then what did that make you feel like?"

He thought a bit and said: "Wow." Then he paused. "You were always
my best friend. I always felt that way. But the truth is I did wonder how
you did it all. I couldn't. I could never do my homework because I always
felt something was bothering me, like I was always distracted. I was constantly feeling like something inside me was agitating me. And I always
wondered why I couldn't do my school work."

"You know, Rowd, it's the same reason that a lot of kids can't do schoolwork. It's usually because when there's something in your personal life, like great difficulties at home, that makes it almost impossible to concentrate—like impossible to focus on objective material like you get in school. You know, for example, in a chemistry class, who cares to memorize that the letters NACL means salt, when at home your father, in drunken rages, is constantly abusing your mother? Things like that. See?"

"Oh yeah, that's me. I always had a bad feeling—all the time. I used to dread going to school. Never had any homework done. I just couldn't get it together. I guess it must have been that my mother was gone, then my father—but maybe even much more. You know, I was full of my grandfather's terrible stories. He even told me that I was the only one he could tell his stories to. I never told you this, Al, but I used to go around thinking that I was an assassin like him, but in my case I was only killing bad guys. And I had this bone disease, you know, a lot of stuff. I also compared us. Your uncle and aunt were great. My mother died. Because of my physique, I wasn't successful with girls the way you were. So, I felt that everything came easy to you but not to me."

"I was aware of it Rowd, and I felt bad about it."

"You don't have to say anything about it, Al. None of it was your fault."

"Okay, Rowd. For the moment, let's get back to Jean. Do you and Jean talk to each other? I mean we both know she's a juiced-up talker, even more than you and me put together. So maybe my hunch is that she wins because of the fact that she's a real manic talker. She's also older, and maybe you back off because she's got your grandfather's ear."

"You wanna know about Jean, Al? How about this? My grandfather bragged to me that she was the one who killed Klaus Gruber. Shot him with the silencer. They planned it so that my grandfather would be coming out of the theater with the crowd and would be completely in the clear as the killer. And I'm glad I'm telling you. Yeah, I'm definitely angry at her. But that's all besides the point. The main point is that I myself do kind of strange things. Nothing serious, but sometimes I just try to figure out how to spend the day, and before I know it it's nighttime. Sometimes it's really lonely so that while I'm walking alone, I'll pick out someone in the street and I'll follow them like from a distance—sometimes for blocks and blocks. It's because I have nothing else to do. I think I'm feeling tired now, Al."

"OK, Rowd, I get it. I think that what you said here today is your liberation. I'm not sure how many people, even those sitting in the next room listening to us, would have the courage to tackle what you've done here today. In my opinion, you've untangled yourself from a strait-jacket."

Even though I thought Rowdy was losing his energy, he surprised me by continuing the discussion.

"You know, Al, I always wondered what this thing is you have about thinking or feeling that you've done something wrong. It's me that's done the wrong or stupid things, not you. I've even had the thought that your feeling of having done something wrong had something to do with me, like we used to kid around when we were young saying that we channel each other. Remember that? You know, you sensing the whole wrong thing in me and transferring it to you."

"Rowd, the first time all those years ago when you said that to me, I thought that might have been the smartest thing anyone ever said to me. I'm not kidding. I think the channeling idea gave me tremendous insight into my problem. It may have been my empathy for you as well as my tendency to want to rescue people, and so my feeling for you was to rescue you from your devils, your problems. My solution? I probably decided to suffer it so that you wouldn't have to. This whole new slice of it will be very interesting to Dr. Martin, the shrink that I started to see."

"Al, you're seeing a shrink? You've been seeing a shrink? I never knew that."

"I didn't get a chance to call you. I recently started."

"Al, I really gotta stop now."

"OK, Rowd, let's meet the others."

I held my finger out to Rowd indicating that I was about to talk into the tape recorder.

> "Chief Garelik, if you don't have further notes for me
> then I think all of you should come in and meet Rowdy
> and ask him whatever needs to be asked."

I looked at Rowd, and he nodded yes.

*   *   *

Quickly, Garelik and a small group entered the room. A few seconds later, the rest followed.

"Rowd," I said, "let me introduce you. This is a group of police chiefs and other police personnel who come from all over the place. All of them have been involved in trying to solve the killings that you know something about. So here we go."

I then introduced everyone and told where they came from. Of course, our group was from several countries—Sweden, France, Italy, and the United States

Tess jumped in. "Rowdy," she said, "even though we just met, I feel we've already known each other. Know what I mean? Congratulations and thanks for coming here and doing this. It's going to help all around."

Rowdy looked at her, smiled a somewhat awkward smile, and he mumbled something like a "thank you," in a gesture of appreciation. Then Garelik took the floor.

"Mr. Quinn, and I hope you don't mind if I address you as Mr. Quinn, I agree with Dr. McFarland, uh, Tess, and can assure you that the information you've provided and might still elaborate on is essential to our understanding of this, shall I say, unfortunate opera in which many people got killed. By the way, could you tell us how you acquired your surname, Quinn?"

My mother was Austrian, and her maiden name was Rostmann. My grandfather, Marcus Rostmann was her father. My father was Irish, and that's the Quinn."

"Also, it's interesting how your grandfather knew about Dr. Cole.

"Well, like I always told him all of the stories about Al and me—Dr. Cole and me—and so he then knew about the condition that Dr. Cole has. When I realized that grandfather was seriously playing with Dr. Cole's mind, and that it was becoming dangerous to Alex, that's when I knew that I should not be involved any more with my grandfather's things."

I interrupted. "Rowd, that makes sense out of Jean's call to me. Her message was from your grandfather. In it, as Chief Garelik said, Jean taunted me by describing my concerns expressed in my enosiophobia, or as you say: my 'enso' thing—about my doubts and my guilt."

Garelik picked it up again: "Mr. Quinn, so you're saying that you got religion when you realized that your grandfather would do anything, including threatening your best friend, Dr. Cole—even with delight in scaring Dr. Cole or keeping him in a state of doubt?"

"That's right," Rowdy instantly said.

"Is that when your grandfather decided to kill someone in Dr. Cole's presence so that Dr. Cole would be more confused about these killings?

"Yes, I think so."

"Mr. Quinn," Garelik continued: "I need to know something more about how your grandfather and his squad got their hands on the money from that bank in Bremen, Germany."

"Grandfather told me that they broke into the bank and took the money. They didn't know the bombing was coming but they were lucky because they had transferred the money, I guess it was in trucks, about two or three days before the bombing. They hid the money in the basement of the Cathedral in Bremen. He said it was like millions and millions of dollars. The basement was like a fortified bunker."

"Mr. Quinn. What do you think is your grandfather's greatest fear? Do you have any idea about that?"

"Oh yes, that's easy. His worst nightmare is to be caught. That's for sure."

"Do you know if he has any weapons in his house?"

"Yes, he does. He has the pistol with a silencer, some knives, and also other guns."

Garelik looked around the room as though giving anyone else a chance to question Rowdy. None responded.

"Mr. Quinn, we're going to take you to the precinct first. You'll be in a separate cell until we straighten out some things. At that point, we'll keep you in what we call a safe house where no one else outside our little group will know where you are. In that way, your grandfather cannot get to you, like getting a message to another prisoner and then bribing that person with the promise of a fortune of money if he would do you harm."

"You mean like killing me."

"Yes, I'm afraid that's what I mean. You know that Dr. Cole has spoken to me about trying to arrange for you to be let off based on your cooperation here. He says that you were dragged into it at an early innocent age. It's a good thought, but I can't promise it. But I think it's possible that if we can't do that then we can at least do something close to it."

Rowdy looked as though caught in the headlights. He was staring. Then he looked at me. I nodded and smiled. It seemed to relax him. Garelik motioned that it was time for everyone to depart. At that point the five of us, me, Tess, Garelik, Stein, and McBride went with Rowdy to his next destination.

PART 5

BERLIN

· 9 ·

AXIS OF EVIL

As far as "destination" was concerned, Rostmann's house, at 25 Hope Street, in Hempstead, Long Island, was surrounded — but Rostmann was gone. Our working hypothesis was that Rostmann must have had a scheduled meeting with Rowdy, the purpose of which was to discuss how to get me to some destination, presumably and simply said, to end my life! I imagine that that was the last straw for Rowdy. Rowdy couldn't assimilate the thought that his grandfather was actually planning to kill his lifelong best friend. This pushed Rowdy's loyalty to his grandfather too far. This one was too real. After the story Rowdy told of his grandfather's odious activities I was frankly in a state of dread. Rostmann likely wanted me dead because he figured that Rowdy told me about his evil deeds, and that meant be able to help the police identify him as the assassin — even though my testimony would be second hand.

When Rowdy didn't show up for the arranged meeting with Rostmann and didn't call him, Rostmann, in his acute vigilant stance, surely knew that something was terribly wrong and that to flee became his only imperative. Of course this imperative to flee included fleeing with the money stored in the walls of his basement at 25 Hope Street in Hempstead, Long Island.

Dave Stein and Jack McBride didn't accompany Garelik, Tess, and me to Rowdy's safe house where he had been transferred. Instead, Garelik changed his mind and sent them both to join with and lead the police contingent that surrounded Rostmann's house. Later, we realized that Rostmann must have been in a panic and had worked feverishly with Jean to extract all that money from his hiding places and escaped, presumably by the skin of his teeth. Then Garelik had that click, that sixth sense. He felt that, as far as Rostmann was concerned, Rowdy was no longer to be trusted. Garelik even imagined that Rostmann could feel it—he could feel Rowdy talking to us.

The bottom line was that when finally the house was surrounded, yes—Rostmann was gone. The detectives saw a man walking his dog and asked about seeing anyone leaving the house owned by Rostmann at the 25 Hope Street address. The man answered yes, and offered that the man who owned the house was with a women, and, he saw them hurriedly lugging packages into a truck. He saw it from the corner, and when he returned from walking his dog the truck was already making a right turn at the next corner. He couldn't remember the make of the truck except that it was dark green. He simply described it as "a regular truck."

While this witness's Q & A period was taking place, McBride appeared with a search warrant, and police entered the house from the front and the back. The front door wasn't even locked, but they broke the back door down, which led into the basement.

Rostmann, and very probably Jean, simply fled. Now the house was practically gerrymandered with police turning it upside down, inside out. Prints were taken in any number of places on any number of items, but McBride casually but pointedly said that the prints were meaningless.

"So what if we have prints," he said. "The man lived here. Of course his prints are all over the place. And in the basement where the plasterboard is movable and there's no asbestos in the walls—so what? What does it prove in a court of law? There's no trace of money, even though, truthfully, I'm actually able to smell it.

"'Oh,'" McBride continued, "you can smell it,'" a judge is going to say. "You can smell the money. I see. So you actually think we'll convict him on your olfactory receptors? Is that what you mean to say?"

"See?" McBride continued, "What we have here is nothing. Absolutely nothing. So that it's not that Rostmann, along with Jean, are *apparently* gone—no, that's not it. What it is is that Rostmann and Jean are *actually* gone!"

* * *

Tess and I got settled in our new digs prepared for us in advance, the location of which we were sworn not to reveal. We weren't there for twenty minutes or so when Garelik called. He recited the entire episode of Rostmann's house being surrounded and that it was likely that because Rowdy didn't meet with his grandfather at what might have been their scheduled meeting time, or that because Rowdy hadn't called him, to set a time and place to meet, then Rostmann, was for sure paranoid about it. This time, with great accuracy—and he cleaned out his money. He was gone. Garelik then said he'd be in touch, with a plan.

If there was a humorous story in all of it, it was when one of Garelik's detectives thought that Rostmann would be worried that he wouldn't be able to sell his house. After all, he was on the lam. The answer Garelik gave was that Rostmann couldn't care less about the loss of the house. Moneywise it meant nothing to him. He dropped the house like a hot potato. It was only, he figured, maybe at the most, worth about $125,000. Cigarette money to Rostmann. Compared to the amount of money he was dealing with, $125,000 was inconsequential.

*　*　*

I wasted no time and called Dr. Martin. He was able to pencil me in that same day. I had several hours before I saw him. Again, of course, I was accompanied by one of my shadows. The other one was responsible for Tess's safety so he stayed at our new place.

The moment I entered Dr. Martin's treatment room I filled him in on my adventures, including the whole story about Rostmann and Kluge, as well as on Garelik's information regarding how they tried to get Rostmann at his house.

The first thing Martin said was:

"It's a lot. You've been around."

"Yeah," I sardonically answered, "around the world! But at the moment I need to talk about Rowdy, the ghost in my dream with the raincoat over the canvas bag with the bank's money. I've had additional thoughts about it, actually a very important one that Rowdy himself brilliantly suggested. I think the whole thing means that it was my way of unconsciously knowing that Rowdy had some kind of similar unconscious thing going on as I had. He didn't have an enosiophobia like mine, but he was overwhelmed by anxiety feeling like he was always concealing something about, let's say, 'wrongness.'

"It could be that's why I dreamed he used his raincoat to drape over the canvas bag with all the money. I originally saw it as a dream representing my oedipal competition with my father for my mother's affection. Right? But now I'm adding this idea that I was also channeling Rowdy by reflecting how Rowdy was constantly concealing something. Now we know what it was that he was concealing. It was all about his grandfather and all the assassination stuff."

"Not bad, Dr. Cole," was his shorthand as a friendly supportive response. "No," I continued, "the whole thing's an example of how everyone's unconscious mind is on the genius level. So from the time we were in high school our channeling theory and everything else tells me what I've always known—that Rowdy's naturally smart. The whole channeling thing probably contributed to my enosiophobia. When we began the analysis and first discussed it, we came to the conclusion that it was about my parents. OK. I've recently thought that I may have been angry with them for abandoning me, but I didn't even know I felt that way. Of course, we both know what happened to them, how they were simply made to be helpless and then eliminated. When I was a kid, I used to think that they still might be alive, but they would have no idea of how to find me. It was my wish for them to be alive. But, because of what happened to them, I'm sure I blamed myself. I think I felt that if I wasn't bad, or maybe if I hadn't done something wrong, nothing would have happened the way it did. But really, I couldn't buy it. I knew I did nothing wrong.

"But the proposition that I was channeling Rowdy would then imply an additional twist to what comprised the enosiophobia. The twist was that it was a way of rescuing him. And so, Dr. Richard Martin, I think my basic personality, buried deep in my unconscious since I was five, has been a lifelong urge to rescue—period. And, I think I, was the first person to be rescued. Who by? By me. By myself. I did it by keeping myself away from commitments because, because, because."

"You know," Dr. Martin said thoughtfully while he was ignoring my becauses, "trauma at an early age—without a doubt—will affect people for the rest of their lives. With therapy it can get better, but that means that such a person will need to engage the struggle, and then continue to struggle better, and then better again, and better, and then again better.

But we need to be realistic about life, and that means that each struggle is part of a lifetime project. The good news is that with a better and better struggle, the trauma loses a lot of its power."

Dr. Martin was a smart guy, but his psychoanalytic mode of thinking at this comment took on a genius cast. Here's what I mean. He had an afterthought and becoming informal addressed me as Alex.

"You know, Alex, when you said that you would need to find your parents because they wouldn't know how to find you, I had the inkling that, without knowing it, you were referring to the drama that's currently in play that you told me about Rostmann and the other guy. It's the drama of Rostmann's disappearance, the thing about that guy, Kluge, and what you said about how this Kluge would be worried that Rostmann would be coming after him.

"My thought was that Rostmann probably wouldn't have any direct route to him, probably wouldn't be able to find him, and that therefore Rostmann would accept possibly never finding him. However, my companion thought was that it would be Kluge who would feel the need to find Rostmann before Rostmann might find him—just like you would need to find your parents because they wouldn't be able to find you."

The session ended on that note and after I left the office I thought: 'Martin, baby, you are a genius.' I knew I would need to tell Garelik that perhaps he should start looking for any clues to the whereabouts of Kluge as well as searching for Rostmann. And, if Martin was right, I thought we might be entering a world of crisscrossing assassins, each looking to erase the other.

Immediately after the session, I called Tess and told her I was on my way. She wasn't frantic, but she was agitated. She told me in no uncertain terms that I could not *do* "not contacting her" for such a long period of time. She actually said: "I need to hear your voice."

There was no misunderstanding Tess! Besides, she said that Garelik informed her that where we were now was a safe house. No more Waldorf and no Gramercy Park apartment either—and who knows for how long?

*   *   *

Wolfgang Kluge had been working as an engineer in a factory that specialized in manufacturing locks and fittings. It was in Velbert, a small town—population about seventy-five thousand. The company was located in the middle of a remote region in North Rhine-Westphalia. It was a good place to hide in plain sight. No one would know him especially by his nom de guerre—his assumed name of Herr Ludwig Aachen. This nom de guerre would be fitting, because he was going to be in a fight to the death. Yes, Herr Wofgang Kluge, aka, Ludwig Aachen, after reading about the most recent death of Walther Koertig, of whom he was fond, but hadn't seen since 1945, thirty-four years earlier, finally convinced him that Rostmann was the assassin. He knew it couldn't be Koertig. He knew Koertig didn't have it in him to be an assassin.

Apparently, just like the others may have been, Kluge was always reading the daily papers for any information of the other nine. And, one by one, he saw subtraction—this latest comrade, in thievery and mass murder by allied bombardment was an example—this time, however, by age alone. That's how Kluge finally was sure that Rostmann was the assassin. He now also knew, without a doubt, that Rostmann would be looking for him.

That was his first conclusion. His second thought was also instantaneous. He knew that in order to get any possible sign of Rostmann, he would need to travel to Bremen, of course under the name Aachen, and wait there. He had reason to believe that at some point Rostmann would show up in Bremen. Kluge didn't need to worry about money. He had plenty of it. The last time he visited the cathedral of Bremen was four years earlier. Now his plan was to rent an apartment in Bremen under his assumed name and wait—no matter how long it took.

Kluge, now Aachen, returned home after work, sat with his wife, Renatta, and told her what the current problem was. She had known about his sordid past—yet their relationship was airtight. He told her he needed to eliminate the impending danger. She understood—nevertheless wept.

He packed.

This idea, this plan to travel to Bremen, was not unique to Kluge alone. Rostmann, as well as Garelik, had the same brainstorm. Bremen was the only place germane to them all. They all, needed to wind up in Bremen. The ongoing suspense, and the trying of everyone's patience, would, of course, be played out in Bremen.

The question became: Who will turn out to be the main character of this drama? It was not a simple answer— one that could be surprising. Of those involved, it would not be the police presence, it would not be

Rostmann, and it would not be Kluge/Aachen in the starring role. In all likelihood it probably would be Herr Torsten Koppel, the caretaker of the Bremen cathedral.

Of course, it had to be Koppel. He was the one who always guarded, monitored, and meted out the money when it was distributed equally to each of the ten. And here's the plus. Over the years he knew each of them well. However, he also knew something was wrong because as time elapsed fewer of the ten would show up to collect their share. At some point it was down to half—only five of them would return to collect more money. Each of the men was always given a specified month for their appearance in Bremen—every four years—and no two ever arrived at the same time, in the same month.

*   *   *

At this point, Rostmann was the first to arrive, even though it wasn't his month. Actually, it wasn't even his year. Torsten Koppel, the enigmatic caretaker, who was in charge of the money that was stored in the church basement (along with several crypts and their mummified centuries-old occupants), was not expecting him this year. But this time Rostmann wasn't here to collect another million or two. This time it was different. Rostmann was not going to be visible.

Rostmann knew the town inside out. Over intermittent four-year periods whenever he arrived, he would scout another part of the Bremen Square—around which stood most of the town's main attractions including the Roland Bremen statue and the town's Gothic cathedral, officially known as St. Peter's Protestant/Lutheran Church, with its vaulted ceiling and vast space inside and its towering twin-peak spires. The church was ultimately identified as Lutheran, named after Martin Luther of the Protestant Reformation—that vile, disgusting, spewing, Jew-hating Luther whom the Christian church still venerates.

The basement, or what is considered the cathedral's lead cellar called a *bleikeller*, was a protected environment that housed not only mummies in crypts but also what Rostmann must have considered all his millions of dollars. In addition, there are reputed to be many skeletal remains in the large crypt holding close to one hundred graves. Remains of former bishops and other church luminaries have been entombed there for centuries.

The cathedral was located between the state parliament and the magnificent Town Hall, along with several other notable buildings nearby. On the west side of the market square stands the Sparkasse bank building, the Rathsapotheke (the apothecary), the customs house referred to as the Akzise, as well as the Deutsches Haus.

Whenever Rostmann visited Bremen, he did not pay any social calls nor did he shop. He was always quickly in and out, trying never to have any significant interaction with town's people—especially interaction that could be remembered.

Now comes the interesting part, because the modern twentieth century history of the town notes that in 1943 an air raid severely damaged the cathedral, but the crypts in the basement (the lead cellar—the *bleikeller*) and all its other stored items were not touched. Eventually the cathedral was rebuilt. Torsten Koppel, the caretaker specifically of the *bleikeller*, was a twenty-seven-year-old man when Bishop Hudal, the influential Odessa personality who, it was rumored, initiated the underground railroad for escaped Nazis, first appointed Koppel as the guardian of this so-called intercontinental underground railroad. From that exalted perch, Koppel was the natural person to oversee a huge cache that would serve to ensure the permanent safety of the ten thieving senior Nazi soldiers nefariously affiliated with this town of Bremen in 1943, and under Rostmann's leadership.

Also, like those senior Nazi officer of the squad, Koppel was in his mid seventies, having spent most of his life loyally and responsibly carrying out the Hudal assignment—glued to the cathedral's *bleikeller*. During those thirty-five or so years that he spent guarding what was in the *bleikeller*, he had outlived two ministers of the church and was now betting that the current minister would pre-decease him as well. Koppel is what is known as a fanatically obsessed ideologue who for those thirty-five years, acted-out his obsessed mission—compulsively.

Of course, Rostmann had agreed that some of the money would go to subsidizing other Nazis who over the years also needed ferrying to distant places in order to avoid prosecution for war crimes. Koppel did that ferrying and subsidizing smoothly and with great mastery.

Rostmann's plan was not to alert Koppel to his presence in Bremen. Rostmann was going to rent an apartment near the town square. Jean was with him, and so she would be negotiating the rental. After she moved in, he would then join her. Then his plan was for Jean to be in constant touch with him because he needed to figure out a physical disguise in the event that Kluge arrived in Bremen. With the help of the disguise, he would be able to spot Kluge, while, at the same time, being unrecognizable to him.

For the first two or three days, after arriving, Jean would be Rostmann's eyes in the Bremen Square looking for an aged man who might be perhaps suspiciously casing the joint—especially the cathedral. Rostmann described Kluge physically. Apparently, Kluge, of average height, average weight, and average everything else, nevertheless, could always be noticed because he had a major scar on his left cheek and also stammered when speaking.

Rostmann was not in the least phased with respect to killing Kluge. Actually, he was aching for the chance. In thinking about it, he felt the sense of thrill, almost as though healed by the thought. At the same time, Jean, with her diagnostic skills tuned, was able to find a suitable apartment and rented it.

Before he knew it, Rostmann got an idea. He decided to don a priest's vestments. It was the perfect disguise because frequently visitors to Bremen were visiting specifically to see the cathedral and visit the cryptorium. These were mostly Christian theologians, other priests, bishops and so forth. Therefore, it was common to see a variety of these sorts of individuals in and around the town square.

Rostmann decked himself out as a Hieromonk, a monk of the Eastern Church. Therefore he was defining himself as a celibate priest. He wore an inner black cassock that was floor length and an outer cassock called an exorason, which was a large flowing garment worn over the inner one. On top he wore a Kamilavka, a stiff hat worn by monastics signifying a mark of honor. Finally, he fashioned a dark beard that essentially covered his face. His disguise was perfect. No one would get the ruse. He became entirely transformed from a paranoid Nazi psychopath to a revered Christian priest—a monk.

It looked as though Kluge didn't stand a chance. Yet, two or three days later, there he was: Wolfgang Kluge, aka Ludwig Aachen, in the flesh, in Bremen. He carried a trim slim Astra 900 7.63 x 25mm Mauser pistol that fit nicely into his pants' pocket. In contrast, Rostmann was loaded for bear. He carried a semiautomatic with a silencer that he had had modified years earlier in order to lock the bolt closed after firing. In this way the escape of gas would be prevented by the suppressor, the silencer. It was a Ruger 22 auto—tailor made.

With all of these preparations Kluge didn't really have a plan. Not even considering renting an apartment, he made a beeline directly to the cathedral in order to engage caretaker Torsten Koppel in what Kluge felt would turn out to be an interesting proposition—to say the least. He knew that the first thing he would do is to share with the caretaker the whole grizzly story of Rostmann's relentless killing spree, which had lasted more than three decades. Kluge was sure that Koppel would understand. He even had the thought that Koppel would want him, Kluge himself, to win the duel, because Koppel then would be ideologically freed to subsidize more and more of these anticipated requests from former Nazis—not meaning any of the original ten. Actually, Koppel was dismayed that many of these hidden Nazis had begun to request financial aid although not wanting to emigrate anywhere.

Kluge always believed that Koppel was true to his Nazi mission of protecting the lion's share of the treasure so it could be equally distributed to the ten (or to however many of them were still breathing). However, Torsten Koppel, together with Bishop Hudal, had a parallel kind of world, salvation-fever characterized by how they needed to continue to financially float the Nazi agenda. This meant that Koppel was assigned the task of being careful about the distribution of the treasure; that is, to make sure that enough remained to finance their underground railroad to former Nazis—those not part of the original ten of Rostmann's squad.

Similarly, Kluge thought that Koppel would consider that, with Rostmann's demise, and his, Kluge's appreciation for Koppel's imagined victory over Rostmann, it would be then that Koppel would feel free to spend the remaining treasure on financially assisting those Nazis whose requests for such help had in fact been increasing. Then again, it wasn't lost on Kluge that, without Rostmann, the entire treasure would be his, Kluge's, and he then could ensure the unending support of his family, certainly continuing into future generations.

Kluge, with no disguise at all, and carrying his Mauser Astra 900 in his pants' pocket, entered St. Peter's Cathedral on the Bremen Square. He was carrying a small travel bag. In it were various items—a number of spare cartridges of bullets and two hand-grenades. Kluge was not fooling around.

* * *

In New York City, at Police Chief Sanford Garelik's office, sat Garelik, Stein, McBride, Tancredi, Grimand, Persson, and the two detectives who had frisked Rowdy at the desk of the Waldorf and then escorted him into the elevator up to the suite where the others were waiting for them. They were discussing how to fit a square object into a round hole. In other words they were at a loss to see how to apprehend two individuals, each of whom had vanished. In the tracing and tracking department, of course, it was known that both Stein and McBride, best friends and colleagues for years, constituted collective genius. In this case it was McBride, the believer, who piped up.

"Hey, guys, I've got it. What are we waiting for. It's obvious like the Chief here predicted. They'll each go where the money is. Follow the money. Let's go to Bremen. It's for sure. There's no doubt they'll both be there. Stein instantly agreed, and the others also saw the light. Garelik nodded knowing he had been right about it.

It was arranged. They would travel together to Europe. Tancredi would need to be in Milan and see what was cooking at his office. Ditto for Grimand in Paris, as well as for Persson in Sweden. They would be in touch by phone and then decide when and how, and with how many, to converge on Bremen. They also wanted to keep Tess and me out of harm's way so at this point we were no longer kept in the loop.

In the meantime, Tess and I had a problem on our hands. We considered getting married right away and then immediately after getting on board to try to have a baby, or, to try having the baby first and then plan about when to get married. We talked about it for a while, when I said, "Let's get married first." Tess agreed, but again she would have gone along with either option. I invited the detective who was sitting outside our safe house apartment guarding it to have a talk. It was not a good talk. I told him we wanted to scoot over to City Hall and get a marriage license. The detective answered in no uncertain terms: "Absolutely not!"

And that was that. The detective was under strict orders. "Dr. Cole and Dr. McFarland are not to leave the apartment," said Garelik, unless there was a good reason for it. The detective actually confirmed it all by saying—"Listen, at this moment, in this time, I don't think Chief Garelik would agree to your request. Now really, do you think he would?" We glanced at each other, both knowing that the only remaining choice for us was to implement Plan B.

*   *   *

How to put the plan in action was everyone's concern. Garelik and his men were getting ready to begin a pincer movement directed at Bremen, Germany. Rostmann, on the other hand, was focused on implementing a fantastic disguise in order to shoot Kluge down in cold blood—and to do it in such a way that one could not know a shooting had even occurred. That's why he took his trusted silencer along.

Of course, Kluge had reached the exact conclusion about Rostmann that Rostmann had reached about him—kill Rostmann!

Although Rostmann had a complex plan set into motion almost as soon as he entered Bremen, it was evident that that was not true of Kluge. Yet, Kluge had already made a quantum step because he found himself much closer to the money and, therefore, much closer, albeit indirectly, to Rostmann. In the meantime, Jean, who stationed herself near the cathedral on Bremen Square, was focused on who entered and who exited the cathedral; and there he was, Kluge, the visitor they hoped would be there. But Kluge first walked around Bremen Square, carefully studying the situation. He was worried that Rostmann may have been lurking. But, he didn't expect a woman to be doing the lurking.

Jean's station was a bench where she was sitting, close to the cathedral, near the Bremen statue. She noticed a man simply walking around the square and looking here and there. When the man approached near where Jean was sitting, he paid her no mind, but she instantly spotted the large scar on his left cheek, and like Rostmann, he seemed to be in his mid to late seventies.

Yes, she thought, it's him, Kluge. She got up from the bench and very casually walked in the opposite direction to where Kluge was walking. Before she knew it, she was at the apartment she had rented. Out of breath and into the apartment she ran.

"He's here. He's walking around the square. He did it twice."

Rostmann phoned the cathedral. At the other end someone answered. Rostmann said two words:

"He's here," and then hung up.

It was then, almost at the same time, that Kluge entered the cathedral looking for the caretaker, Torsten Koppel. Of course they had met over the decades, so they would instantly recognize one another. Kluge followed his own historical steps, which had, over the years, become familiar, so he simply walked to the end of the aisle in the nave of the church, pushed a door open leading to a hallway, then a few steps later to a mailbox, and finally to a stairway leading down to the basement—to the *bleikeller*.

Torsten Koppel was sitting eating his lunch at a desk, like a nurse's station situated directly in the middle of a hospital ward. Kluge noticed that Koppel seemed startled upon seeing him. Koppel stood up and then greeted Kluge in a friendly way, speaking in German.

"You didn't inform me of your visit. I'm not making another distribution for about six more months. Did you want to alter the schedule so that you could find it easier to transport the amount?"

"No," Kluge said. "I came to kill Marcus Rostmann."

"What? What do you mean you would kill Marcus Rostmann? One of our own? For what reason?"

Kluge wasn't sure whether Koppel was pretending to not suspect Rostmann as the assassin. It would be obvious to anyone that Koppel himself was certainly aware of all the killings and therefore aware also of the consistent subtraction of just about each one of the ten. Kluge was certain that Koppel at least inferred that he and Rostmann were the only two left. Kluge, confronting Koppel, incisively stated: "The reason is that he and I are the only two left standing. The other eight all died by assassination or, at least one of natural circumstance, like age. Of the others, I believe Rostmann did all the assassinations. Should Rostmann live beyond this time period, but I not, then something harsh is going to happen to you," he said to Koppel. "Rostmann is the type who worries about the bad things he's done and needs to cover everything up—including, at some point, covering you up—permanently!"

In contrast, he said: "Should I be the one who guns down Rostmann, then you and I can make a deal, because no one else will be coming at us with guns blazing.

"OK, here's the deal. If I'm the only one left, then the entire treasure is up for grabs. I know you have interest in rescuing others among our friends and that you've done a magnificent job in getting that done. Now I'm suggesting that we split the remainder of the treasure that you have so very nicely protected in these quarters. If Rostmann wins, he'll kill you — simply said — and he'll keep all the money. He's paranoid that way — very! However, if I win, then we'll continue to support ourselves in style, of course based upon the wealth accumulated and stored here. Then you'll go your way — perhaps to stay here and continue your work or do whatever — and I'll go mine.

Koppel was listening with great interest. He responded by asking a few pertinent questions. The discussion that ensued revealed Koppel to be prepared to talk. But he expressed concern about one thing. He said to Kluge: "Herr Kluge, how do I know you will not renege on your promise not to attack me? Where is the assurance I need to go forward with this agreement?"

Kluge's answer was again direct.

"Herr Koppel, there's one easy way to accomplish this task. Let's divide the money now, as we speak, and then you can carry away your share and store it in a place that is entirely foreign to me and to all others. You would still be able to carry out your mission with those disaffected or otherwise, let's say, remaining or still undiscovered Nazis Party comrades. Then I, too, will disappear, and we will never see one another again. I would say that's a fetching idea. N'est-ce pas?

But there was another catch. That is, Kluge also considered the possibility that perhaps Rostmann was not the assassin. He thought maybe it was Koppel himself. And, if that was the case, Kluge also considered the possibility that Rostmann was perhaps planning to kill Koppel before Koppel could kill him. In truth, Kluge wasn't sure. His first choice was Rostmann as the *apparent* assassin. But at this point it also occurred to him that Koppel himself might be the assassin, the *actual* one. Because of this obsessive indecision Kluge's further rumination was that Rostmann would, in all likelihood, be coming to Bremen — either to kill Koppel and transport the rest of the treasure for himself, or to kill him or, more possibly, both.

Kluge, however, didn't know what he was talking about. He had no idea. He finally reached the conclusion that the only way not to gamble was for him to kill them both! His thought was: Eliminate Koppel as well as Rostmann and take no chances whatsoever, in knowing of which one he should be wary. Why take any chance at all?! Then, abruptly Kluge told Koppel he needed to make a private phone call. Koppel, of course with courtesy, and without any questions complied with Kluge's request, opening the door that lead to a staircase to the main hall, next to which was a table with a phone connected to the cathedral's switchboard operator. Kluge had no idea that when Rostmann made the call to the cathedral to indicate that Kluge had arrived in Bremen, that Rostmann was talking to Koppel. Apparently, Koppel was playing possum with Kluge and, for the moment, biding his time.

Kluge asked the operator to dial the number and was connected. He said: "Gut morgn, gut nakht" (good morning, good night), and was immediately transferred to someone else. When the person being called answered, Kluge simply said: "One. Same place. Immediately." This was the code that over the decades Kluge used to commission two trucks to arrive in Bremen in the shortest time-interval possible. The supplier, from years of experience with Kluge, knew Kluge paid handsomely for the service and paid immediately. From past experience, Kluge was confident the truck was on its way even minutes after he put in the order for it.

When Kluge reentered the *bleikeller*, Koppel was now sitting with Minister Konrad of the church, who apparently had entered from the main door. As Kluge walked in, he saw they were in what seemed to be a serious conversation. It certainly wasn't casual, and they weren't laughing. The minister rose from his chair and extended his hand to Kluge. Kluge responded, and as they shook hands, the minister with his left hand held a pistol and shot feckless Kluge in the chest. It was a fatal shot, and as Kluge lay dying he muttered to himself:

"Rostmann, you, together. Renatta."

Kluge was gone. The gist of it was that the true contingent of men was actually ten plus two. Apparently, from the beginning, thirty-six-years ago, Rostmann had arranged with Bishop Hudal to have Koppel do Rostmann's bidding—that is, Hudal made sure that Koppel would know that the authority would be with Rostmann. True to their reputations as German Nazis *an order is an order is an order.*

Because of this preplanning, decades ago, Rostmann, it seems, was way ahead of the game. In contrast, in Kluge's obsessive ruminations, even before he had first entered the cathedral as well as reentering the *bleikeller*, he actually considered almost all possibilities as to who was the assassin. Was it Rostmann or perhaps Koppel himself? What he didn't consider was that Rostmann and Koppel were in it together, from the beginning. As to Konrad, the minister of the cathedral, Hudal made sure that the ministerial line of descent would only go to those who in some way were sympathetic and therefore partial to the ultimate plan devised by the three of them—Hudal, Koppel, and Rostmann—and assisted by two former ministers of the cathedral, plus the current one, Konrad, who had just killed Kluge; all of them comprising the real cabal—and, in a church!

The job now was to dispose of Kluge's body. A truck would have been convenient, but alas, there were no trucks on the way because the cathedral operator then called the same phone number that Kluge had contacted and nullified the order by saying: "Kluge—order canceled."

Kluge was no match for Rostmann. That was obvious. Now the question was: Do Rostmann and Koppel work together in the absence of malicious intent, one toward the other, or do we now have a new dilemma as to which one will be the last man standing?

Now that Kluge was history, Rostmann made a brilliant geometric decision. Rather than staying in Bremen, he decided to leave for Berlin. Whatever business he had with Koppel he knew could be taken care of at a later, more propitious, time. Rostmann got to the apartment wanting to talk to Jean. It was noontime, and Jean was napping. He couldn't wait. He woke her up.

"Marcus, what is it?"

"We're going to Berlin. I need to personally take care of some things. First I'm calling Koppel at the cathedral. I want to know what happened. I want to know what happened after he saw Kluge and where Kluge might be. I need to take care of Kluge immediately."

Rostmann made the call, and the switchboard operator at the cathedral switched the call to Koppel. Koppel answered. Speaking German, Rostmann said:

"What happened at your meeting with Kluge?"

"'Kluge' and 'was' are now synonyms. Understood?"

First came a split second pause and then: "Yes."

Without saying another word, Rostmann clicked off. He then told Jean the good news that Kluge was dead and that Koppel would of course get rid of the body. He was happy about it for two reasons. First, it was a victory of the first order because now all other soldiers of the squad were gone and, second, it simply saved him time and effort. However, in a moment of consideration, he cursed the time it took for him to put together the costume of a Hieromonk, which now he would discard. Rostmann was bothered because there were still loose ends and he remained concerned. First, Koppel was still there and, second, the minister was still there as well. And the three of them knew that the centerpiece of the entire cabal, of the entire project, and, of course, of all the assassinations was the responsibility of Marcus Rostmann.

Yes, Rostmann, knew this.

Back at the cathedral, Koppel and the minister, of course speaking in their native tongue to one another, were in deep discussion, the end of which established an agreement that, indeed, the very fact of Rostmann's existence was worrisome. The question was, what to do about it? The minister started: "We know he's not one to share things and we know that he, too, understands that we know that. It simply means that Rostmann on the loose will be highly dangerous."

"So," the minister added: "He'll find us one at a time. The only question is: How do we get him first?"

Koppel knew that the minister was completely rational in his conclusion, and he answered: "We must get him."

At this point there were a lot of "gettings" to be gotten. First, the "him" that had to be gotten referred to Rostmann's getting of Koppel—and also of the minister. Those two were one unit and obviously had to be gotten at the same time. Second, the "him" that had to be gotten referred to Koppel together with the minister's getting of Rostmann. Third, the "him" that needed to be gotten was also Garelik's getting of Rostmann, and, finally, the *who* who needed to be gotten would possibly boil down to Koppel, on the one hand, or the minister of the cathedral, on the other: that is, which one would do it to the other, or would, in fact, one do it to the other?

* * *

No, we must never be unaware of Garelik and his team. As Rostmann and Jean were packing and planning to slip unnoticed out of Bremen, Stein, McBride, and two other detectives of the Persson Interpol team were slipping in. Only they were not trying to be hidden. They checked into the Hotel Classico right on the Bremen Market Square. It was a three star hotel but the most important thing about it was that it was neighboring the famous St. Peter's Cathedral, along with many of the other important historical structures around the square. The Classico was considered to be a boutique hotel with significantly fewer rooms than many of the other hotels. Unlike other hotels of more than two-hundred rooms, the Classico had fewer than fifty.

After the four of them checked in and had dinner, they congregated in a comfortable little nook in the lobby of the hotel and discussed the situation and plans that might be made. The situation was that each of them needed to spread out and try to pick up some information about the air raid during the war, and any information about the squad of men who were assigned to guard the bank. All agreed that that was the thing to do. They then retired for the night.

· 10 ·

BERLIN

In New York City, Tess and I were already working on our special project. We were also interested in leaving our safe house apartment because we were becoming stir-crazy and needed just to get out for awhile. I was especially dispirited about not being in on Garelik's action plan. Both Tess and I knew about Stein and McBride's mission in Bremen.

The fact was that I thought I could be of help based on what I knew about psychology. I felt I could very likely predict various things about Rostmann's behavior. I was an expert in the paranoias: encapsulated paranoid delusions; in generalized psychotic paranoia; and, in a rather subtle prodromal state known as paranoid character. Prodromal simply means possible precursors to a more serious diagnosis. As I was talking about it, and in view of what I was saying, both Tess and Detective Marlow wanted to hear more about what I thought Rostmann would do next.

"OK," I said. "It's actually very simple. You see, an encapsulated paranoid delusion is one in which the sufferer can feel paranoid about one particular thing but in all else seems normal and not delusional. For example, a man might think that the next-door neighbor has designs on his wife. That so-called truth that the man believes real can lead him to begin spying on the other man and generally feel upset. Such a feeling can go on for a very long period of time—perhaps even permanently. Nevertheless, such a man may not display delusional feelings toward anything else.

However, at times his paranoia can break out of its capsule and therefore no longer be contained. When that happens the man would be diagnosed as having a generalized psychotic paranoia where hallucinations and more bizarre thinking emerge so that the specific diagnosis can be a paranoid schizophrenia. In such a case, this person would have what's known as a pathological thinking disorder meaning that everything becomes known only through the self so that reality becomes irrelevant. It's known as a solipsistic state.

I caught myself observing Tess and Marlow. I could see they were interested and following me. I repeated what I had just said, and then continued.

"See, now, finally, we arrive at a very subtle form of paranoia, which is considered a nonpsychotic or nonschizophrenic state. That's the paranoid character. This type of paranoid state is not a psychotic one and we don't get delusions or hallucinations. What we do get is a person who is highly critical about everything. This criticality is designed to keep everything in the world out and, correspondingly, not let anything new in. So, you can see, if someone is constantly criticizing everything then nothing is good enough to incorporate, to take in. And the "nothing" that is never good enough to incorporate can even—and especially—include another person to love. But basically, this paranoid critical mode is used by such a person to deflect any thought that even remotely would suggest something is wrong *inside*. Rather, the critical mode in this person is therefore to *see* that *nothing* is wrong inside, but that everything is wrong out there.

"OK, so now you can see that with a pronounced paranoid characterology—meaning personality—some such individual can break out of this paranoid position, this paranoid character/personality position, and begin to show greater pathology. Like I said, that's what prodromal actually means—something containing the seeds of a possible future, serious pathology."

After a moment or two of silence to let this sink in, I looked directly at Detective Marlow and said, "So my friend, I need to talk to Chief Garelik and try to persuade him to use me as a psychological consultant in the hunt for Rostmann. You know, at the very end, understanding his obsession and his felonious impulses, devoted entirely to premeditated murder, I believe I could be useful in helping to apprehend him.

It didn't take Marlow long. He phoned Garelik and discussed it with him. Very soon after our discussion Garelik arrived with one other detective at our safe house. Garelik saw the sense of it, already had had a dossier on me compiled, and my expertise and reputation impressed him. That, along with all of his dealings with me, he decided that I might indeed help in apprehending Marcus Rostmann.

But Garelik had a dilemma. The dilemma was how to keep me, and Tess, out of harm's way. Despite his instinct to invite me into the investigation of Rostmann, he was acutely aware that Tess and I were civilians so that our involvement needed to be such that in case something did happen to one or both of us, neither he nor the police department would be faulted or held responsible for the less than fully serious accusation of negligent decision-making . . . or even the serious accusation of endangerment.

But there was no stopping this freight train. Garelik was going to go ahead with it, and Tess and I would soon be traveling to Bremen. Garelik then decided to head back to his office, of course taking his own shadow with him. He was going to arrange our trip and would be in touch.

Retiring into the adjoining room, Detective Marlow said he was going to take a nap. And that was the day.

When it was all arranged, I told Tess that I was looking forward to being reunited with Stein and McBride. I repeated that I really liked and respected them.

"You know, Tess, I guess I'm always awestruck with someone's expertise at whatever. And that goes for my feelings about Stein and McBride."

"I see," Tess countered. "Then how about the expertise of a Marcus Rostmann?"

Surprised by her comment, I admitted she had a good point. Nevertheless, I added: "If I can be objective, I do, in a sense, appreciate Rostmann's ability to plan and act-out feats of courage and, yes, danger.

That's a confession—my confession to you. Unfortunately for Rostmann, and for those he killed, all that talent went down the drain because he contaminated it with psychological disease that led to the horror of all those murders.

"By the way," Tess asked, "how's your enosiophobia? I haven't heard you referring to it in a while, and I haven't heard you even mentioning your Jackal diary.

"You're right. I haven't even had a thought about it. As Rowd might say, my enso might be evaporating especially since I now know more about my trauma with my parents, my channeling of Rowdy's concerns, and especially knowing that it was a specific person involved with the wrongdoing. It was Rostmann! It wasn't me! I didn't do it, and neither did Rowdy. What a thought. I might actually be free of it all."

Tess added what I thought was the last inspiration of the day: "Alex, I guess even though your enosiophobia may have been prodromal, nevertheless you've apparently gotten the best of it and it's therefore no longer prodromal. You're now free of psychological pathology."

That gave me an opening for a truly final inspiration.

"The truth is no one is completely free of psychological pathology. We all have our quirks. Idiosyncrasy actually rules the world — especially with respect to what goes into the engineering of one's psyche so that the person gets his basic wish gratified."

Seeing Tess was with me, I squeezed out a final-plus thought.

"The result is that what started out with the basic *wish* of the person's algorithm ends with what that person *wants* to do and then what that person actually *does* in order to try to get that wish satisfied. "And," I emphasized: "Rostmann has a dilly of an algorithm! In our still quite primitive state and stage of evolution, survival is paramount to every creature; to many people it begins to mean that money rules. And so we get Rostmanns in this world who will do anything for money — even kill!"

I looked at her, paused for a long moment, and said: "So, Tess, my residual pathology is probably no longer with my enosiophobia. Now, my main obsession is with guess who?"

She reflexively answered: "me." And she then pushed me onto the bed.

*   *   *

Then, before you knew it, we were all packed. No more safe house. It was no longer necessary because Garelik and his brain trust came to the conclusion that Rostmann was too busy at the moment trying to stay out of sight. They knew he had no fix on my location and surmised that his plan was to concentrate on Bremen and the loot and, nothing else. They considered the high-level probability that in Rostmann's zeal to achieve whatever his goal was, some people might be killed.

The bottom line, however, was that no matter how many factors were interacting, we all believed that Rostmann would ultimately be found in Bremen. That's where the final curtain would likely fall. But before the final curtain would fall, Act III was just beginning.

It was arranged for Tess and me, plus another detective in addition to Marlow, to fly to Bremen. We were confirmed at the Hotel Classico, where Stein and McBride, and who knows how many others from Garelik's contingent, were as well.

My new friend Tancredi would be arriving in a few days. Persson arrived first before we got there from New York City. The next day, Grimand appeared. He was accompanied by Philippe Marcel, apparently Grimand's secret weapon. We spotted him as he was walking into the hotel lobby. Finally, several days later, there was Tancredi. I was happy to see him. We talked a bit and then headed to the bar for a drink. Just the two of us. Tess took a break and rested in our room. The only person missing was Garelik. Whether he would show up was iffy because at one point in New York he stated that as long as Persson from Interpol was present, that his presence would probably not be necessary. Garelik had confidence with his tracing and tracking genius-duo there on the scene, as well as having Marlow and another detective on the case.

Now we needed a plan in order to understand how to make logic out of a very complicated puzzle. Here we were in Bremen, Germany, and we don't know a soul, Rostmann is not visible to us, Rostmann's Jean is only a "maybe" so we decide to check on the situation at the cathedral. Next we needed to interview several people from the town about the air-raid bombing during the war. Our target group was people who were in their seventies or older, who'd lived there at the time.

McBride had a good idea. It would be important to tap into the grandchildren of these people in their seventies, or even older, because grandchildren may have heard stories about the war, especially about the bombing. McBride added that it's very typical for grandparents to need to tell their stories. I agreed, adding that frequently, after so many years of keeping silent, people need to open up with information that for whatever reason they didn't even tell their children. Stein had told us about his interview with the minister of the cathedral in Bremen, who was fluent in English, so without a doubt, that minister needed to be revisited.

We knew even before we traveled, mostly because of Rowdy's comments, that the caretaker of the cathedral was likely an important chess piece in this game, a game clearly of death objectives. Torsten Koppel, the caretaker certainly knew a lot about the bombing of Bremen and, according to Rowdy, also knew about the stolen money. That was crucial information. Rostmann surely would be back to collect the money that was probably hidden in the cathedral.

We started to plan how to proceed. We would start the interviews with the elderly Bremen population as well as with their grandchildren. Not being fluent in German we needed a translator. Tancredi found someone at the hotel who spoke both German and English. Stein and McBride told me that, under Garelik's orders, Tess and I could not be involved with anyone or anything without our shadows. Wherever we went we would be accompanied by two detectives—one was Detective Steve Marlow of the New York City police department. These shadows were filled in about the plan and why they were protecting us.

Tancredi would be working with a female officer who accompanied him from Milan. When I asked Tancredi why it was a woman and why she was there, he told that me that each of us needed to have some security protection. He added, "Maria, is the smartest person in my unit and is also courageous."

"She's also gorgeous and she speaks English," I added.

He smiled and simply said: "Maria, Maria."

All told, our little, but growing unit was populated by twelve members—each an expert in his or her field. McBride and Stein were the first to leave unaccompanied. Their immediate job was to collect as many eyewitness reports of people who were along in their years and, if possible, interview grandchildren as well. And very importantly, before they departed, Grimand noted that interviews with the minister and caretaker of the cathedral interested him most. From the moment of Rowdy's description of things, especially of the cathedral personnel, Grimand, said he had a funny feeling about everything related to the cathedral. Then he added—with some emphasis: "We're not all in the dark here. It's the cathedral, the cathedral."

That's all he said—and then without pausing, repeated it again. After that, everyone began to implement their particular task. Tancredi and Maria along with Tess and I were escorted by Detective Marlow and his partner as though we were a group of tourists. Tess was selected to lead the group as a tourist guide and point out various places of interest while we perused the grounds of the Bremen Market Square. But Tess protested:

"What? I don't know a thing about the place. How am I going to explain anything? And I don't speak a word of German."

To which Detective Marlow answered: "Just mumble something. No one will know the difference anyway. You'll be fine."

Tess looked at him and reluctantly nodded as though to indicate that she saw his point but was still skeptical. The job Persson, accompanied by his own bodyguard assigned to himself, was to station himself inside Town Hall on the square. There he would pick up on the work Stein and McBride had done when they first visited Bremen and where they spent a great deal of time at the Town Hall checking historical records.

Grimand would stay at the hotel and be in constant touch with his people in Paris who were compiling as much data as they could find regarding the men who had been assassinated. Philippe Marcel suggested this task because he was particularly interested in whether the data they were searching for would include the travel histories of these assassinated men. Marcel believed that there was a chance that all of them had reason, at one time or another, to travel to Bremen. He even mentioned that if it could be proved that the one who died of natural causes, named Walther Koertig, also traveled to Bremen, then we would have it. Of course this would necessarily lead to the question of where and who in Bremen they visited.

Grimand was chosen to keep up the information flow to Garelik in New York. As for Philippe Marcel, he remained glued to Grimand at the hotel and became, at least temporarily, Grimand's research associate in a task that could be titled *Information Gathering*.

Now it was all go.

*　*　*

Marlow was right. Tess handled the tourist thing with great elan. She was expressive and demonstrative and she mumbled as directed. The Market Square was bustling with people and no one could tell what in the world she was saying over the din. Alex thought she was a natural-born star. However, that didn't matter, because no one in Alex's group spotted anything of interest at the Market Square. With one exception — they saw McBride and Stein enter the cathedral.

McBride and Stein considered their Town Hall mission to be not quite as important as when they first visited the cathedral. Now they would pay a first visit to the minister of the cathedral, and only then to the custodian-caretaker-gatekeeper, Koppel. They surmised that this protocol would follow the formal chain of command of the cathedral. Of course, since they'd already interviewed these gentlemen during their first visit to Bremen, they couldn't see how they'd be refused for a second. It wouldn't be polite for them to be refused, moreover it might look suspicious.

After Alex and his group saw them entering the cathedral, McBride and Stein followed suit unannounced, not having called in advance to schedule the meeting. Inside the great hall, a few people, obviously tourists, were milling around and assessing the magnificent structure. After seeing them, the minister left his pulpit and approached them.

"Oh, hello, detectives. What a surprise. Nice to see you. What brings you here?"

"Well," McBride started, "we're still interested in the episode during the war when the bank in town was bombed. The truth is that not just you, but many others have told us that it is common knowledge that a fortune of money had been stored there and was either destroyed in the bombing or was simply taken—stolen."

McBride paused, and it was obvious to him the minister seemed to experience an awkward moment, and was at a loss to know how to reply. Stein waited a moment but then said: "You see, minister, here's what we know. There was a squad of soldiers guarding the bank and we also know that after the war many of them were killed—actually assassinated. We think that one of these guardians of the treasure at the bank, may have been one of the assassins or even a lone assassin."

"That's a lot to digest, sir," the minister said. "I'm not sure I follow it."

"Well, it's a lot to follow," answered McBride. "At the moment, we're basically interested in knowing whether the money was in fact stolen, and, where it could have been stored."

"Oh, yes, we have quite a lot of space here in the cathedral and a very capacious basement in which are stored crypts with mummified corpses of former notables who have historical importance. You know, bishops and such. You're welcome to follow me down to the basement, the *bleikeller*. It's the lead metal basement directly below the nave."

They all descended to the *bleikeller* where they spent a little time looking it over. McBride later told Stein that he was trying to smell the bouquet, the scent of money. He swore to Stein after they left the cathedral, that he could tell how money smelled. They both laughed at the remark, but, Stein believed him.

Shortly after, the minister excused himself to return to his pulpit in order to review various papers held there. He said they could remain as long as they wished and to familiarize themselves with the *bleikeller*.

"Always be comfortable here at the cathedral my friends, and come visit with us anytime. Please excuse me."

After the minister left, Stein commented:

"He couldn't wait to get the hell out of here. I could feel it. No doubt."

"Right," McBride agreed.

McBride shifted over to one of the crypts and, in a split second, pried it open a bit to see if it was housing any money. Nothing—except what looked like a mummy. He tried another casket. Again nothing.

"Dave, if there's any money here, it's not keeping these mummies company. I don't think the money is in the cathedral any more even if Rowdy told us it was. My hunch is that they've moved it."

"I got it too. They've moved it."

At that moment, Torsten Koppel, the caretaker, walked in and, with a kind of surprised, look, greeted them.

"Hello, hello, hello" he said. "Welcome. Minister Konrad asked me to accompany you. What can I do for you? Do you want to review the bombing story that we talked about the last time we met?"

"Yes, that would be good," Stein said.

They talked for a while but nothing new materialized. It's what both Stein and McBride probably predicted beforehand without even talking about it. Both the minister and the caretaker were stonewalling. You couldn't be on the police force as a detective for all the years they were on it without being able to diagnose a stonewalling effort. Stein said it later:

"They're in it up to their eyeballs."

"And how," McBride again agreed.

In another one of the Bremen venues, two of the interviews conducted by Persson and translated from the German by someone Tancredi sent over, generated the information that in the past few days three trucks pulled up to the cathedral's back entrance and several men were transferring a lot of cartons onto these trucks. A young man of about twenty-five said he was sitting nearby at night with his girlfriend for at least an hour, and the activity went on without stop. He didn't know when it ended, but he did know it was feverish activity.

* * *

Later, our entire Garelik contingent met back at the hotel. After dinner, all but Grimand and Marcel talked it over. Grimand and Marcel sent word that they would be late because they were putting something together.

I described Tess's performance as Oscar worthy but said there was nothing much to report, and added—more to the point, we hadn't located Rostmann.

Then Stein and McBride described their meetings with the minister and caretaker. McBride pointed out something odd. He imitated the caretakers greeting:

"Hello, Hello, Hello." Look, guys, his name is Torsten Koppel, and after he greeted us with these "Hellos" three times, my thought was that one hello would have been enough. He didn't need three. But the guy was nervous—I could feel it, and Dave agrees.

Persson piped up and described the interview with the twenty-five-year-old man whose story was corroborated by a second witness as to the feverish activity at night when the trucks at the cathedral were being loaded.

The moment Persson finished, McBride, jumped in.

"Listen, guys, I have no doubt that the minister and the caretaker are in on it. Rowdy was absolutely right. Also, there's no money in the cathedral. It's been moved. Trucks. There's no chance that the cartons of money are hidden in the steeples of the cathedral because there would be no way to bring it all up there, especially in so short a period of time. Oh yeah, it's been moved all right."

Everyone agreed.

"So," Stein continued, "first, we don't have Rostmann and, second, we haven't found the money. We're right back where we started"

It was Grimand who rescued it all when he and Marcel rushed in.

"We've got a new lead. As we were poring over the files, Marcel noticed that Alois Amsel, the one knifed in the hotel elevator when Alex was at the hotel in Paris, paid numerous visits to Berlin. Then we came across the same travel schedule to Berlin, made by Horst Kabkow, another one of the ten who was recently stabbed to death. The clincher is that Hans Milch, also recently stabbed to death, similarly, made several trips to Berlin.

"I think we're onto something. We've been examining the files of each of the squad that was killed as well as the notes on Walther Koertig, the one who died a natural death. And we now know for sure that they were all over forty during the war when they first started guarding the bank. It was Marcel here who distilled this travel information. Guess what? Marcel found the travel itinerary of Koertig and was practically shaken. Koertig, as was his Germanic manner, kept detailed notes on everything. You all are probably guessing about what's coming next. Here it is. Koertig's travel excursions took him to Berlin on three different occasions over a ten year period.

"And here's the killer, sorry, I mean the unifying theme of it all. They all registered at the historical Rocco Forte Hotel de Rome in Berlin, located on Behrenstrasse 37, close to the German Historical Museum. We're thinking that all of them, not just these few, visited that hotel at one time or another. We've contacted the German Secret Service, the BND, and I've spoken to the deputy chief who I know. He assures me that the Hotel de Rome has attracted many former Nazi officials, most of whom had avoided prosecution. He added that there was a group of hotels in that area, near the Rocco Forte Hotel de Rome, that have also been target destinations for former Nazis. I don't see any reason for this cluster of hotels to be attractive to this demographic — except the obvious.

"So there you have it. There's no doubt that Rostmann was also there. We need to have members of our unit represented there. Who should go?"

"Call Garelik," I blurted out. Let's see what he has to say."

Garelik was filled in on the entire story. He suggested that since nothing was found at the cathedral and Rostmann was still at large, there was no longer any use in staying in Bremen. He suggested that we all go to Berlin and check into that hotel.

When Garelik's rationale for his Berlin option was considered, Grimand again was the first to rush in. "He's right, let's get the hell out of here and get to Berlin — to the Hotel de Rome."

And that was it. But we all agreed: Philippe Marcel was becoming indispensible. While everyone dispersed and retired to their hotel rooms, Marcel made all the flight reservations to Berlin, plus he also nailed down the hotel accommodations.

*   *   *

Rostmann was already in Berlin. But he was not staying at the Hotel de Rome. That would be too conspicuous, because he knew that other former

Nazi brass could possibly recognize him. He avoided recognition because Rostmann's first rule of engagement was *not* to engage. Better would to be as hidden as possible. Thus, he was holed up with Jean in a little rental unit on the fringes of the German Historical Museum. Rostmann had business at the museum and none at all at the Hotel de Rome.

*   *   *

The next day, we all traveled to Berlin and settled in at the Hotel de Rome. Of course we faced the same problem we faced in Bremen, although in Bremen at least we had information from Rowdy as well as Dave and Jack that the cathedral was a sure-fire lead. Here we had no such clue and weren't even sure how to proceed. The only thing we could rely on was the solid information that the Bremen Squad of ten all had contact over the years, and each one, on more than one occasion, was in touch with some of the others and at this hotel. Something was brewing here, and someone at this hotel knew something, and possibly more than one person would know what that "something" was.

So here we all were starting at point zero. But now it was Tancredi's turn.

"Gentlemen and ladies, it's pretty clear that we need to do all we can to engage the help-staff at the hotel, especially with trying to get any information on Marcus Rostmann. This hotel in Berlin has the same importance to our case, to our quest, in a way that's analogous to St. Peter's Cathedral on the Bremen Market Square. The information we need will be unearthed at this hotel."

"Right," I blurted out. "Absolutely."

Grimand turned to Marcel: "Well, what do you think? What do we do first?"

We all respected Marcel, so that Grimand's question to him actually represented our collective agreement.

"I was thinking," he said, "that at this point perhaps we ought to consider the dubious hypothesis that any help-staff at the hotel who speaks English might be more amenable to engaging with us, so that we can develop the conversation and steer it in a direction that will be productive. So, we do everything we can to locate English-speaking service people. That goes for waiters, maids, those at the front desk, bellboys, room service personnel, and others—even guests."

Stein, in something similar to one of McBride's out-of-the-box brain-storms then added:

"About guests, Philippe's idea about speaking to guests as well as to others jogged a thought. See, in some hotels there are guests who live there permanently. It might be a good idea to see if we could identify anyone like that who's always here."

We all agreed that that was a good idea. We then started working out at least a tentative plan on how to interject ourselves into the life of the hotel to blend in with the other ghosts who haunt it.

It was lunchtime and we joined together for a meal sticking to conversation only about personal issues, taking care not to reveal who we really were. After lunch, we spread out to all parts of the hotel, and went to work. We were looking for any information, particularly about Rostmann, but also about any stories regarding former or present Nazis who may have frequented Hotel de Rome or even some of the other hotels in the area. We were interested in identifying possible allies at the hotel in our information-gathering phase of the operation.

Tess and I, plus Tancredi and Maria, became a foursome—two couples, friends who traveled together. We were happy and talkative and engaged any hotel personnel we happened to run into. And there were many such encounters, and many of the staff spoke English. We would ask all sorts of questions and try to develop the conversations, although with a great deal of indirection. I had told the group that there could be some hypnotic effects when a conversation is peppered with indirect references to things. It tends to invite, actually stimulate, the other person's stream of consciousness. I assured all that when one's stream of consciousness is stimulated, things will emerge that could be highly significant. They all got it, and felt my comments were interesting.

* * *

Stein and McBride started it. Both had a great way with repartee and being handsome and macho types were finding a willing audience. They were having an animated conversation with one of the desk clerks. She was an attractive woman of about thirty and it was clear that she was flattered at the casual and yes, flirtatious manner of the two of them. And she spoke English very well.

"So," Stein said: "How long have you worked here?"

"Two years," she answered. Her name tag read: *Astrid Neumann.* "Astrid, I like that name. Beautiful. Nice sound to it." It was McBride knowing exactly what to say and how to say it. Astrid really liked it. Later on, McBride made Stein laugh when he said: "But I wasn't crazy about the Neumann."

They didn't need to keep the conversation going, because Astrid was very open in her responses. Her conversation was the kind that needed a response from the other person. And boy did McBride and Stein step in!

Stein said it. "You know, I once lived in a hotel for a while in New York City, and at that hotel — it was a residential hotel where people could have their own room as an apartment — I met two elderly ladies who had lived there for at least forty years. That's the truth, forty years. After that I used to wonder if that was also the case in all hotels. You know, I mean are there always some people who live at the hotel permanently?"

Astrid answered enthusiastically, "Oh yes that is also the case here. We do have also two ladies who have been living here for many years. One is, I think, only middle age, but the other is quite elderly." Guessing, she added, "I'm sure they've been here probably also about perhaps twenty years, or maybe more? They always sit in the lobby and read their papers and sometimes talk to one another. You know," she added, "they didn't move when the rooms were renovated so that each of them still has a little kitchen on the back of one of the walls of their room, and they're able to cook in the room."

Dave continued. "I thought that might be the case in all hotels, especially if the hotel was built decades ago, like this one."

"Yes, this hotel has been here a long time."

McBride was amazed that Dave kept the conversation going quite naturally and, threw in all sorts of indirection just as Alex had suggested. It seemed to work because Astrid was beginning to add a lot of detail. The question was how to get the information they needed. But, without saying anything, they both obviously thought: So far, so good.

"Tell me Astrid, I would love to talk with these ladies. I'm very interested in a person's history and I'm sure they must have fascinating stories. Do you think you could point them out to me?"

"Yes, of course," she said, and she looked around in the lobby. "There's one right there. She's sitting on the leather chair in the far corner. She likes that chair because she says it's comfortable, but I think it's really because it gives her a full view of the entire lobby. She loves observing people."

"That's great. Jack is going to try his best to keep you company—I can tell he loves talking to you—I'm going to try to talk with, uh, what is her name?"

"Her name is Frau Krause. Please address her that way and tell her that you wanted to know more about the hotel and that I suggested she might be a person who could help you. I'm sure she'll be thrilled to talk with you. You're lucky because she tells everyone she meets from America that she lived in a city in America from the time she was a little girl until her family moved back to Berlin many years ago. But just one thing. Be sensitive with her because although she is still a youthful woman, there is something wrong with her memory and even with the way she sometimes thinks and talks."

Dave Stein made a beeline directly to Frau Krause. Frau Krause was, at one time, one could see, a rather stately woman, now probably close to fifty if not more. She was a bit frail, as though she were suffering with some malady, and her age, despite its still relatively youthful calibration, wore on her. She spoke in a tremulous way with a high pitched voice.

"Excuse me, Frau Krause."

"You want to talk to me?"

"Yes, the desk girl, Miss Astrid Neumann, said you might be able to help me."

"Yes, of course. I can tell you're American by your way of speaking. You know, I lived in America from the age of five till I was about eighteen. Then we moved back to Berlin."

Then Frau Krause started on a roll. Her English was fairly good.

"I was born in 1930, and I'm in my late forties. I know I look older. I'm not ashamed of it. That's the way it is! It's that, physically, how shall I say, I think I'm a little compromised. What do you want to know, young man?"

"Well, first, my name is Dave."

Dave confessed later that he didn't want to say "Stein" and especially not his full Jewish name, David Stein. After all, it was Germany, but even more than thirty years after the war he wouldn't take a chance to ruin the possibility of landing a big one—especially on the first try. So he continued:

"Well, I'm very interested in history, and Miss Neumann said you know a lot about the history of this hotel. Is that right?"

Frau Krause became invigorated. You could see she wanted to talk, to tell her story.

"Oh yes, I live here, and I've been here since 1960, since my parents died. They were killed in a car crash here in Berlin. Now it's 1979. They were killed almost twenty years ago. I was always good with numbers. I was five years old when my parents left Germany in 1935. My parents moved back to Berlin only a few years after the war, in 1948. My father was democratic and hated the Nazi movement, which was gaining power in 1935. So he took us to America, to Pittsburgh where he had relatives. So from 1935 to 1948 we lived in America. Of course that's how I know English. My father became rather wealthy in a relatively short period of time, and so I inherited his wealth, and that's how I can live happily in this wonderful hotel."

"That's very interesting," Dave said.

"Oh yes, I think so too. Thank you. Did I tell you that I lived in America? That's important because it shows that my father was not a Nazi. He left Germany and only returned when the Nazis were defeated. Of course Hitler made a terrible mistake because he used too many troops to guard Jews and he did those terrible things to them. If he hadn't used so many troops for that reason, he could have used them to fight the Americans and British and then we might have won the war. Don't you think?"

Man oh man, was she talking to the wrong person. Dave was alert to anti-Jewish feeling, and he noticed that she said "then 'we' might have won the war." Yes, she said "we." It revealed that in her sentiments she was allying herself with the Nazis. Dave later asked Alex what that meant — that at first she seemed proud she was with America and then, unconsciously, made what Dave immediately identified as "a Freudian slip."

*   *   *

When Dave told us about it, I answered this way:

"Dave, it's like this. Apparently the lady has some cognitive deficit, kind of like either a memory problem or something like a bit of early organic brain problem. So what happens in a case like that is some impulse is set free in the person's stream of consciousness so that unconscious material begins ever so slightly to mingle with conscious material."

"Well," he said, "does that mean that underneath she sympathizes with the Nazis?"

"Maybe yes, maybe no," I answered.

"You see, Dave, her father was anti-Nazi. But it could be that, underneath it all, in order for her to feel independent and not controlled by him, she may have harbored what might be called oppositional tendencies. He says 'day,' she might unconsciously say 'night.' He's anti-Nazi so she might underneath it all, and just to be contrary, identify a bit with the Nazis."

"Yeah," Dave said. "She even had a strategy for Hitler winning the war by not bothering Jews and using the soldiers who guarded Jews to fight against the allies. That also bothered me."

* * *

And that was that. When Frau Krause asked Dave what he thought about what she said, he answered that it was interesting, knowing full well that there was no use in discussing the Nazi thing or the Jewish thing. Anyway, Dave was obviously right. Don't mess with the on-target narrative. Besides, she didn't seem to give it much thought that, when he introduced himself as Dave, it might be Jewish.

"Frau Krause, you are an interesting woman. May I sit here alongside?

"Of course. I like you. I'm pleased with your company."

"By the way, are there others who also return here often because they like the hotel so much? You must have noticed them because I can see that you're very alert to everything that happens in the lobby and in the hotel. I guess sometimes good and at other times bad, or maybe sometimes something positive and at other times something negative. Know what I mean?"

"I know exactly what you mean. The truth of it is that my father would turn over in his grave if he saw the Nazi riff-raff that frequent this beautiful hotel."

"My my, Frau Krause, how do you know they're Nazis? That's so interesting. Real Nazis? I thought they were a thing of the past."

"No, no. They're not a thing of the past. They do actually stay at this hotel. I pretend not to know it, but I do. I hate Nazis, just like my parents did!"

"Truthfully, about almost ten years ago, maybe about 1969, when I think I was about in my late thirties, a Herr Hans Milch, who was then married, even though I never knew it, still in all, stayed at the hotel, and, while here, he asked me to dinner. We went, and he was gracious and expressed warm feelings toward me. At that time I was still quite attractive. I was often told that I was statuesque and beautiful. Can you tell?"

The only reason Dave paused was because he heard the name Hans Milch. Dave knew he was about to get an earful.

"Oh, yes, very definitely. You have a very nice way about you, and I can also see what Herr Milch meant. Certainly."

"Thank you. I'm always susceptible to flattery even though I arrange to elicit it. Anyway, Herr Milch was quite wealthy and he couldn't stop talking about how rich he really was. He confessed that he was in the army during the war. He wouldn't tell me how old he was, but I could see he was probably about seventy, or even more, and here I was something like thirty-five or so. That's something like a thirty-five-year difference. I know my numbers. I was not considering anything other than dinner—you understand."

"What did Herr Milch do at his age?"

"Quite frankly, I never found out. He wouldn't talk about his personal business, although he did say that, whenever he stayed at the hotel, friends of his would also arrive, and they would hold meetings at the museum nearby, in the room devoted to plants, you know those that are hearty and can survive under most circumstances, in contrast to those that can't.

"The curator of that museum, uh, it's the Historical Museum near the hotel here, is a man who also frequents this hotel. I know his name. Let me see. Yes, yes. His name is Manfred Bauer. He's the curator of that Historical Museum, near to here—oh yes, I said that. You see, I do know a lot about the history here."

"Did you ever meet any of Herr Milch's friends, those that he met here?"

"Yes, of course. As a matter of fact, Herr Milch met a man named Torsten Koppel here, and I was introduced. Herr Koppel I think he told me he was either the curator or maybe he said the caretaker or gatekeeper of a cathedral in Bremen. It's north. Once when I was sitting in this very spot, the three of them walked through the lobby and out into the street. They were so engrossed in their conversation that they didn't even notice me. Can you imagine that?"

"You mean the curator, Herr Bauer of the Historical Museum, here, near the hotel in Berlin, was also with them when they were all together walking out of the hotel?"

"Yes. Yes. Exactly."

"The history of it all is so interesting. All these people and their stories," Dave continued.

"Did you ever hear the name Marcus…." Before Dave had a chance to say "Rostmann," she said it.

"Oh yes, Marcus Rostmann, he was really a Nazi. A swine. Herr Milch knew him, too. Herr Milch told me that Rostmann was a captain in the army and was very strict; that he had people severely punished who were not doing what was commanded. I did not at all like to hear about Herr Rostmann."

Dave tried to get more information about Rostmann, but Frau Krause had nothing else to give. Dave knew he had amassed a treasure trove of important information. However, as he later remarked, it troubled him that he felt low, by not being authentic in his conversation with Frau Krause. He knew it was in the greater interest, but, as usual, that sort of thing made him feel manipulative, and he basically didn't like it, even though as a detective he had done it numerous times in the past.

* * *

When we all met in the evening Dave and Jack were the only ones who had anything new to report. We were all tired and demoralized. Then Dave and Jack laid it on — how they lucked out with Frau Krause and how she had actually named Milch, Koppel, Rostmann, and the new guy, Manfred Bauer.

Yes, we all started from point zero, but now, as Marcel suddenly exclaimed: "It's obviously the museum. That's our next stop. It's got something to do with the museum and that curator, Bauer."

I said, "Hallelujah." Tess hugged me.

* * *

Rostmann was at the museum doing his favorite thing. He was not counting out hundred dollar bills. Rather, he was counting out stacks of such hundreds bound by what looked like adhesive strips. At the same time, Manfred Bauer, the museum's chief curator, was tracking the tally. They were in the subbasement of the museum where all museum equipment was stored along with various displays of former museum exhibits. In the furthest back room of the basement was a large, heavily bolted room—a room as vast as a ballroom. In it were stacks and stacks of hundred dollar bills wrapped in those adhesive or what looked like paperlike strips. This had been the new repository for the stash. Now the cash was being loaded onto large carts. And witnessing it all was Inspector Maria Oliva sitting tied in a chair. The two men who had taken her were the ones wheeling the carts out of the room. Obviously, the money was going elsewhere.

Yes, they had Inspector Maria Oliva, Tancredi's love. They got her in the corridor of the hotel, just like that. And now she was tied in the chair, although not gagged.

On the Rostmann side, it was clear that at least in the recent past he would not harm Bauer because it was Bauer who decided who could visit this museum site and who couldn't. And even if Rostmann wanted to kill him—which he probably did—with all that money in that particular museum safe house, how was Rostmann going to get it out? Even though the money was recently transferred from the cathedral in Bremen to this museum in Berlin, Rostmann knew that Berlin was getting too hot and therefore the money needed to travel again. But how in the world did Rostmann know that the scene in Berlin was getting too hot?

Obviously, someone tipped him off. And it was probably someone at the hotel.

At first, Bauer felt safe, and, in fact, was safe, because since he was the gatekeeper of the money and the museum, it was only common sense that Rostmann wouldn't do a thing. In fact, it was the only situation about which Rostmann needed to accept a recessive role. He was furious. He was made to feel disempowered! Helplessness! Impotent! It was his worst nightmare because he felt stopped—in contrast to his need for unending highly stimulating action.

Here Bauer was the boss of everything including and especially the money transferred from the cathedral. No one knew how it got there, but for sure it must have been a Herculean effort for it to be relocated so efficiently. Rostmann knew that Odessa did not just transport people but could transport anything and do it well.

Rostmann was initially confident that the money was safe in this particular ivory tower, this museum sanctuary. But now he felt this safety feature was possibly compromised. Now they had Maria. Rostmann knew that with Maria's absence, the museum was vulnerable to a comprehensive police search. Therefore, despite Rostmann's original plan to spend much more time visiting this museum in Berlin, now, though Rostmann knew not to stay at the Rocco Forte Hotel de Rome or in any of the other hotels immediately surrounding the museum, his entire focus was to get the money the hell out of the museum.

* * *

We were still tooling up our team and needed to decide a strategy for getting us all into the museum so that we could spread out and not leave a stone unturned. Grimand reminded us that if anyone suspects that one of the people there is Rostmann, not to do anything—that it's obvious Rostmann would certainly be armed.

"Rostmann doesn't go around without a weapon, and his gun is always loaded," Grimand said. "Let's keep it in mind. We don't want anyone hurt."

The fact was, Marcus Rostmann was never concerned about hurting someone. His preoccupation in life was to do just that. Now that he was in Berlin, it was almost predictable there would be a dead body found somewhere. We could all feel that Rostmann was nearby. The museum was a short walk from the hotel. We didn't know if he had a place to hole up at the museum or whether he was in some sort of a hideout of an apartment.

Stein piped up: "OK, I think this is a job for Jack and me. We'll be the first ones at the museum. Maybe we'll have beginner's luck like we did with Frau Krause. The key is to make some contact with Bauer, the curator, and see whatever we can see. Hopefully we'll run into Rostmann. We kind of know what he looks like from photos Jacques had, showing him when he was a soldier of about forty.

"Remember," Marcel said: "He was a captain and had been a career soldier. The photo was probably taken in 1943, 1944, or maybe 1945, when he was about fifty. Let's take the middle number, 1944. That would put him in his mid to late seventies. He was described as a six-foot-two man who had sort of a limp or a funny gait. Figure with age, and with that gait, he would probably look shorter. And let's not forget that he might be balding, or at least gray."

Persson said that Dave's and Marcel's points were very good. He also suggested that we all scour the neighborhood close to the museum by fanning out in pairs but certainly not looking like one group. Some should look like tourists. Everything should be casual and easygoing.

"I'm not sure about you and Tess, Alex," he said. "I think you both need to remain at the hotel, along with Detective Marlow. You might also do some investigating here at the hotel."

Then, speaking to us all, Persson said that after our museum excursion we should all meet for dinner at the hotel at 6 p.m.

*   *   *

And that was that. Tess, Marlow, and I stayed behind while the others headed for the street. We were then on our own. We sat in the lobby of the hotel. Tess was asking Marlow about his police work. I was sitting as if in a dream world. I guess I was just tired. Almost at that moment, a tall man with gray hair, looking to be in his mid seventies and walking with a slight limp, passed right by us. For a second it didn't register and then bang went my heart. I was alarmed and amazed.

"That's gotta be Rostmann," I said to Tess and Marlow. Looking at Marlow, I said: "He even looks like Rowdy. It can't be anyone else. Look, he's stooped, age-wise exactly right, and he's got an awkward gait caused by that limp."

They both gasped and sat up straight, just gazing at him walking toward the elevator. He stood with these other seemingly random people waiting for the elevator and along with the others, entered the elevator. The three of us walked quickly over to the elevator. It stopped on 3 and on 5.

Marlow said, "We need to get a complete list of who's on 3 and on 5. We also need to check floors 2, 4, and 6, because he's too smart to ring his floor. He'll probably either walk up a flight or down one. That means we need a complete list of everyone booked on these five floors. My bet is that he'd rather walk down one—so my bet's on four—assuming of course that he got out on five rather than someone else getting out on five.

But we can't get that information through the concierge desk. We don't know if there's someone working in the hotel on his payroll or a fellow-traveler—you know, someone allied with his mission. We need to find out another way."

"How about Astrid, that young woman at the concierge's desk that Dave and Jack told us about," I suggested.

But Marlow was a real detective, not a maybe-one like me.

"No," he said, "not good. Even though she's located at the desk, we can't be sure. Remember, would we have guessed that the museum curator was in on it? No. We've got to get it another way."

We all tacitly agreed that Rostmann would never want to be seen at this particular hotel, assuming of course that he had been there many times before. Therefore, if he was trying not to be seen, he wouldn't have a reservation here. But, it's for damn sure there he was. The room would not likely be in his name. It could, however, be in the name of Bauer.

We were talking in the lobby when Dave and Jack walked in. They spotted us and walked over. Dave then saw Frau Krause sitting in her chair against the far wall where she had that panoramic view of the entire lobby. Their eyes met and Dave reflexively got up and walked over to say hello to her.

*   *   *

"Oh, hello, sir. Thank you for coming over."

It was a bit awkward because Dave never gave her his surname, so the way she greeted him was quite skillful.

"How are you this evening?" Dave said.

Then Frau Krause began her review of her day's events. Here and there Dave got in a comment. Then, surprising us Frau Krause said: "Oh there goes Herr Manfred Bauer, the curator of the museum. He lives here on the fourth floor."

Wow, Dave thought. Now we've got the floor that Rostmann's on. We need the room number.

*   *   *

Dave bade Frau Krause a respectful farewell and came back to sit with us. He excitedly told us what he learned, and Detective Marlow took it from there.

"Maria is the one to do it. She needs to put on a maid's uniform and get to the fourth floor with towels in her arms and a pistol in her hand that's tucked into the stack of towels. She has to walk back and forth until she spots either one or both of them leaving Bauer's room. That way we'll know the room number. We'll give her a description of Bauer. She's knows all about how Rostmann looks.

Marlow said, "There's something very important going on in that room for Rostmann to walk into the hotel and risk being noticed. Once we get the room number after they both leave we'll have it tapped."

Marlow was excited. "Having it tapped is the first true inroad into Rostmann's inner life, into Bauer's role, and into the relationship between them. What a break!"

PART 6

DECEPTION

· 11 ·

DECEPTION

Philippe Marcel, rushing, practically tore open the door and ran past the maitre d'. He disregarded other diners and shouted:

"They've got Maria. It was a trap all along."

With that, Dave and Jack ran out of the dining room — with Dave taking the stairs and Jack, the elevator. Both had guns drawn. They met on the fourth floor. The fourth floor corridor was empty, and, as in most hotels, it was absolutely quiet. All one could see, up and down the corridor, were doors. No Maria. Other than Dave and Jack, it was Tancredi who exited the elevator. He was ashen.

"I knew it," he said to them. "I shouldn't have permitted it. Maria. Maria Oliva" — he repeated her name. Tancredi was beside himself. He knew she was taken. "They saw through her maid's uniform. They got her anyway."

Jack McBride added: "They got her all right and there's no way they're still in the hotel. There all kinds of ways in or out of the hotel — even a basement exit. They're gone."

Looking at Tancredi, Jack continued: "We both know, Aldo, we'll hear from them. And they won't hurt her because she's good for some kind of trade. Rostmann's dangerous, but he's not stupid. As far as we know he's only killed members of his squad, not police personnel."

Tancredi, Jack, and Dave met back in Philippe's room where we were all wondering about how it happened. Without any of us having a clue, Philippe Marcel, who in his unwavering belief in detail had been checking each and every person that any of us had come in contact with for even a minor conversation. Once he had that person's name, he made brief investigations on each. Thanks to his thoroughness, it included checks both on Astrid Neumann and Frau Krause. In believing that the devil is in the details, and his mantra, "details needing to be specific" as not really a redundancy, he touched base with every secret service organization on his radar and finally got the information that electrified him.

"OK, here it is," he told us. "I realized that getting to Frau Krause through Astrid Neumann happened too coincidentally and too fast. It bothered me. Sure, it could have been pure luck, but it still bothered me. Her first name, which she didn't give you, Dave, is Ilsa Krause. You were worried that you masterfully avoided telling her your last name, but the truth is that she deliberately avoided giving you her given name, Ilsa.

Frau Ilsa Krause, did live in America, and her father, who had traveled widely in America, was a member of the German Bund, a Nazi organization that, by the way, once held a rally at Madison Square Garden in New York City. Frau Krause is not in her late forties; she's fifty-five. At the age of twenty-four, when she lived in America, she was in the employ of the same Bund. She worked as a translator. The FBI even faxed me her picture. It's the same woman, just thirty-one years older.

"I think, Dave, that her wobbly voice, and her tendency to repeat a phrase or two, was put on. You may have been feeling guilty that you were duplicitous with her, but she was completely deceptive with you. And I mean completely. There's real treachery here. And the whole business with her slip of the tongue regarding the Nazi thing, the thing that Alex had theorized about, was also a ruse, to make you believe that she was a little mentally scattered. She's obviously a first-class operative. And that's why she's living at the hotel, probably paid by Rostmann or Odessa. She was here because these hotels are where people like Rostmann congregate. It's the same with the rest of the hotels near the museum. Apparently, they're all hotbeds of Nazi intrigue, and they need to have eyes in all of them."

"OK," Dave said with no reaction. "What about Astrid Neumann?"

"I did a check on her as well, but she's absolutely clean with the FBI, Scotland Yard, the BND, and Interpol. Nevertheless, innocent or not, she's not to be trusted."

"So," Dave said, "when Frau Krause fingered Rostmann and Bauer, and mentioned Milch, she was baiting the hook." Thinking further, Dave said: "Of course, that's why Rostmann walked through the lobby of the hotel, very blasé. He knew Frau Krause would be there to spot and announce to all concerned whoever it was in the flesh, and she did it that way, no doubt, because we were there to hear it and see it. And she announced Bauer, and of course Rostmann, who just strolled by."

Meanwhile, I was sitting there, listening to all of it, every once in a while glancing at Tess. I was feeling a bit embarrassed that I had made up such a ridiculous theory about Frau Krause and her unconscious slip of the tongue as well as other interpretations that I now thought wound up being psychobabble—like the stuff about her relationship with her father. Man, oh man, live and learn. "OK," I joined in, "my theory about Kraus and her father was ridiculous. What happens now?"

With that, Marcel repeated that he was sure Maria was not in mortal danger—at least not at the moment. "Rostmann wants something. There's no doubt they have her at the museum."

* * *

Marcel was right. Maria was at the museum. She had been sharing that capacious back room in the museum basement with many millions of dollars—tied to a chair. And she watched every second of Rostmann, Bauer, and two other men transferring the stacks of money out of the museum. It was a job that required tremendous effort, but the four of them managed to do it by filling up large carts with stacks of money and wheeling it all out. Maria estimated that it must have taken about a couple of hours for the job to be completed. She counted the carts as they were filled and wheeled out and arrived at a rough figure of more than sixty full of stacks of money. Maria assumed they moved the money by truck. She had heard Tancredi and the others talk about trucks as the perfect mode of transit for this kind of a job.

But now, she was thinking of how she had been subdued on that fourth floor of the hotel. She reviewed it in her mind—exactly. Before she knew it, and as she was passing a door in the corridor, it opened quickly and she was subdued by two men. How they knew who she was or why she was there was a mystery. But they knew! One of the men held a gun with a silencer to her head while staring menacingly and with intent directly into her eyes. She submitted. Didn't make a sound.

They led her to the back staircase into the basement and out the service entrance door, directly into a station wagon. They then traveled a short distance and parked the wagon at the side entrance to the German Historical Museum.

It was the situation, so professionally done, and obviously with such precision, that convinced Maria to be the perfect captive—entirely compliant. However, Rostmann, as well as Bauer, were also sure she was a competent police officer and that, given the slightest chance, she would try her best to destroy their plans. Of course, they weren't going to give her any chance whatsoever.

Maria was not blindfolded, was not unconscious, and not muzzled. She could see, hear, and talk. Rostmann knew that Maria, was aware that her life was hanging by a hair. But she also knew not to dare scream. In any case, the room was probably soundproofed. Screaming wouldn't have helped, even if her life wasn't being threatened. But she was keenly aware of the danger because she was seeing and hearing everything.

Now she was tied to a chair and in a subbasement.

Rostmann spoke evenly—showing no emotion at all.

"Miss police officer, don't make me hurt you. Answer my questions directly and everything for you, at least for now, will be peaceful. What is your name?"

"Maria, Maria Oliva."

"Were you here because of the money?"

"Yes."

"Is that all you're here for?"

"No."

"Please tell me what else."

"We know you were involved with that bank heist in Bremen when you were captain of the squad protecting the bank."

"I thought that was it. How many are with you?"

"I'm not exactly sure, but I think about ten."

"All from New York City like that officer Dave, with the absent last name?"

Maria instantly knew that Frau Krause was part of it all. "No, not all. Some are from European capitals who work in police affairs."

"So they know about me—yes?"

"Yes."

Maria was thinking that he knew everything or at least had guessed it, so she felt she had done no harm by answering his questions directly and honestly. As a matter of fact, Maria realized that Rostmann would not know what to ask if it wasn't already something he suspected. Therefore, Maria's answers were truthful. In fact, Maria could see that Rostmann's approach was simply to verify his suspicions.

Rostmann persisted:

"Do they have Rowan, Rowdy?"

"Yes."

"Did he talk?"

"Yes."

"So they think they know what I can do?"

"Yes."

"But it's all hearsay. They have no proof that I've done anything wrong. Right?"

"I'm not sure about that, but you may be right."

"Do they know about Jean?

"Yes."

"And they know about the museum?"

"Only somewhat."

"Do they know where the money is stored?

"No, not really, but they probably suspect it's here at the museum."

"Where do you work—which police department?"

"Milan."

"Milan?"

"Yes."

"Where are the others from?

"Sweden, France, America."

"Very interesting," Rostmann said. "They even have Interpol involved. I know the chief of Interpol is from Sweden. Persson."

"Do they know anything about Kluge?"

"I'm not sure, but I don't think so. I haven't heard about that."

"You realize Kluge and I are the two who survived, and I plan to keep Kluge away from me. He's the one who's been doing the killings, not me. Do you understand?"

"Yes, I understand what you just said."

"Meaning you're not sure you believe me?"

"Yes, I'm not sure."

"You're smart and you're honest. I can see that. I admire that."

"Thank you."

"Even with this money transfer, yes, I'm an accomplice but I'm not in charge. And I have no choice except to be an accomplice because quite frankly, they would kill me in a second otherwise. Do you understand?"

"Yes."

"But you still don't quite believe me?"

"I'm not sure."

With that, and at the end of the money transfer, they escorted Maria out of the museum and into the back of one of two panel trucks waiting at the curb. In the truck, Rostmann sat with Maria while one of the other men drove. Cartons of money practically filled up the entire space of the back of the truck. Bauer and a driver were in the front cab of the other panel truck.

Both trucks began to move.

Rostmann spoke quietly with Maria.

"You see, officer, Oliva, I'm innocent. Kluge is the culprit. He did it all, and now he knows that I know he's the one in charge and he knows I didn't do anything. Understand?"

"Yes."

"I'd like you to say more than 'yes.'"

"Well I think if there's no direct evidence against you, then you might very well get off. However, that fact about your defense as an accomplice—even an unwilling one, insofar as you might claim you were really forced into such a role, then you still would be vulnerable to some sort of trial. I can see that your presentation of the material sets your case as one of insufficient evidence against you. And, further, if this other person, Kluge, is not apprehended then your case is obviously stronger."

Maria was no fool. Everything she said and did made it less likely that he would hurt her or even kill her. She could see that he was building a case against Kluge, whom she felt had most likely already been disposed of. But the way Rostmann was talking to her, actually had some appeal.

Maria was startled when the trucks parked on a deserted warehouse corner. Everyone got out and milled about. At one point Maria noticed that Bauer and Rostmann were facing one another as though in an animated but quiet and discreet discussion. Suddenly one of the other men brandished a pistol and pointed it at both Rostmann and Bauer. Rostmann pulled Bauer around in front of him as a shield, and the other man put three bullets into Bauer. Bauer fell dead on the spot. Rostmann then shot and killed the shooter. Now there were only three left: Rostmann and his driver and, of course, Maria.

Rostmann left both Bauer and the shooter dead on the sidewalk, and he, Maria, and his associate drove away.

Maria was a witness to it all. In this case, Rostmann was the out-and-out winner, the savior; that is, it was Rostmann who shot the shooter. But Maria couldn't help being a police detective. She immediately fixed on the issue of whether the entire thing was planned so that Bauer would not live. In other words, the shooter may have been in league with Rostmann, but then Rostmann double-crossed and killed him. As a result, Bauer was out of the picture and so the only other person that could have fingered Rostmann as the architect of the entire scene was gone—except, of course, for Rostmann's driver—and Maria.

Maria said to Rostmann:

"You saved the day. I feel you saved me."

It was the smartest thing she could have said because Rostmann, whether he believed her or not, was: a) in the clear, and b) had an irrefutable witness to his heroics.

Now Kluge was gone, Bauer was gone, and, lo and behold, back at the ranch, Frau Krause could no longer be a witness against anyone because one of the porters emptying ashtrays in the crowded lobby of the hotel saw her slumped halfway down in her usual chair while her head flopped to one side. She was dead. And so now Frau Krause was also gone, as were the minister and caretaker at the cathedral in Bremen. But, Rostmann knew that both the minister and caretaker had absconded and were probably already in Rome at the Vatican.

Man, oh man, there was no doubt that malodorous Nazi effluvia pervaded that hotel.

One by one, all affiliates of Rostmann were being eliminated—except for Jean. At this point Jean was the only one who could be an eyewitness to Rostmann's actions, including many of his homicides. Jean could not keep track of the exact number of assassinations Rostmann had accomplished. She thought it was five or six, but it could have been as many as seven.

The truth was that Jean always felt a sense of safety in the presence of Rostmann even though he was an out-and-out killer. Perhaps she felt that sense of safety because of precisely that—that he *was* an out-and-out killer; that is, she actually liked being with him. Or it could have been a psychological trick, actually a self-deception she'd been playing all those years being with him, living with him. The self-deception may have been that deep down she was terrified, but used denial as a way of not permitting the terror to surface into consciousness.

In contrast to Jean's denial, Maria was hoping that, because she felt that Rostmann actually liked her — maybe he would let her go. Or was Maria in denial as Jean had possibly been?

*　*　*

Just as Rostmann's house at 25 Hope Street was surrounded, so too, was the museum. The instruction from Marlow was that Alex and Tess would remain behind. The entire team spread out and entered the museum from the three entrances. They fanned out all over, and now the team included investigators from the German BND — its secret service.

They were looking specifically for Manfred Bauer, the museum's chief curator, but, first and foremost, they wanted to get Maria in their sights. They were told by a museum docent that Bauer would likely be found in the museum basement, in the room with museum preparation displays that will eventually become the final museum exhibits. The docent said it was a large room that they couldn't miss. She was about to say more, but one of the BND said to her in German:

"Never mind that. You come with us."

Down they rushed, with the docent leading the way, and with Tancredi following. Of course, no Bauer and more importantly, no Maria. They scoured the entire basement and then went down into the subbasement. Nary a soul was found. Stein and McBride were on the second floor of the museum, and they, too, found no one. Finally Grimand, Marcel, and two other BND inspectors regrouped in the lobby. They didn't have the slightest idea what to do.

And just then, suddenly, Maria appeared. She casually walked in. They were all astonished. Tancredi rushed over and embraced her, and the rest applauded.

*　*　*

"Where were you?" Tancredi entreated. "Where were you?"

"I was held by Rostmann."

"What? How'd you escape?"

"I didn't escape, he let me go. He actually bade me farewell, kissed my hand, and simply let me go. He's basically not afraid of you—any of you. He claims he's innocent of all and any potential charges against him and he believes that none of us have a thing on him that can be proven. From what he told me, I know that Frau Krause was in on it, so maybe she could be the main witness against him, provided of course that what he told me is false. So, I suggest we get to her immediately."

"Too late for Frau Krause," Tancredi inserted. "She's been poisoned by a drink she ordered. Cyanide. She died sitting in her favorite chair in the lobby. Just slid down half off the chair and was found dead."

Maria shook her head. "What a conspiracy," she said.

At that point Tess and I also arrived despite the instruction for us to remain at the hotel. And I immediately made my presence felt.

"Do you think Rostmann had it done, had it arranged?" I asked—meaning the Krause killing. When she was found, people in the lobby were aghast.

I knew of course, that Tess and I had become rather useless in this adventure, but I still felt that when the time was right I might be able to add something of importance. Maria answered that of course she didn't know whether Rostmann had Krause killed, but someone knew that Krause might have been the only one able to finger Rostmann, assuming Rostmann was actually the guilty party.

"Maria," Marlow asked, "do you think Rostmann is the assassin and the one running the show."

"I quite frankly don't know. It could be. But Rostmann is convincing, and, believe it or not, he can be charming—and he can be a gentleman. He indirectly implicated Rowdy in all sorts of nefarious activities—he calls him Rowan—but says he knows for sure that Kluge actually did the assassinations. We had a discussion when I was held in back of the truck that was transporting the money. It was there that he called Rowdy a sociopath and claimed that he, Rostmann, personally prevented Rowdy, from ever being hospitalized in a mental institution. But in the end, he gave me quite a run-down of all the factors that in his telling, reveals him, Rostmann, to be in the clear."

As Maria went on for a while but could not tell us where Rostmann was and what he was doing or planning to do, Tancredi got me off in a corner and asked what I thought. I told him that Maria's encounter with Rostmann sounds similar to the phenomenon found all over the world where the criminal was good to the captive or rather, the hostage, and, in return, the hostage felt so appreciative that such a person could practically feel love for the criminal.

I wondered if any part of that might be relevant to Maria's feelings, and especially to her judgment of Rostmann, even though she reported being skeptical of his explanations. It was obvious she was a bit charmed by him and grateful he had not hurt her.

Maria saw us talking. She could sense it was about her, and of course she was right. At that point Tancredi asked me to tell her what I had just told him. So I did.

She said: "Could be. I can see where it could be. He doesn't seem like an ogre. And I know that on one level I would like to believe him but on the other hand I probably don't believe him. There's some kind of a thing going on here, but I can't put my finger on it. I'm both afraid of him and not afraid of him. It's something like that."

"That's very perceptive, Maria," I commented. "You see, when someone is in that kind of helpless situation they feel afraid. However, underneath, in the unconscious mind, pressed down deep, they're angry, furious, rageful. But they can't show this rage – especially toward the person who has a life-and-death power over them, and because of their need to seem calm they can't even acknowledge the rage to themselves. So, Maria, underneath it all, you are, I'm fairly sure, furious at Rostmann for having you in a helpless situation, but you don't really know it. As you say, and in the sense that you're hinting at the truth to yourself, it goes something like this: You're consciously "not sure about it," but nevertheless, underneath it all in your unconscious mind, you are absolutely sure about it.

"That kind of rage is worse when the captive's life's at stake. With Rostmann, I'm sure you felt your life was at stake, but you didn't want to face it in those stark terms, so, instead, you did the opposite thing by persuading yourself that basically he might be a nice guy. It's when the hostage expresses an alliance, and even an affection, with their captors. And, Maria," I added, "make no mistake about it, you were a hostage! It's called the Stockholm Syndrome, named after a situation in Stockholm, Sweden that happened not too long ago, maybe about 1973 or so. It was there that in a bank hold-up the hostages expressed sympathy with their captors. It's a situation of abuse versus kindness.

"When you feel the alliance with Rostmann, the empathy with him, it's equivalent to feeling that when he experiences your agreement he will then no longer see you as the enemy; therefore the implicit threat to your life would vanish, so you would be relieved and also feel grateful."

I turned to Tancredi. I was thinking, and I then said: "Let me continue. I've known this Rowan, Rowdy, practically my entire life. He is not crazy, nor was he ever crazy. It's not in him to kill anyone. But, I agree, he has led a very idiosyncratic life and, as we know, he has implicated Rostmann, his grandfather, in all the wrongdoing. I believe Rowdy, and as a professional interpreter of personality I'm able to assess character. I can't emphasize this enough: Rostmann is a very dangerous person.

"It's true that we haven't gotten a lead on Kluge, so that some pieces of the puzzle don't jibe. Is there an outside chance that Kluge is really the one we should be looking for because he is the assassin? Yes, maybe. It is an extremely slim one."

As we were being joined by the others, Maria thanked me. Then Philippe Marcel wanted to know the basis of Rostmann's rationale for his innocence, so Maria started listing the things that Rostmann enumerated, as best as she could remember it.

"He first said he was innocent and that Kluge was the killer. He said that Kluge is especially cunning. If Kluge is dead he asked, where was the body? And, where's the proof that he, Rostmann, killed Kluge? Rostmann also said it was quite the opposite, because he never killed anyone, and, since he and Kluge were the last two to survive, he knew it had to be Kluge who was the assassin.

"Now the museum curator, Bauer, is dead, shot by Rostmann, in self-defense, turning it into a self-defense action for all of us remaining there. Those who remained standing were me, Rostmann himself, and one of the other men who was part of the crew helping Rostmann and Bauer move all of the money into the truck.

"Of course I don't know how Rostmann knew it, but while we were in the truck he mentioned that the caretaker and the minister at the cathedral in another town in Germany had also disappeared. I guess he meant that they might have been able to shed some information on everything—that is, in incriminating him, but now that would not be possible. He also mentioned that the house where he lived is clean, meaning that there is no possibility of finding anything incriminating there. Therefore, no one could convict him on a clean house. Now we hear that Frau Krause has been killed, so that, again, as far as anyone knows, there is no person known to the police to connect Rostmann to anything.

"He also said something very important. Referring to Rowan, Rowdy, he said that Rowan was grandiose and also homicidal; that Rowan always wanted Rostmann to tell him adventure stories about assassins — especially as it related to World War II. And he added that Rowan was especially interested in assassination stories that he, Rostmann, had to continue to fabricate for Rowan's pleasure.

"In addition, Rostmann was not at all trying to avoid admitting to being one of ten men who figured out how to get the money from the bank in that German town. But as he was telling these stories to Rowan, and mentioning the names of certain individuals who were in the squad of men ordered to guard the bank, Rowan was engrossed. According to Rostmann, Rowan couldn't get enough of these stories. At first Rostmann concluded that it must have been either Kluge or Rowan who did the assassinations; Kluge, because he knew of the money, and Rowan because he was acting-out some adventure fantasy about being a CIA agent with a 007 sanction to kill. But then he said it was Kluge. That's almost word for word what he said."

I interrupted her to ask whether Rostmann had ever mentioned Jean. Maria answered in the negative. He never mentioned another woman. No Jean.

What Maria was telling us, therefore, also told us she was right; that, in conversing with her, Rostmann was setting up a scenario in which he could proclaim his innocence. He was making everything point to Kluge or to Rowdy.

"Could it be," I said to the assembled, "that Rostmann is considering simply giving himself up — thinking that because no one could prove anything he then might be cleared — especially if he's already disposed of Kluge? He might think some deal could be made to trade off for his participation in the wartime criminal activity of stealing money for a pardon. In return he would tell us whatever he was asked — of course never confessing to anything.

* * *

Rostmann's whereabouts were always a secret. Yes, Kluge was gone, the minister and caretaker of the cathedral were gone, no money was found, and generally what they had on Rostmann was practically nothing of any importance. At the moment he had transferred a great deal of money from the museum to a large private garage in a commercial district of Berlin. Apparently, Rostmann had decided to use the garage as a bank vault. He had cameras installed that ran 24/7. He had the wide doors to the garage bolted shut. Without blinking an eye, he also killed the remaining man who had worked both with him and Bauer in transferring the money into the trucks. He couldn't let Maria see him doing it so it was then that he released her. Yes, he released her. He did it in the most humble way by apologizing to her—actually saying he was sorry.

This all happened after his associate was busy bolting the wide door to the garage floor from inside the garage. Then he, Maria, and this other associate left through a side door of the garage. The side door led through a narrow vestibule into the main building of the garage. Then in the rather small radius of the building's lobby, he paused, looked at Maria, and, to her surprise, rather than taking her further into the bowels of the building, he hesitated, looked at her, and escorted her through the building's front glass doors, into the street. It was at that point that he kissed her hand and bade her farewell.

Rostmann then motioned for his associate to come out into the street. He had the associate drive Maria around Berlin for half an hour. He asked Maria to keep her head down and try to not look at street signs or anything else. But it was a request. She was not blindfolded. It became obvious, both to Maria and to Rostmann, that she had developed somewhat of a passive and almost nonjudgmental attitude toward him. Rostmann could see it.

They drove for about twenty minutes, zigging and zagging away from this commercial warehouse district and into a more populated area congested with pedestrians as well as a great deal of traffic. The driver pulled over, instructed her in a polite manner not to look at the car's license plate, and just to keep walking in a direction away from the car. Maria did what she was told. When she finally did turn around, the car was gone.

Returning to the garage, Rostmann was waiting for the driver at the entrance to the building. Rostmann entered the car on the driver's side and his associate slid over. Then with swiftness Rostmann shot him and killed him. Yes, Rostmann was a cold-blooded killer. Clearly a psychopath. He drove the car close to the Spree River into a cul-de-sac. At the end of the cul-de-sac Rostmann opened the door on the companion side and literally kicked this former associate out and onto the pavement. He backed the car out of the cul-de-sac and blithely drove back to the garage.

Now what Rostmann had always dreamed became a reality. He was free and clear—but, then again, not quite. He knew he was only actually almost completely free and clear. There was not one person except Jean who could be a witness against him. He knew that Koppel the caretaker at the cathedral and Konrad, the minister were safely emplaced in the Vatican and in airtight Vatican security. They were home.

Jean, however, knew everything about him. He did in fact, love her, and they'd been together for all those years. She was, he would admit, "an excellent companion." The only problem was that Rostmann was afflicted with an abnormal claustrophobic sensation regarding his freedom. The very thought of being incarcerated left him horrified. Whenever he thought of it, he needed to instantly shake out of it.

He kept thinking about Jean.

Jean and Rostmann had an apartment she had rented at the Karl-Marx Allee Street, about a mile from the museum and very close to where the two trucks were kept. Rostmann finally arrived there, and for the first time since Jean and he had become a team, he didn't talk about killing Bauer or the other helper. He didn't talk about killing anyone. Also for the first time that he could remember, he found it difficult to talk to her and started making the kind of small talk that he would ordinarily detest.

The problem was that it was difficult for Rostmann not to talk—and especially about something exciting. Rostmann needed that constant external stimulation. This stimulation enabled him to compensate for an impoverished inner life. It was the external stimulation that allowed him to feel the vitality of life. Thus, Rostmann led a life of risk, danger, and provocative acts, because such excitement made him feel alive, in contrast to how he would have felt otherwise. Without such stimulating events, Rostmann would have felt as though he were living on a solitary planet as a solitary individual. As I explained to the others, with psychopaths it's always too terrifyingly quiet inside, so they need to think wild thoughts—and do wild things.

Apparently, one of the ways Rostmann achieved such external stimulation was by utilizing his grandson as a convenience; that is, as a person who would listen while he could weave all these exciting stories. That's why he kept telling Rowdy all those stories and repeatedly went back to them and, over the years, told them to Rowdy again and again.

Rowdy claimed that at first, he loved to hear the stories, but that at a certain point he had heard them so many times that he simply indulged his grandfather and, without interrupting him, let him repeat the stories, although it had by then become tedious.

No, it wasn't Rowdy who was the disturbed one. It was Rostmann. Define him as a sociopath or a psychopath. That sort of distinction just doesn't matter.

Rostmann, of course, kept thinking about Jean as the only other person to offer him some excitement; in addition, she would always listen to his stories. So now here he was, still needing to tell Jean what happened. But he didn't. It was killing him, but he kept silent.

As would be expected, Jean asked him what was the matter.

*   *   *

We were all back at the hotel. Tess seemed preoccupied. I asked her what was on her mind. She said she'd like to return to Milan. She felt unneeded and really needed to get back to her work. She knew I was secure here with all of this police protection and added that Tancredi would make sure I was always safe.

"Are you having feelings about Maria and Tancredi and me? Could it be that you're feeling a bit competitive with Maria, and it's making you angry? You know, I think I'm flattered."

Tess was truthful.

"Yes, that's how I feel."

"Tess, it's only you—only you. Maria is a valuable, attractive, intelligent woman, and I think Tancredi's in love. But me, I'm in love with someone else. See what I mean?"

She smiled, and we embraced.

"But, she added, "I do need to get back to Milan. I'm feeling so guilty that I left them flat. I know they'll understand, but I need to finish the year there. At the beginning I needed only to be with you, but now with all that's happening here I'm really a third wheel and I feel useless. It's best I go back."

I then asked Marlow to call Garelik, get the OK for Tess to travel back to Milan, and asked for him to make the arrangements. We made love that night and slept warmly in an embrace. The next day Tess packed and took the flight from Berlin to Milan.

*   *   *

I was without Tess, but then again the conclave formed, and I was distracted from my sense of temporary loss. I was asked what I thought about Rostmann's information and what prediction might I make purely derived from that psychology. I was glad to contribute a theory about what we could expect from Rostmann—whether or not we would ever have evidence to validate it.

"OK, here's the theory," I said. "It's that, given what we know about Rostmann, including how what Rowdy told us rounded out the picture, and now knowing what happened to Maria and how Rostmann tried to mesmerize her with kindness, and how, now, with Bauer's death, and the death of the others, including even Frau Krause's demise, it seems apparent that Rostmann feels he's in the clear. Given that assumption, here is what I believe to expect. If Jean is still alive, it might not be for long.

"The point I'm making is that from what we now know, and especially from what Maria has told us, all those around Rostmann who could possibly incriminate him are gone. All but Jean. If Jean is alive, I believe there's a good chance he'll kill her. Plain and simple. You need to understand that with a true psychopath—especially one who feels cornered, and whose pathology is embraced by an underlying psychosis—the only thing more important than inviting an unrelenting flow of external stimulation is the terrible fear of vulnerability to being caught. And being caught means, being *stopped*. And being stopped is the core issue of this or any true psychopath's worst nightmare.

"It all means that if you physically stop the psychopath, then he believes he has nothing left. It means that the psychopath's inner silence, in the deepest structural core of his mind, really makes him feel dead inside. In Rostmann's case, in order not to feel dead, he needs to make someone else dead. That, to him, is stimulating. It's action and it's doing. It's the external stimulation compensating for the inner absence of stimulation—that is, eliminating any consciousness of the inner silence.

"Therefore, stopping him physically means a definite end to the continual momentum of his consistent need to create such external stimulation. In Rostmann's case it essentially also refers to the stimulation of all of that money sitting where he knows he can find it, and concerns his knowing of what he felt it took to keep that money safe and then to maximize his ownership of it. His metric was that the more he had of the money, the greater his stimulation. So killing the others simply increased the stimulation of thinking about the money as well as constituting the stimulating dividend—of killing.

"Therefore, the bottom line is that, from a psychological point of view, Rostmann's entire killing spree was not about being the richest. Rather, his entire killing spree used the stolen money as a personal ruse. Yes, I say a personal ruse, because primarily, he could use this ruse to justify the killing, and to justify it each time. More of the exciting stimulation would then be comprised of escaping, and then planning, and then doing, and then, therefore, it was all in the service of creating external stimulation. No more, no less.

"Jean/Gina, at this very moment, if she's alive, then, as I've suggested, imminently she won't be. And that's not a weak guess. I say that because, despite the fact that I believe Jean's role in his life has been to be the pivotal person who can share his many exploits, giving him someone with whom he could continue to review his actions, his excitement, nevertheless, because she alone could be the one person to stop it all by testifying against him, that would, in the end, force him to kill her. And, believe it or not, he wouldn't even blink. Let me also put it this way: The intensity of Rostmann's fear and hatred of being incarcerated and thereby stopped, is hugely greater than the intensity of his love for Jean.

"Very much, unlike Maria, who Rostmann sees as the vehicle that could create testimony for him, in his favor, therefore in his mind she becomes a person who will possibly be able to keep him free. Maria is unquestionably considered by him to be an asset, and a valuable one at that—in contrast to Jean, who now fills the precise opposite possibility—that of not keeping him free.

"Rostmann's need for complete freedom will always be more important to him than any personal relationship. Look what he said about his own grandson—trying to pin it all on Rowdy. Despite that, he might love Rowdy. Nevertheless, if Rowdy can be a witness against him, the personal relationship would have no bearing on this psychopath's decision to even kill Rowdy. Or, in this case, because he can't get his hands on Rowdy, then to kill him by incriminating him.

"Everything I've just said defines the true psychotic psychopath. It's a person who doesn't blink at killing. He is ominous, malevolent, even demonic. And please keep in mind that such a person is nothing but an encapsulated corrupt psychotic psychopath. This means that he still gets up in the morning and puts the same color socks on, and knows to put his right foot in his right shoe and so forth. Such a person can look perfectly normal in any number of ways—as, for example, in how charming he was with Maria—but nevertheless, at the same time, he still maintains his focus on the one pernicious, even sinister thing that keeps him stimulated. It's only a trained eye that can see the hollow man through the social pretense. His entire approach with Maria proves it. Yes, Rostmann, when he wants to, can embody himself with social pretense."

After a moment or two of silence, Marcel repeated the sentiment he had expressed before.

"We're glad you're with us, Alex. Really glad."

Tancredi, still holding onto Maria, expressed what we were all feeling. It was obvious that none of us knew what to do. The only word that came to mind was *helpless*. My thought was: Not only is Jean, in all probability, in a helpless position, and either does or doesn't know it, but all of us, in our collective guise as a superhero group—as a Justice League, a group of illuminati—are just as helpless. Not one iota less.

· 12 ·

DESPERATE ACTS

Yes, Marcus Rostmann was desperate. He was desperate because he had made a choice based upon his natural reflex, in moments of important decisions to become detached from his feelings. More, when such decisions became an imperative, then he became compartmentalized, meaning he could function one way in his personality approach to things, but, whatever the particular approach was, it had absolutely no influence on another compartment of his personality. And neither would ever bleed into the other.

Yes, he loved Jean, and yes, he needed Jean, but no one could threaten his security, not even Jean. He needed to stay unrestricted and, by all means necessary, not to be stopped. It's exactly as I had it psychologically pinned down. Bona fide psychopaths, underpinned by a psychotic delusional system, are also basically paranoid with respect to worrying about who could potentially harness them in one place. That was intolerable for Rostmann because to be on the move and to constantly create stimulating conditions is, as I've proclaimed, for the psychotic psychopath equivalent to breathing.

As I had predicted, Jean was in a very precarious position with respect to her life. She always knew that Rostmann would be capable of killing her to cover his tracks, but, like in the Stockholm Syndrome, whereby captives fell under the spell of their captors, she was in a profound denial. She was actually denying her fear of him. Instead, she fell in a faux love with him, and was under his control in a dire and corrupt life.

*   *   *

"Marcus," Jean persisted, "something's bothering you. What is it?"

Rostmann simply told her he was tired and needed to sleep. When he appeared to be asleep, Jean had a lightening stress reaction. She instinctively knew that something was definitely bothering him and his reluctance to share that something with her, instantly awakened her and, also instantly dissolved her denial. In fact, there was no more denial. Rostmann would never want to sleep instead of sharing some exciting detail. She knew that for sure. Her terror led her to quickly pack a bag and for the first time since the fateful day they met, she severed the tie with Rostmann. In a life saving split-second, she slipped out of the apartment — sight unseen, she thought. But Rostmann was not actually sleeping. He wanted to know what she would do. He let her leave, quickly went to the window, and saw which way she was walking. He knew what she was doing, what she might ultimately do, and then, of course, what he had to do.

Rostmann exited the building, jumped into his car and headed in Jean's direction. Within thirty or so yards he spotted her walking at a deliberate and quickened pace. He gradually drove toward her, pushed the automated window lever on the passenger side, and the window side slowly opened. As the car caught up to her, he fired off two rounds from his pistol. He needed only one. The first shot hit her directly in the head. Her head exploded as she crumpled to the ground. Blood and brain tissue all over. Rostmann jumped out of the car, quickly snatched her bag, got back into the car and was gone in a flash. No witnesses. But even if someone saw the action, what would such a witness report seeing, a man jumping out of a car and jumping back in, and then speeding off? So what? It would mean nothing. Rostmann knew it would mean nothing. His experiences in life taught him that chaos rules and people are generally unreliable, especially during tense or traumatic moments.

As he drove away, all emotional connection to Jean receded. It was replaced by a sense of security, melting over him like a warm sunny day. Now, he experienced a sense of freedom — in bold relief — Jean or no Jean. No. It was, simply, no Jean!

Rostmann instantly shifted his thinking. He thought about Torsten Koppel, the caretaker at the cathedral in Bremen, and Konrad, the minister. It gave him a sudden bad feeling. But, again, he quickly shifted to the truck. He had already gotten a second truck. He knew it was important for one of the trucks to remain in the garage in Berlin. Then he would have time to arrange for the money to be transferred to the Rothschild private bank in the Cayman Islands where he had retained his numbered account, a contained accommodation known as a crib — actually a full chamber in the bank's mother vault. Later, he would move half the money that was now in the second truck to a private bank in New York City where one could rent an equivalent chamber within the bank's major umbrella vault. Shifting the money from that truck to New York City was easy for him. He had done it before. The Caymans was another story. No, he changed his mind. He would not leave one truck in Berlin!

He also knew that caring for Rowan and for Jean was something of the past. He knew it, but he didn't or couldn't feel it. And, without feeling it, it didn't matter! It would become something of the past, some memory from another world. He could almost think of it as existing the way it was, the way it used to be, while at the same time also denying its passing. It's a trick of a person's schizoid psyche that enables one's personal horror not to be, in any way, engaged. The feelings are anesthetized and remote. Actually, and diagnostically, *schizoid* means remote, alien, aloof, and cold.

And so it was with Marcus Rostmann. No other horror bothered him. The only horror that could possibly affect him was something self-referenced — something personal to him alone that resonated with his idiosyncratic and psychotically paranoid psychopathic pathology. In that respect Jean could have her head explode by a bullet — his bullet — and Rowdy could also disappear. How? It didn't matter. The only thing that mattered was his own freedom from restriction.

And yet, in thinking about the trucks and Jean and Rowan/Rowdy, he undermined his good feeling by suddenly thinking about Koppel and Konrad. After all, he reasoned, they have a ton of money, and he was sure that they had preordained their plans with Odessa, to be able to transfer the money to Rome, to the Vatican department identified as the *Department of Grants and Appointments*. Of course, Rostmann knew that this so-called *department* was a veneer, a shield for its real purpose: Odessa!

Yes, Rostmann knew with high probability where the cathedral money would be. But he further reasoned that neither Koppel nor Konrad could tie him to any of the killings or to anything else other than accepting money. However, he also realized that it was Konrad, at the cathedral who told him over the phone that Kluge was dead. Then he thought that even if such a revelation would come to pass, all it would mean was that Konrad, as well as Koppel would be incriminating themselves of murder, unless, of course, they would blame the murder of Kluge on Rostmann himself. Yet Rostmann's logic would not let it rest there because he could likely make the challenge that any such accusation would be a transparent attempt on their part to exonerate themselves.

He felt better.

Again he comforted himself that it was only Marcus Rostmann for Marcus Rostmann. He also was sure that even if he surrendered, nothing could be pinned on him. He would again be free because there was basically no evidence of any massive irregularity, save the specific one of his being an accomplice in the original theft of the money. He was already planning the deal he would make. A trade-off; that is, surrender and give the authorities a chance to question him, but the charge of theft of the money from the bank in Bremen would be dropped. And that would be the trade. He was also counting on the possibility regarding the issue of statute of limitations. But he would need to look into that.

He drove back to the apartment and fell quickly into a dreamless sleep.

*   *   *

The BND unit from the German Secret Police were now in on it. They wanted to take over the investigation, but Persson, the chief of Interpol, said no. Persson stated he was glad the BNDs joined them, but, since our "Justice League" had been on it from the beginning, and had a good amount of data that we had personally collected, and, experience already in smelling and tasting the ins and outs of it all, we were the ones who should still be in command. The truth was that since it was on German territory the BND could have easily insisted on their own leadership, but in the end, the BND saw Persson's reasoning and were agreeable to be part of the team. I later asked Persson about it, and he confided that he wasn't sure that each and every person of the BND could be trusted. He knew, as did all Europeans, that there was still much sympathy for the Nazi past among various Germans in parts of the country. Then he further qualified his remark by saying that, by and large, he felt that most Germans today do not hold such Nazi ideology in any high regard.

The only question now was — Where was Rostmann?

I asked to speak to Garelik. I had the thought that Garelik should tell Rowdy that I would be calling him from Berlin. My thinking was that Rowdy might know something about Bauer, or the museum, that could clue us into making an educated guess as to where Rostmann might be. After all, we knew that Rostmann continued to tell Rowdy all his stories. Could it be that Rowdy omitted anything about Bauer, the museum, or even where in Berlin Rostmann lived — assuming Rostmann, in fact, lived in Berlin?

It was the only thing I could think of because, except for Rowdy, everyone connected to Rostmann might have already been eliminated. Marlow didn't wait for anyone's permission; he jumped right to it. He left the hotel and called Garelik from a phone that he knew couldn't be monitored by anyone at the hotel. He brought Garelik up to date and told him that my plan was to speak to Rowdy. Garelik said it was a good idea, but that I shouldn't call from the hotel because who knew who these telephone switchboard operators were? Marlow reassured him saying he was calling from a phone away from the hotel. They then arranged the time for the call to Rowdy. Garelik said that Rowdy would be available at that particular specified time to take the call from his safe house where he now lived.

Marlow then set it up for us to call from the phone at the Berlin Railroad Station. It was a bustling place with so many people rushing here and there at the station that it would be impossible for someone to overhear the call. I was worried about all the ambient noise, which I imagined must be constant. I hoped I could hear what Rowdy was saying.

We arrived at the station with fifteen minutes to spare. Marlow and I talked about what I was going to ask Rowdy. I actually had not written anything down to ask, but of course I generally knew where to go with it. And where to go with it, was to ask Rowdy about Rostmann.

Marlow made the call and handed me the phone. It rang once, and Rowdy answered right away.

"Alex? He was obviously expecting the call that Garelik said would be coming.

"Hiya, Rowd; I'm calling from Berlin. We've tracked your grandfather to this place but we've lost his whereabouts. My hunch is that he may have told you something about Berlin. Am I right?

"Yes, of course. I know a lot about his visits to Berlin. He usually has two apartments there. One apartment Jean rents temporarily each time they're in Berlin. The other apartment is a permanent one on a street that's named after Karl Marx. I don't know the exact street name but I do know that it's not far from the History Museum and fairly close to the German cathedral that my grandfather talked about. Oh yeah, also not far from the City Hall. Grandfather talked a lot about streets in Berlin because he owned a few garages there and also a few buildings. But that's about all I know. I've heard those stories many times."

"OK, Rowd, is there more?"

"No, that's it. If I remember anything else I'll call Mr. Garelik. I have his number and he said I could call him any time day or even night. He's a nice guy."

"OK, Rowd. You've been very helpful. Thanks a lot. I'll be in touch with you again. As soon as we land in The Big Apple, I'll come to see you. Bye."

That was it. It didn't take long, but it was a valuable phone call. We now guessed that it was likely Rostmann was still in Berlin, that he had an apartment in the street named after Karl Marx that a BND inspector told us was Karl-Marx Allee — which he said would be the only street resembling what Rowdy told me. Karl-Marx Allee was a wide street with lots of traffic and large classic-style old Soviet residences on both sides.

That was good news and bad news. The good news was that we felt at least we had something and that the something we had would enable us to encircle the few blocks that contained the residences on Karl-Marx Allee. The bad news was that even though we were relatively certain that Rostmann was there, we didn't know exactly where. What we were sure of was also not such good news; that is, Rostmann, if there, would not have rented an apartment in his own name.

But, we had Karl-Marx Allee. So it meant we had something — something.

* * *

Rostmann was awakened by a night terror. This kind of night terror becomes physiologically generated even in the absence of an actual dream.

His first thought was: Rowdy knows the street. He's heard me mention Karl-Marx Allee.

With that, Rostmann jumped out of bed. He was in a panic. He ran to his closet, packed all his things in a large suitcase, gathered his keys and other IDs with his alias of Roland Bremen, quickly surveyed the rest of the apartment, not wanting to leave anything incriminating behind. Then, satisfied that he was in the clear, he left the apartment and the building, walked to his car and drove away.

Rostmann decided that in order to let things quiet down, he would live in the back of the truck at the garage. There he would be safe. He also owned the building where the truck was now safeguarded, and had a two-room office there but never used it. Even though it was furnished, he didn't want to sleep in the office. It felt too vulnerable. At the garage he would be locked in, but with a key to the door in his possession that led from the interior of the garage into the building. He had the sense of freedom because, at will, he could come and go. He also just felt good sleeping with the money. He knew the money in the truck remained invulnerable to anyone else, but he still worried about it when he wasn't actually there to guard it.

This was the second time he needed to abandon his living quarters. First he left his home on Long Island, and now the one on Karl-Marx Allee, in Berlin. Just as he didn't care about losing the money on the house when it would be sold for lack of payment of real estate taxes, here too he was not at all concerned about leaving, and therefore breaking the lease that Jean had signed. He knew that he could never return to the apartment.

Rostmann arrived at the garage. He walked into the building using his keys, entered the doorway leading to the garage from the inside of the building, unlocked the door into the garage, and breathed a sigh of relief.

The relief was temporary. He was a fugitive on the run, but one with millions of dollars in cash yet nowhere to spend it or, at the moment even to know how to implement his next step. How was he going to arrange to get the money to the bank in the Cayman Islands?

He had an important underworld contact in the Caymans. This contact was someone who could get practically anything done, and in record time if necessary. It was common knowledge that the Caymans were a secondary place that fugitive incognito Nazis traveled to even before the war was over, especially those stampeding out of Germany during the bombing of Berlin. These rats, were, so to speak, the first ones off the ship. Of course, the primary place Nazi fugitives escaped to were the Canary Islands. The Canaries touched the tip of Africa. But Rostmann chose the Caymans because it was one of the best off-shore banking havens, closer to Cuba and Puerto Rico and therefore not that far from the good ole' USA where he knew that money was truly understood. Rostmann's plan was to reach the USA where he would ultimately live. He was sure of it because he also knew that even in the worst of outcomes, the legal system in the U.S. would and could protect you.

But thinking about protection quickly turned to focusing on where he now was—on the run—and remembering that Rowdy knew where he might be. It was then that it hit him. Rowdy knows this is Number 1 Gasse. He immediately thought to phone his contact in the Caymans and use him, as he had in the past, as a conduit, so that a series of steps, a veritable network could be fashioned that would get underway and successfully move the money to the Caymans. Rostmann was a strategist of the first order. From feeling frantic just a few hours before to suddenly knowing what to do, feeling relieved, and in turn feeling dread, could have been his trademark—the template of his life. External stimulation after external stimulation! That was his psychopathic creed.

He left the building and quickly walked to a commercial establishment that sold general household items. Situated at a far end of the store was a snack counter with a half dozen seats This part of the store was seen as a service to customers so they could relax with coffee and perhaps some dessert. Adjacent to the counter was a pair of phone booths. Stepping into one, Rostmann reached his contact in the Caymans and set into motion what needed to be done to get the money and himself immediately relocated to the Caymans. And Rostmann meant immediately!

Grand Cayman was his destination because, of the three islands that comprise the Caymans, Grand Cayman is by far the largest, with the greatest population as well as a location displaying its wares—a whole variety of banks, including the one considered to be his own bank. It wasn't really his bank, but it was so private that he always felt a proprietary sense about it.

The Caymans are British territory of the British West Indies, located in the western Caribbean, somewhat surrounded, yet south and distant from

Cuba, on one side, and northwest of Jamaica, on another. The other two islands of the Caymans are Cayman Brac and Little Cayman. On Grand Cayman Rostmann had a little place he kept in George Town, in West Bay, on the southwest coast.

In discussing the transfer of money with his Cayman contact, Rostmann talked about a voyage at sea, which they had done in the past. Even while on the phone, Rostmann's contact was able, with assurance, to answer Rostmann's urgent concern. The contact could arrange a ship immediately. Since Rostmann always offered huge sums of money for whatever he needed done—especially done quickly—he mentioned to his contact a number (meaning payment), the contact could hardly believe.

The number was about five times what anyone else would ordinarily pay for that kind of job, but, nevertheless the contact was not particularly surprised, since they also agreed that the ship needed to be undocumented, the voyage also undocumented. Apparently the contact could and would, and with pleasure, do both—no documentation anywhere. Rostmann decided to take both trucks rather than trying to put all the cartons in one truck. He would personally accompany the cargo and, at the other end, he would need this contact to arrange a reliable driver to drive one truck and he himself would drive the other. The contact said, "Done." In addition Rostmann ordered another driver to be sent to his garage immediately. Rostmann gave him the address.

A small merchant ship was required for the voyage. Rostmann would need to deliver both trucks to a set area at the Spree River where the ship would be waiting. The contact promised the merchant ship to be there within the next three or four hours. Rostmann arranged that the merchant ship this contact promised would be waiting at the appointed place on the Spree River where it was structurally possible for vehicles to drive onto the ship. The ship would then ultimately dock at its destination—the George Town southern port of Grand Cayman, a short distance from the Royal Water Terminal, where it would be possible to manage this kind of surreptitious landing. From there Rostmann ordered that the trucks would disembark, again at a spot where vehicles can drive off the ship. The cargo would travel to one of the largest, most private banks in Grand Cayman—the Rothschild Bank—private banking.

Rostmann, by phone, assured his contact that the amount he suggested paying was real and also expressed strongly that everything, meaning *every-*

thing had to go — urgently. Rostmann's contact did, in fact, immediately set it all up. The contact couldn't wait to count his windfall.

Rostmann, also, as usual, was moving swiftly. He would be out of Berlin and on the merchant ship with all the cargo that day, within hours. In the meantime, Rostmann unanchored the front gated door from its bolted positions so that the trucks could be driven out of the garage. First he himself drove one truck out and parked it a short distance from the garage. Then he hurried back and did the same with the second truck. He needed to get away from the garage altogether. He wasn't worried about the trucks in the street because his garage was on a street of warehouses, and few people were around. Besides, he was carrying his trusty silencer and knew how to use it. He was awaiting his newly arranged driver.

* * *

It happened fast. The BND enlisted a squad of officers from the German police precincts they could trust. They were planning to fan out in pairs along Karl-Marx Allee, criss-crossing avenues and streets. They all had Rostmann's physical description — an older tallish man with a limp and a funny gait. No mustache, no beard.

Of course, it was all for naught since Rostmann was already a distance away from Karl- Marx Allee, holed up outside and also a distance away from his garage with millions of dollars to keep him company. After a day of scouring the Karl-Marx Allee and its surrounding area, the search was called off.

Our group knew we were in the dark. Since the Rowdy situation led at least to something, it was decided we should be in touch with Rowd again because, at the moment, it appeared as though Rostmann had fallen off the face of the earth.

PART 7

BRAINSTORM

· 13 ·

BRAINSTORM

Thank God for Philippe Marcel. Grimand gave him to us before he, himself, returned to Paris. Marcel exclaimed: "Rather than trying to find Rostmann and trying to follow him, it may be more efficacious to concentrate on trying to follow and find the money. The question is, Where is the money? Where could it be, and how might we trace it, are questions I've been asking myself. My first thought was if Rostmann wanted to put distance between him and us, he might think of getting the money and himself out of Berlin—assuming the money was stashed in Berlin in the first place and also assuming he's still here.

"If Rostmann and the money are no longer in Berlin, then let's think of offshore locations. Where do millionaires stash their money when they want to hide it? Well, it's common knowledge that the offshore places to hide money include the British Virgin Islands, the Bahamas, the Cayman Islands, the Canary Islands, Cook Islands, Belize, Singapore, several others, and of course, the most famous, Switzerland. The immediate question, though, is: Who would know about Rostmann and the money? Rostmann probably has a numbered account in some private bank in one of those locations. And he would want to transfer the money in a clandestine way that would be practically impossible to trace; that is, how to get the money there without it going through legal channels. Switzerland might be more difficult, but some of the islands could be a

better way to go. For the longest time now, Geneva has been under an
Interpol microscope. So that leaves, I'll bet, any island that has a major
private bank. Singapore is simply too far. Rostmann would need a private bank and particular code numbers to access the account. Grand
Cayman Island is one that has some of the largest private banks. Rothschilds is one of them. But then I thought we should go back to the well.
Let's tap the well."

I immediately saw what he was getting at and shouted:

"Call Rowdy and discuss the stories Rostmann told him."

"Exactly," Marcel said. "Right. Rowdy's the well. Whenever we talk to
him we anticipate getting a lead, and we do. He might know something
that he himself doesn't realize he knows. Whatever it could be hidden in
one of the stories Rostmann told him or even in some recollection Rowdy
has, provided, of course, that he ever traveled with Rostmann."

At that moment Jack and Dave rushed in, with McBride leading the
charge and bursting with the news.

"We just got word that a woman was found on Karl-Marx Allee in the
middle of the street with her head blown off. Shot dead at pretty close
range. In her vest pocket they found the telephone switchboard number
for her building. The building is a residential hotel with the address on the
Marx block. They described her physical appearance to the doorman and
he immediately identified her and her apartment number. Her name: Jean
Adele. They raided the apartment. Empty. Prints were taken."

"It's Jean; I'll bet he killed her," I said. "You know, I never even asked
Rowdy what Jean's last name was. But it's Jean. No doubt. We're talking
about the sickest of the sick. Someone he lived with and probably loved in
his sick way, and who kept him company all those years. And what does
he do? This cold-blooded psychotic psychopath simply blows her head off.
And why? Because she's the last person in the world that could incriminate
him in murder—except, of course, for Rowdy. So, to save his own skin,
even if he wasn't in immediate danger, or perhaps even if she was definitely
completely loyal to him, he kills her anyway. Just like that!"

"OK, Marlow said. "Alex, let's go to our favorite phone booth at the
station and make the call to Rowdy."

Everyone agreed. As it was ringing, we both hoped Rowdy would pick
up. Rowdy picked up on the second ring and Marlow handed me the
phone.

"Hello," Rowdy said.

"Rowd, it's me. We need to talk to you more about your grandfather and possibly get some idea about where he is, maybe by what he had told you in those stories."

"I'm not sure what to tell you, Al."

"Was there anything he said in those stories that might give us a glimpse as to where he is or where he might go?"

"I can't think of anything, Al."

"Well, OK Rowd. We just thought that you might know something."

"Al, I had a bad dream."

"Oh yeah, like what?

"Well, I was somewhere in a house and then I was in another house. There was a man there who had work clothes on. He said his name was George Casey. I remember that exactly because I don't know anyone with that name. He was asking me whether I had wished for my grandfather to take me there again. The problem was I didn't know what he was talking about. I didn't know where he meant that my grandfather should take me. I didn't know what to say at all and I had the feeling in the dream that something was wrong. Then we started to argue and I got scared. He said: 'You're scared.' And without even thinking about what I should say, I yelled out: "You, killed him, not me!" Then I started running and I woke up scared. Al, I don't know why I yelled like that about *him* killing, but not *me*?"

"Rowd, you said you didn't know who George Casey was. Right?"

"No, I never heard that name.

"First of all, Rowd, let's get something straight. We both know that you never killed anyone. Therefore, the dream is about something else that's on your mind. And I need time to figure it out. But tell me one thing right now: when have you heard someone say, or maybe you said the sentence yourself — 'You killed him' — forget about the end of the sentence where you said 'Not me' and just try to think about the 'You killed him' part. Anything come to mind?"

"Wait a minute. I once had another dream where my grandfather had taken me to one of his garages somewhere. I'm not sure where. I think I knew where in the dream it was, but the dream was a long time ago. In the dream, there again we started to disagree, and I got the same feeling that something was wrong."

There was silence on the phone. I was waiting for him to continue, but he didn't.

"Rowd, where were you and your grandfather when you had the feeling in the dream that something was wrong? Were you both in New York City or in Hempstead, where he lived, or how about where you now live? Or maybe it was in another country, a foreign country?"

"No, wait a minute. It was in a foreign country, not New York. The garage of the building had big glass doors, and the number on the door was, I think, number 1, something like Grosse or Gasse. I think it meant street or maybe, avenue. Wait, now I remember. My grandfather even told me—this is not the dream, this is real life now—he told me he liked the address because it was number 1."

"That's good, Rowd, that's very good. Anything else come to mind?"

"I don't think so, Al. No."

"Think a bit more, Rowd."

Rowdy spent another ten seconds or so thinking, but nothing came to him.

"OK, Rowd, I'll get back to you. I also need to think more about the dream."

"Al, Al, don't hang up. When will you be back in New York?"

"I'll be there pretty soon now. In the meantime we'll be in touch. Take care."

I hung up the phone and turned to Marlow.

"I think we have an address in Berlin—number 1 either Grosse Street or Avenue, or number 1 Gasse Street or Avenue."

*   *   *

It was actually 1 Gasse. I was left behind, with Marlow as my body-guard, while the rest encircled the building at number 1 Gasse They pried open the garage door that had been previously bolted and then unbolted and rolled it up like an accordion door, even though it was originally meant to be impenetrable. The place was vacant. Paint brushes and other sundry things were around, but that was it. Thus the hopeful lead from Rowdy went nowhere.

But Philippe Marcel wasn't finished. He surmised that Rostmann had already beat it out of Berlin, and to one of the safe harbors, for his safety and for the safety of his money. Marcel's first choice was Geneva, but he wasn't sure how Rostmann would get that kind of massive load to Geneva, with all the checkpoints he would need to face at borders. On that basis, he eliminated Geneva. Then he hypothesized that the smartest thing Rostmann could do would be to smuggle it all into another country by boat. He thought that by boat all sorts of headaches with cargo and checkpoints could be minimized, actually eliminated, and that for sure Rostmann would accompany the loot on a boat. At sea, relatively speaking, Rostmann could relax. And that confirmed for him what he had thought before. By boat!

Then again Marcel revalidated his thinking. If it were to be one of the islands, it would need to be the Caymans because of the Rothschild private bank there. He also knew that Rostmann was probably willing to pay off any numbers of officials or private individuals for their help—and their silence. He also surmised that in the Caymans that might be easy to do. That was a sticking point, because Marcel added that asking questions of strangers would not be possible. One couldn't be sure in whose employ they were.

* * *

Back at the hotel, we sat in Marcel's room to plan. Marcel said: "The best we could do is to take a chance and monitor the Rothschild bank to see if we could ever catch a glimpse of Rostmann. But, he added, "It's all speculation—maybe just hopeful guesses—and, if I'm wrong, to get all of us to the Caymans could be a terrible waste of time and effort—even an embarrassment."

"Nope," I said. "Hopeful guesses, yes, but also educated guesses."

Then Marcel really surprised us, and at this point the "us" meant me, Marcel, Marlow, Jack McBride and Dave Stein. Persson and his bodyguard, Tancredi and Maria, and Grimand all returned home. The "us" was five people. Our original crew of twelve or at some point fourteen or so was now less than half. The good news was, of us all, no one had been hurt. But Marcel's surprise was a whopper. He dropped it on us.

"When we do decide to talk to someone because we think we might have a lead, we'll need to transport that person, even against his will, to some safe house and restrain him from leaving. The person would need to be tied down and muffled. We might even inject him and let him sleep it off. Remember, once the cat's out of the bag, we're doomed for failure again. You can be sure that if Rostmann's there he has the place covered. When we get Rostmann, we then release whoever it is we've taken.

"On that note," Marcel continued, "even given my doubts, I believe we should all leave for the Caymans. We'll need to put Grand Cayman Island under close scrutiny because like I said it's Grand Cayman where the Rothschild Private Bank is located. My hunch tells me Rostmann's roosting somewhere near the bank — that he actually lives somewhere near that bank or one of them: First Carib., Cayman National, Merrill Lynch, Fidelity, or a number of others. Rothschilds is located in George Town on the southwest coast of Grand Cayman."

Suddenly, hearing Marcel say George Town hit me like a ton of bricks.

"W a i t   a   m i n u t e, I said, with the intonation both Rowdy and I always use when something hits either one of us. "George Town!" I exclaimed. "In Rowdy's dream, which he just told me, the guy's name was George Casey. Rowdy said it was 'a man' whose name was George Casey. Rowdy said "a man." I think Rostmann's in George Town. Here it is. The *George*, the man's name, could be a reference to George Town. The *Casey* is possibly a compound word from Cayman — especially if you put the *man* after the Casey as in *Caseyman.*"

"Or Cayman," Marcel shouted.

"That's right," I said. "And Rowdy told me that his grandfather would take him on trips. I've got to call him back to confirm if he ever accompanied Rostmann to George Town in Grand Cayman Island. Wow! But listen, guys, I know it sounds like improbable psychobabble, but trust me, this is really how dreams work. Not only that, but there's usually a ghost in everyone's dreams. In this case, in Rowdy's dream, the ghost trying to tell the dreamer what it all means is this man named George Casey. Following that lead can usually uncover where the key is. In this case it leads us to George Town in the Caymans. You see, it's good always to try and identify the ghost."

* * *

Marlow and I immediately headed for the phone at the Berlin station. Again, Rowdy picked up on the second ring.

"Rowd, it's me."

"What's up, Al? You sound excited."

"Right. Listen Rowd, did your grandfather ever take you on a trip to the Cayman Islands, like Grand Cayman on the George Town side, on the coast?

"Yeah, I went with him when I was about ten or eleven years old. I remember he did something there. I never knew what it was. Once he scolded me because he told me to wait in the room until he got back but I didn't. I remember I was hungry and went out to find a store with some candy or some kind of food, but I don't even remember if I had any money on me. But I recall wandering around. It was when I got back that he was angry, and, no matter how I tried to explain why I did it, he still scolded me for disobeying him."

"That's great, Rowd—very helpful. By the way, I believe the George in your dream could be a reference to George Town, and the Casey could be a reference to Cayman, as in Cayman Islands. You even said there was 'a man' there and you felt some wrongness that led you to yell 'You killed him.' You know, if you put the 'Casey' together with the 'man' it gets pretty close to Cayman, and, as far as your grandfather's stories go, you know he's killed people. That's what you accused the man in the dream of doing. You yelled at him: 'You killed him.'"

"Really?" he said.

"Yes, really, Rowd. At least that's what I think. Stay steady, brother, I'll get back to you."

With that, Marlow and I returned to the hotel. We rushed up to Marcel's room. Looking for us, Jack and Dave tried Marcel's room also, and there we all were. In the meantime I looked at Marcel and smiled.

"Marcel," I said, "we're all going to George Town. Rowdy was there when he was a kid. Rostmann took him there. It's for sure. It's all starting to gel."

When Jack and Dave joined us, we told them the news. But I wasn't through with thinking about the dream. Still, I thought, Rowdy's phrase in the dream, "You killed him," was what he was thinking he really wanted to say to his grandfather but couldn't. So, instead, he screamed it in the dream. It tells me that Rowdy was frightened about the stories his grand-

father was telling him. That led me to the absolutely logical but horrifying thought that if Rostmann could kill Rowdy, he would. And wow, Rowdy knew it. Definitely. And it was also certain that Rostmann was sure that Rowdy knew too much. And then I began to think that given Rostmann's diagnostic personality profile, he would surely want—and need—to kill Rowdy.

Marcel interrupted my rumination and started to hypothesize about the route from Berlin by sea to Grand Cayman Island.

"You see," Marcel said. "The only way out by sea is on the Spree River. The Spree flows to a place that just about touches the Czech Republic and then to the River Havel on the border of Portugal and Spain before flowing into the Atlantic. Then the boat would need to cross the Atlantic to the West Caribbean directly to the Caymans. It's definitely a merchant ship, a small one. And no use trying to find it during the trip it's taking because the rivers are cluttered with boats of all sizes, and the Atlantic is too vast to try to find it.

"We'll reach Grand Cayman way before he does, and we won't see him docking because, without a doubt, they'll dock in some godforsaken area so that the situation is not observable. I suggest we get ready to go. I'll make the arrangements for the flight. We'll have plenty of time to set up before he arrives. The more I think about it, the more sure I am that Rostmann already has a numbered account there—already for many, many years—and that he's on his way to the Caymans."

We all retired for the night thinking about preparations for the next day's flight. Arrangements were made and the flight was uneventful. The five of us deplaned at Grand Cayman's Owen Roberts Airport. We had talked so much about how to handle the situation, that our group was all set. It only took several hours and we got going. We began reconnoitering around Rothschilds. Our reconnaissance was turning out to be very good insofar as we targeted various vantage points from which we could take in the scene of large swaths of the surrounding area and at the same time have a view of the bank. Of course, we were especially interested in spotting a rather tallish, somewhat elderly stooped gentleman with a limp who would be visiting the bank. We had agreed that if we saw Rostmann, Jack and Dave would be the ones to disarm and subdue him—in whatever way was called for.

* * *

Rostmann's plan was unfolding like clockwork. He stayed, nervously with the trucks, but remained out of sight in the cab of one of them. The new driver showed up sooner than Rostmann expected, and then, after confirming the deal and payment, the driver drove the first truck according to Rostmann's directions. Of course, Rostmann paid him a handsome sum and promised an equally extravagant amount once they got there. Rostmann also promised him another hefty sum if he would be willing to come along on the voyage so that when they reach their destination, the driver would drive the truck off the ship and this time follow Rostmann to the destination which in Rostmann's plan was the next haven — the Rothschild Private Bank.

For Rostmann, the journey was endless, but he was determined not to let it get to him. He busied himself with obsessional money-counting rituals and also contemplated highly detailed steps regarding how to get the cartons off the ship and how to navigate it all in order to safely get the numbers of cartons of money into his private crib at the bank.

At the journey's end, when they finally arrived at Grand Cayman, Rostmann's contact had arranged for two panel trucks to be used for the last leg of the trip. Each of the trucks was an official car of the Rothschild Bank, so indicated with lettering on the doors. The original panel trucks remained on the ship but the cartons they carried were wheeled down and loaded onto the panel tucks parked at the dock exactly as Rostmann had envisioned. Rostmann's driver drove the second panel tuck, and Rostmann led in the first one. Rostmann led because he knew the driver in the other truck couldn't break away even if he wanted to divert the vehicle with whatever he imagined was in those cartons. There would be nowhere to go. Even on the ship heading for the Caymans, Rostmann got the driver to stay in one of the staterooms on the ship, but for the entire trip, Rostmann himself, although assigned a stateroom, hunkered down with the trucks.

Yes, it all worked. They arrived at the Rothschild bank. At that point, both the driver and Rostmann, along with two other workers at the bank, loaded the well-packed cartons onto dollies and had the dollies wheeled into Rostmann's private vault room within the bank. Rostmann supervised the entire operation and didn't let the cargo out of his sight. His vault contained similar cartons, which had already been there, and with the newer ones stacked, one upon the other, the cartons filled more than half the space of this compact yet capacious room. After these newer cartons were all stacked, and with a great sigh of relief, Rostmann felt the job was successfully done and he was finally safe in George Town, on the southern west coast of Grand Cayman.

All five of us in our sleeper-surveillance spy roles were already there and very excited that we spotted the trucks and felt we had finally located him. There, we thought, was Rostmann himself! With the panel trucks. At the bank. We had already been situated near or around the bank, either sitting at cafés or seeming to window-shop. However, the problem was we were blocked by the panel trucks and although we were certain it was in fact Rostmann, we couldn't confirm who it was that was unloading cartons from the back of the trucks into the bank. But, again, we were sure it was him.

Stein was the one who decided to go into the bank as if to open a new account. When he did, he spotted someone who he could swear was Rostmann: tallish, elderly, stooped, and with a slight limp. He didn't want to take the chance of confronting Rostmann alone, because he was sure Rostmann was armed and he was worried that people would be shot. Rather, he picked up some literature on the bank's history, which was stacked neatly on various countertops, and walked out. When he got out on the street, he motioned for Jack McBride to follow him. They convened nearby at a little café somewhat removed from the bank. They entered and were met by slow dance music and many women dancing together. It was obviously a lesbian bar so they reflexively walked out. They both looked at the neon sign. It announced: *The Nutcracker Suite.* They actually didn't have even a moment to laugh together, when Stein said: "It's definitely him."

As they were about to make a plan to take Rostmann down, at that very moment, on that very spot, both panel trucks drove past the café. Stein and McBride just stood there watching the trucks drive by. They couldn't follow the trucks because they had no vehicles, so as the trucks receded into the distance, they stood there helpless and hapless.

"Not to worry," Stein said. "He's here to stay. We'll get him tomorrow. In the meantime, we need to monitor the main dock and the airport. One new question I have is this: who's driving the other truck?"

*　　*　　*

Rostmann owned a small house on the island, but first, before heading for the house, he had another job to do. Based on the original deal for this kind of a job, he paid his driver far more money than the driver ever expected. But, alas, even in the face of such generosity, Rostmann was still not to be trusted, especially because he had become accustomed to erasing anyone who could possibly incriminate him.

He took the driver to a café at the other end of the island. They had something to eat and drink. Rostmann himself ordered the drinks from the bar, and when the bartender set the drinks on the bar Rostmann took the drinks to their table. While doing that, Rostmann slipped a tiny fraction of a cyanide capsule into the driver's drink—just enough to make the driver sick and drowsy, inevitably feeling a little pain in his chest along with a sensation of heavier breathing. When that was accomplished, and after they had sandwiches to eat, they finally toasted to a journey well traveled.

The bit of cyanide began to affect the driver, and as they walked out of the café Rostmann helped the driver into one of the trucks, for the time being abandoning the other truck. He then drove the truck into the woods. There, with the driver practically expired, Rostmann finished the job by pouring the remaining cyanide down his throat. He pulled the driver out of the truck, took out a shovel and then dug a grave as best he could. He dragged the driver toward this newly arranged accommodation and, at the last moment before shoving him in, rifled the driver's pockets and removed all the money he had given him along with all identifying information the man had on him. Then it was all over. Rostmann rolled him in, filled in the grave, patted it down, and covered it with brush. Rostmann, even with his age and infirmity, was still strong enough to do it all.

He then drove the truck to the back of his house and parked it. The first thing he did was to peel off the letters on the truck that identified it as a Rothschild Bank vehicle. His plan was to have the panel truck repainted in the next days. At this point he was in no hurry. He quickly cleaned up, picked up the other panel truck and drove it back to Rothschild's where he returned it to one of the bank's custodians.

Rostmann again walked some distance back to his house, locked his door, and before he went to sleep reminded himself that, except for Rowdy, no one would or could know anything about what he did—ever. His contact who arranged all of it, with whom in the past he had had several other dealings, and who resided in Grand Cayman, had never met him and therefore, as far as Rostmann believed, never even knew what

Rostmann looked like. Some years ago, one of the conspirators of Rostmann's original squad, whom Rostmann eventually killed, was the one to
recommend the contact to Rostmann, but only through a phone number was Rostmann ever able to reach him. The phone number apparently
could not be traced. Therefore, even though, over the years, they had made
several illegal arrangements with one another, nevertheless, they actually
never personally met.

Now Rostmann considered Grand Cayman as a good place to retire.
But, he thought, Rowdy was in New York City. Rostmann thought about
it more. He then fell into a deep sleep.

* * *

The next day, we were all ready for him. We discussed it carefully, but,
as we were about to wrap it up, Philippe Marcel, our genius, said something that floored us.

"Just a minute," he said. "There's something here we need to seriously
consider. You see, the government here in the Caymans, like any government,
will want to prevent any incursion of its sovereignty. In order for us to get him
out of here and back to New York City without any government interference,
is probably only possible if we do what the Israelis did in 1960 when they
drugged Eichmann and slipped him out of Buenos Aires. This means we're
going to need to disarm him, bring him to a safe house that we don't yet have,
hold him there, question him there, then drug him and do like the Israelis
did. In this case we'll need to slip him out of George Town's Owen Roberts
Airport into some kind of a plane—a private plane—and off into the wide
blue yonder. And we're going to have to get him onto the plane with no questions asked. "Anyone here have any idea how to do that?"

We all looked at one another for suggestions. But Marcel thought we
might call Persson in Sweden to ask what Interpol would consider appropriate. Marcel made the call from his room, not really worrying about
some Nazi spy listening in. Persson said he would immediately send a
trade delegation to the island from Sweden, with the intention of opening
up more trade to all three of the Caymans. It would be in that plane that
Rostmann could be slipped in without any interference—similar to how
the Israelis got Eichmann out of Buenos Aires. He also said he would send
some drugs that could be used.

Naturally we all felt we were in it now, up to our eyeballs. I asked Marlow what he thought of the plan, and he said he actually liked it. He said he thought it could work. Marcel then volunteered to find a safe house. He put on his jacket and left—promising that within the hour he would rent something.

In great haste we stationed ourselves in the positions we had the day before. I, of course was always teamed with my other new friend Detective Marlow. It was obviously Marlow's job to keep me safe. This time, however, no one said that I needed to be left out of the hunt. Now, even if we spotted Rostmann, our job was simply to note his movements and where he went. We would need to wait for Persson to send the official trade delegation and of course, the drugs.

· 14 ·

ABDUCTING ROSTMANN

Of course, now we didn't need to worry about kidnapping two or three people, questioning them, and drugging them in order to keep them quiet until we left the island. Before, we were definitely going to do it, but now we wouldn't have to. The only person we'd be trying to abduct will be Rostmann himself. And the strategy was going into effect the moment Persson sent the so-called trade delegation—along with the drugs—hopefully the next day.

Marcel appeared and told us he had the safe house all ready. It looked like we all agreed that if anyone was a better strategist than Rostmann, it would be Philippe Marcel. Marcel figured that since Rostmann successfully transferred the money to his private vault at Rothschilds, and was able to slip out of Berlin, then why would he want to leave George Town? He wouldn't. Marcel further concluded that it looked to him like we were going to spoil Rostmann's new world in George Town, where his persona—whether he wanted it or not—would have gradually become known to the citizenry as a familiar face among the many steadies in town.

He further added that our group could take time in order to be able to strike at the propitious moment. Thus, according to Marcel, no rushing and certainly no panic. As a postscript, Marcel acknowledged that simply walking in town, here and there, over several days would not be easy, especially because we probably all felt the same thing—impatience, stress, and anticipation.

Marlow then received a call from Persson, who told him that Garelik called advising him that Grimand would be flying in from Paris and that Tancredi, along with Maria, would be flying in from Milan. We were all excited to hear that all the main members of our team would be together again, the very actors we could count on. On the other hand, here we were, five of us, and it wouldn't be easy to do this moseying around town without being conspicuous. With the five of us, it just about could be done. But now we were counting five plus four. That meant planning how to be inconspicuous for nine people. It wasn't going to be easy.

* * *

Rostmann had spent a very busy first day in George Town. What with a smuggling operation, a murder, a spectacular transfer of a fabulous sum of money, an abduction of a panel truck with time to spare to neuter it by peeling off the Rothschild markings and returning the other panel truck with nary a cry from the Rothschild's administration, he had a very busy day indeed. It was pretty clear that Rostmann had a special relationship with certain individuals at the bank. Some of the administrative personnel at the bank must have been getting "gifts."

The next day, Rostmann wakened, completed his morning ablutions, left his house, and ordered breakfast at his favorite café. The owners knew him as a fine gentleman, and one would never be able to diagnose him as a pathological psychotic psychopathic killer.

At the *Seascape Café*, Rostmann was as friendly and as charming as could be. He was not at all tense. As a matter of fact, at the café he was quite relaxed. He seemed finally to be right at home. The *Seascape Café* was sort of a hangout for boaters, and fisherman. It was a down-home place, entirely unpretentious, and without fail there would be a few inebriated types at the bar. It was a place where one could be a face in the crowd—no one cared who you were.

But as a "regular" he was recognized. Yes, they knew him there. The waitress asked him if he wanted his usual. He nodded to her and answered that he did. They laughed because of the familiarity of it all. He ordered what could be considered a standard American breakfast; orange juice, bacon with eggs over, home fries, toast with jam, and coffee. This sort of breakfast was also the tip-off for Americans visiting Grand Cayman, and hunkering down in George Town, that the *Seascape Café* was the place to be for a down-home feeling and a down-home meal.

It was obvious that Rostmann felt like staying there—at least for a while—at the *Seascape* as well as in George Town proper. And at this point Rostmann knew just what to do for inviting some companionship. He was in his mid to late seventies, but his virility was still very much intact, and he could feel that it needed exercise.

This part of it all was easy for him, and it didn't bother his sense of masculinity one bit that the waitress at the café was always, and really, thrilled with his extravagance. That is, he knew he was buying her. He would always leave her a gratuity that was more than the total check for the meal. How much evidence does one need that she would light up whenever she saw him entering or even approaching the café. With her typical salary and tips she was probably only making enough to live week to week and month to month. She had no choice, and maybe didn't want a choice. She was tired.

Although Rostmann had not invited her into his lair before, now he felt he needed her. He needed her specifically for sex, but generally, of course, for his fix—his need for uninterrupted external stimulation—in all forms. It was the fuel that kept his psychopathic fires burning.

Her name was Akilina. He didn't know her last name but he knew she was Russian. She spoke with a distinct Russian accent. Apparently, she'd been in George Town for a number of years, and periodically, when Rostmann visited his money there, he would have his meals at the *Seascape*. On those visits they always had a friendly interaction. He couldn't speak Russian, but he knew more than just a few Russian words. Luckily for him, he knew the word for "beautiful." It actually translates as "extraordinarily beautiful." The word is *krasavitza*. And that's what he said to her. They were both speaking in English—he with his German accent and she with her Russian. It was then that he called her *krasavitza*.

Akilina was excited that he knew the word, and she practically squealed. Rostmann asked her to come to his house sometime where they would cook dinner together, and Akilina said she would love to. She told him she was surprised he could cook because he always had his meals, it seemed, at the café. But Rostmann confessed that when they would cook together, she would see that all he really could do was prepare the salad. With a smile, he told her that she would really need to be the one who actually did the cooking. He said he hoped she didn't mind—that all he liked to do was cut. And he repeated it, about liking to cut vegetables. They both laughed, and without any hesitation, they made the where and when arrangements. Now, Akilina knew where and when, and Rostmann had something to do and someone to do it with.

Akilina knew she was going to get tipped, get paid somehow. Sex was all right with her, and both Rostmann and she tacitly knew that she would not only be paid, but be handsomely paid—rewarded actually. She was ready for love and sex and was of course excited that he was going to give her either something like money or jewelry or some such thing or maybe, she thought, both money and jewelry. She knew it was a sure thing, and without a doubt, felt grateful for it. She didn't care at all that he was probably more than thirty years older than her.

The "where," of course, was Rostmann's house, and the "when" was to be that night. Rostmann knew absolutely that Akilina would have canceled any other commitment she may have had in order to comply with his wishes. It was Rostmann's unshakable belief that his money made it possible to buy anything. And as far as he was concerned, Akilina was "anything." But, apparently, she was in no danger for her life because she knew nothing about any of Rostmann's undertakings, nor did she really know anything at all about his life outside of George Town.

In any event, Rostmann was not planning to leave the island anytime soon. As long as he felt safe and relaxed in George Town at least for the time being, Akilina was just fine—safe.

*   *   *

Persson's trade delegation (and the drugs) were flown in two days after it was promised. Because the Caymans were a British territory, Persson had contacted United Kingdom officials who needed to approve this ostensible trade mission. This was accomplished in due haste. Instead of British officials however, the pilot and crew were all Interpol and were fully aware of the mission. Jack McBride met them at the Owen Roberts International Airport of Grand Cayman The jet was a private luxury plane—a jet-setter type—designed for flamboyant living but reinvented as a Swedish government plane. Five Interpol so-called "trade-delegates" deplaned with carry-on baggage plus other items. One of them had a briefcase loaded with documents to share with Cayman government officials ostensibly detailing the Swedish array of plans for various reciprocal vacation concepts to be negotiated between the Cayman Islands and Sweden.

Persson was afraid that Rostmann might have confederates stationed at the airport that he would be paying to keep an eye out for suspicious arrivals. Thus Persson made sure that the Interpol people passing as government personnel from Sweden included material with them, particularly these specified documents.

The first thought McBride had was: Uh oh, another five — four men and a woman. The woman of course would take the role of secretary. That makes nine of us and five of them. Fourteen! He further thought: We'd better get this job done fast. His experience told him there was too much going on. The Interpol five had hotel reservations at the five-star hotel, *Deep Water Cay Club*, befitting their official standing, We, on the other hand, were located at the four-star *Grand Lucayan Bahamas Hotel*, not far from Lucaya Beach. Persson had decided that the Interpols should not be with us at the same hotel. Too conspicuous.

It was agreed not to use hotel phones. Any communication would need to be done by sending couriers one to the other, and, at the final hour, we would all need to disperse and locate ourselves in predetermined positions. Our positions were also decided in advance according to where Rostmann might be when the word was "go." We had the *Seascape Café*, Rostmann's house, the *Rothschild Bank*, and the *Owen Roberts International Airport* in our sights. Each one of these locations were mapped out as to where exactly each of us would be positioned. And, of course, each of us would be armed — except me. The objective however, was at all costs, to capture Rostmann alive.

Again, I was not left behind, although I was weaponless. Marlow felt I might be useful during any situation that might explode that would require someone to persuade Rostmann, during such action, to surrender peacefully. I went along with it although I was never trained in hostage negotiation or anything thing like that. Should the time arrive when I would be put in that position, I knew I would need to be in it by understanding the mentality of a psychotic-psychopath.

I was fully aware of the psychodynamics of such a person and how such psychological and emotional construction figured in that person's behavior. But, the truth is, despite what I knew clinically and academically, translating it all into a spontaneous interactional situation with complete non-scripted extemporaneous and excited verbal confrontation is a transition not easily made. That was what was worrying me—the transition between knowing and doing.

The first order of business was to stake out the *Seascape Café*. It was decided that the Interpol agent, the woman with the trade delegation, Amy Hazen, would team up with Dave Stein as a couple on vacation and spend some time at the café, having brunch or dinner. They would then depart to Dave's hotel and stay together in Dave's room. Dave's room was planned in advance for two.

Second, it was decided that Maria needed to stay completely out of sight for obvious reasons. She couldn't even leave her room. And her room was now known as the safe house. Meals would be sent up. Third, McBride was exiled to the airport. That's how he felt—exiled—even though it was he who volunteered. And that was McBride—nothing was more important than that which was, indeed important. And, therefore, he put himself where he thought it would be important to be. Nevertheless, to his dismay, he felt out of the action. One of the Interpol agents accompanied him. Fourth, two Interpol agents posing as members of the trade delegation would slowly walk along looking at the sights in George Town near the bank.

That was it so far.

But that wasn't it for me. I was pining away for Tess, but I wasn't allowed to make phone calls from Grand Cayman. Tess and I had spoken many times after she returned to Milan, but in the past few days what might be considered my phone privileges were forbidden.

*   *   *

The next day, beginning at about 9 a.m., we started our mission. Ever so gradually, we trickled out into the day. Everyone knew what their positions were, and by 10 a.m. we were all out and about and in position at various locations, all of which had a common target—the Rothschild Private Bank.

But, as fate would have it, our locations didn't correlate with reality. Yes, there was Rostmann in the flesh. He was finishing his breakfast at the *Seascape*. Apparently, he was an early bird and was having breakfast by 8 a.m. when the café was open for business. The café was an open eating area with tables and chairs outside so that people could have a choice as to whether to sit inside where it was not as public—of course where Rostmann dined—or out in the open under an umbrella to shield the sun where many others sat.

And here came Rostmann, his breakfast finished, sauntering out of the café. Dave Stein, half of the great tracing and tracking team, made the first move. He was accompanied by Amy Hazen of Interpol and, in the here and now, of the bogus Swedish trade delegation. They made a beeline toward Rostmann. Rostmann felt it. He saw it coming, especially because Tancredi, spotting Dave and Amy, made a bold move and came in from his own position, which unfortunately was very much in Rostmann's field of vision. Rostmann drew his revolver and backed into the café.

He made a beeline to Akilina and held her as a hostage shield. He told her not to worry because he was bluffing and would give himself up. Akilina didn't understand it at all and was terrified about what was going on. Dave and Amy also had guns drawn, but another two of the Interpol agents together shouted for all in the street to hear: "No shooting." Dave looked at them and waved, meaning "OK." At that point people all around were running here and there, but the café was surrounded by our entire contingent.

A momentary funny exchange occurred when Persson said alarmingly, "It's got to be done now. We need to avoid the police." Rostmann heard him say it and pushed Akilina out in front of him into the street. He said, "I will surrender and not fire a shot, but I will only surrender to Inspector Maria Oliva. Where is she?"

Persson answered, "OK, no shooting. We'll have her here momentarily." Word must have instantly spread that there was a commotion in the street near the café.

We kind of surmised that because of the many people who began converging at the scene. And almost at the same time, Maria and one of the Interpol agents appeared. She later told us she could see it from her window at the safe house. She rushed up to Tancredi and at the same time saw Rostmann partially shielded by a woman. She shouted directly at Rostmann:

"Mr. Rostmann, please don't hurt her. I know you're able to be heroic. Now's not the time to spoil it. Let's talk. Remember, I know you want to talk because you want to clear your name. I know we both remember what you said."

I thought Maria was brilliant to use the reference "We both remember," with a focus on the "We." It was then because of what Maria said, and how she said it, that just about made it impossible for Rostmann to back out of the deal.

"All right," he shouted. "But first even once you get me, I need to say a few things. Is that agreed?"

With authority, Maria answered: "Absolutely."

With that he dropped his weapon and also instantly released Akilina. Akilina ran into the café. Our Justice League surrounded Rostmann and cuffed him. He was further frisked and quickly led away. Persson commandeered a car, and Rostmann was positioned in the back, with Tancredi rushing in on one side and Stein on the other. Amy Hazen drove the car with Maria sitting in the companion seat. The entire "Eichmann-like abduction" lasted no more than a minute, and there was no sign in that time of any George Town police. Philippe Marcel was left behind only because he wasn't nearest to the car, so that when Tancredi, Stein, Rostmann, Maria, and Amy rushed into the car, Marcel simply remained standing there. Marcel walked casually to the safe house; he didn't want to invite onlookers.

It took another minute or so for the five of them to reach the safe house only about forty yards from the café scene, to exit the car and usher Rostmann into the house. It was a house located down a little turn from the main street.

Rostmann was treated in a civil manner. Our Justice League all knew that Maria was in charge. A knock, a pause, and then two knocks, then repeated, told us the others had arrived.

Then Marcel arrived. The room was full of our people. And there was Rostmann. We had him. The question was, what really did we have?" However, I, especially, was privileged to be there. I'd never been an observer of this kind of inner drama with police interrogating a vital suspect—in this case someone who might very well have been the person looking to kill—me.

Rostmann was offered a cigarette, and he accepted. Maria ordered the handcuffs removed.

Maria started: "Mr. Rostmann, OK, you surrendered, so we all want to know what you want to say."

"First," he said, "I'm glad you were here because in order to defend myself from some gang that wanted my money, I would have had to begin shooting. I took a guess and hoped that perhaps it wasn't a robbery of my money, but that it might be the police—especially those who were your comrades, you know, police from around the world. I know you all may think I'm a terrible person who has committed terrible crimes, but it's not true. As a matter of fact, I'm afraid of a man named Wolfgang Kluge, so that I actually feel safest here with you. It's because of this Kluge that I carry a firearm. I know he wants to kill me because of the money we took from that bank in Bremen, right before the night of the bombing. I know you all know about that.

"Kluge is the one who's been the murderer, and when just the two of us were left I then knew he was the murderer. I may have even said that to Inspector Oliva. Looking to Maria, Rostmann said:

"OK, here's the deal I'd like to make. I'll tell you everything about the robbery at the bank, the thing about the bombing and the light that gave the signal for the bombing, the cathedral people who were involved in guarding the money, and how and where the money is now located as well as how it all got there. In return, I want you to drop any charges regarding that initial robbery so many decades ago and let me stand trial for anything else. I'm innocent of anything else and I want to take a chance on American justice. I don't want to be tried in Germany or anywhere else. That's the deal I want, and I think it's a fair one.

"I'm not asking for any leniency on any other matter that may arise. Justice, I believe, will be on my side, especially if my association and involvement in the initial robbery from that Bremen bank is legally neutralized. I believe I can prove that only two people could have accomplished all those killings. I can identify them and possibly offer you information about where they can be found.

"I think that kind of deal is fair, and I hope you will concur. Otherwise I will not utter a word about anything and will simply take my chances with a jury."

Rostmann was obviously very smart. Persson decided we needed to have a pow-wow in the next room while four of the other Interpol agents remained with Rostmann, again rehandcuffed in the room. Rostmann was told just that—why we were exiting to the other room—and he actually thanked us.

* * *

Persson, Tancredi, Maria, Stein, and I, and, of course, Philippe Marcel, who had also just arrived, were included in this private police discussion. And, of course, McBride also came in—not knowing anything about what had happened. He joined us and was excited to see that we actually had Rostmann.

Persson led it off. He first said that Rostmann's act of surrendering in the manner in which he did was as edgy as the sharp side of a sword. "He's very very smart," Persson added. "He thinks he can get away with it all because he's sure we have nothing on him except maybe the stolen money from that bank heist in Bremen. My hunch is that he would not be convicted on that score anyway—at least in the sense of prison time, and other than his confession that he did, in fact, participate in that robbery, we have no proof that he actually did. He could recant saying that we pressured him."

We then talked it over. We asked Philippe what he thought we should do.

"Well," he answered, "even if it happened—meaning the robbery—and continued as a cold case file, especially a thirty-five-year-old cold case file, the case does qualify as having a good chance to come to trial. But—and it's a big but—a robbery that happened all those years ago is not going to stimulate the same kind of a need for justice, especially if the state does not have witnesses to verify and validate the accused as intrinsically responsible for the crime. In such a case, the accused might get minimal jail time or, even more likely, a suspended sentence. It's a roll of the dice. In this case with Rostmann, I don't think we have any hard evidence against him.

"On the whole, we can't prove he stole the money or was the leader who instigated it all. Second, we can't prove he killed Jean in Berlin. Third, we can't prove he killed any of the others. Even with his use of the name Bremen. So what? He could say it was a more convenient name to use for business purposes. It's done all the time. He could say anything, like, for example that he's a student of history and after seeing the Bremen statue on the Bremen Square, and admiring—who was it, Charlemagne?—he then adopted the name Bremen. He liked it, so he adopted it.

"There's nothing we can prove. Even the Cayman bank account. He'll simply say that it was given to him against his will as his share of the money stolen, which he was against in the first place. And if we make the deal, even that won't be permissible in court because our part of the deal would be to not pursue accountability for the robbery. It would be a dead issue. And to top it off, as a consequence of the deal, Rostmann would wind up keeping the money. We may not have a choice here but to agree to his condition and put him only on trial for murder of the others—in the hope of gathering new hard information. But otherwise, without such hard information, he's going to walk."

Grimand then asked Philippe whether he had any further thoughts about Kluge.

"Oh, yes, I do," he answered. "You see, the core of it all with regard to Kluge is why in the world would Kluge want to kill Jean. He probably never met her and, more, probably never knew there was a Jean. No, it was Rostmann who killed Jean. He was trying to eliminate anyone who could implicate him in murder. So, I think—and I hate to say this because also of you, Alex—that Rowdy's also in danger. I'm sure this has not escaped your attention. As far as Kluge is concerned, my hunch is that Kluge is either dead or in hiding. Of course, if alive, he knows that Rostmann is the culprit. So either Kluge is in hiding or else he's out to get Rostmann before Rostmann gets him. One or the other—assuming, again, of course, that he's alive."

With that, Marcel said he wanted to hear what I had to say—from a psychological point of view. My newest friend, Aldo Tancredi, seconded the motion.

"Well," I began, "I've been thinking a lot about it—less about any potential trial and more about Rowdy per se. It's clear to me that Rostmann is setting him up—setting Rowdy up as the guilty party to the murders. Rostmann's deranged to the point of not only killing his companion, Jean Adele, who had been at his side for decades, but also in planning to set up his own grandson. And all of it is or was premeditated. I think, at any trial, Rostmann will paint Rowdy as an inadequate personality.

"This diagnosis has been widely used as a diagnostic reference. It means that such an individual is basically underdeveloped in all spheres of functioning, although not necessarily in intelligence. What with Rowdy's history of not doing anything, of not going to school, and of not having any other means of survival except that offered by Rostmann, a court appointed mental health professional such as a psychologist or psychiatrist will necessarily, and on the basis of Rowdy's history, declare him to be competent to stand trial with respect to his sanity, but also necessarily brand him diagnostically as an inadequate personality. In such a case, Rostmann emerges in the ascendancy as someone with all his marbles, but Rowdy is consigned to a rather defensive position — one that paints him as only a likely suspect in all the murders. In that sense, I don't think a trial will solve anything, and Rostmann will walk out a free man.

"My hunch is if we go in and discuss it further with Rostmann as to who he thinks is the guilty party, that he will tell us exactly what he would say at a trial. He'll incriminate Rowdy further. So, I say, let's give it a try. Let's talk to him some more. But one thing is fairly certain. I believe that even if the inadequate personality thing doesn't stand up in court, Rostmann could no longer take the chance that Rowdy lives. If the court should dismiss the case, I believe Rostmann will find Rowdy, and kill him. As we all know, with Rostmann, we're dealing with a cold-blooded killer who refuses to permit anyone to live who might be able to testify against him. And to top it off, I might be next. He knows that Rowdy shared everything with me. And if he actually doesn't know it, then he assumes it. That's for sure.

"Further, he also may be afraid that I could puncture whatever testimony is given by either a psychologist or psychiatrist regarding Rowdy's ostensible diagnosis of inadequate personality. If that were so, then my supportive testimony in Rowdy's favor could keep the case going. Or, if the case gets dismissed, then my potential testimony in Rowdy's favor might enable the prosecution to reopen it. Rostmann's not going to be able to take that chance. Rowdy's first on his list — and I'm next.

"I'm predicting here that, if we go into the next room and ask him to tell us what's on his mind, his entire speech will be an indictment of Rowdy and maybe of Kluge as well. There's no doubt about it."

I stopped and looked at Marcel, who continued.

"All right, I say we go in and test Alex's theory. And if Alex is right and Rostmann tries to fry Rowdy, and to that we'll still not be sure about what to say or do, then we all agree to return to this room for a continuing discussion, while making no further promises to Rostmann."

With that, we all headed for the door to the next room.

*　*　*

Rostmann was sitting handcuffed but slightly rocking from side to side in his chair. Grimand ordered the handcuffs removed.

"Mr. Rostmann," Grimand started but instead of giving Rostmann a chance to invent whatever it was that he was going to say, Grimand rather directed him. "Please tell us more about Kluge and about your grandson Rowan."

"There is no doubt that Kluge is the one. I've already told that to Inspector Oliva. And I believe Kluge will need to kill Rowan, my grandson, because he thinks that that will flush me out. If not for my fear for Rowan, I would probably spend the rest of my life in hiding because I know that Kluge wants me dead. He's killed the others. I'm the only one left."

"But, Mr. Rostmann," Grimand interrupted, "you were involved in stealing the money from the bank and in the bombing of Bremen."

"Yes, I was captain of the squad, but it was Kluge, from the beginning, who decided we should shine that light. Each one of us agreed to take the money, yes. What should I have done — said 'No?, They would have killed me on the spot. I kept on reading about the others getting killed. I've been in hiding from the killer, whoever he was, all this time. Now I know it's Kluge!

"And I know he's going to try to find Rowan and try to kill him. And the police can't protect Rowan because no threat has been made. He wants to kill Rowan because he wants me to seek revenge, so that my need will bring me out into the open. Then he'll make it a point to find me and try to kill me. With me out of the way, Kluge is in the clear because no one can be a witness against him."

Again, Grimand continued. "Mr. Rostmann, what if your grandson Rowan states that Kluge wasn't the assassin. What about that?"

"That's ridiculous. He's my grandson. He knows that it had to be Kluge because only Kluge and I remained. But, Rowan is an underdeveloped person. He dropped out of school because he couldn't keep up with the work. He also has a delusion that he's a CIA operative, kind of like a James Bond character.

"Rowan has never worked at a job. He even admitted to doing strange things like stalking people for no reason. He told me he would stalk people by spending hours and hours following them in the streets of New York City. I never knew if he did any of these individuals any harm. It could be that he did. And besides all of this, I've been financially supporting him for his entire life. I've been taking care of him, keeping him nourished and in good health. Like I said, he could never hold a job, so I had no choice.

"Of course, you can understand that the only thing I couldn't do is cure his mental disturbance. As a matter of fact, he would become upset if I didn't create stories about spying and things like that. And he would ask me over and over again to tell him such stories. It was his obsession. The stories all concerned his favorite theme, which, I'm afraid to say, was assassinations. I believe he got that idea because he knew I was worried about who it was in my squad that was obviously killing our other comrades. Just about all of them were suddenly, over the years, assassinated. And, as would be the case with such immature minds, Rowan latched onto the assassination story and definitely over-identified with it.

"That's about it. That's about it."

Rostmann sunk into silence, staring at us, but he looked forlornly at Maria.

"Mr. Rostmann," Maria kindly stated, "we will discuss this some more in the other room. I don't think it will take long."

At that point, those of us who gathered in the adjoining room earlier again reconvened.

Grimand said: "Alex, you were right. He's implicating either Rowdy or Kluge as the assassin — or even assassins." Then Grimand turned to Marcel and asked him to sum up.

"Look, everyone," Marcel said decisively. "We've got no choice here. Let's make the deal about the robbery and get Rostmann prosecuted in New York City for the crime of murder. We've got witnesses who saw the tallish man with the stooped posture and funny gait. At least it's something."

We all reluctantly agreed, and the deal with Rostmann was reluctantly struck.

* * *

Travel arrangements were completed, and the next day Marlow, two detectives, Rostmann and I boarded the plane that brought the Swedish trade delegation to the Caymans, but now took us all to New York's Kennedy International Airport. All the others dispersed to their European cities, including Maria. She said her good-byes — also to Rostmann.

Tess met me in New York, and we settled into my Gramercy Park apartment. But I was preoccupied and disturbed.

"What is it, Alex."

"OK, here it is. They essentially have no hard evidence against Rostmann with respect to the murders, and it looks to me that he'll be acquitted or the trial will be thrown out. The penalty for the robbery has already been neutralized by our deal with him. So he'll be a free man, and an enormously wealthy one. I'm concerned about Rowdy. Rostmann's going to kill him. And he's going to do it in a way that can't be traced. Rowdy's life isn't worth a plug nickel.

"Rostmann's psychopathic vigilance will get the best of him because he'll probably remember that he'd told Rowdy some incriminating information, and so killing Rowdy would be a given. As we all know, there's been no threat to Rowdy's life from anyone, so Rowdy can't ask for police protection. I'll now also want to financially support him otherwise he would wind up living on the street. He knows his grandfather will try to kill him. And, Tess, after Rowdy, I'm next. I have to stop it."

"What does that mean, Alex, you've got to stop it? What does that mean? Like you've got to stop Rostmann yourself?"

"It means Rostmann's got to be stopped! Simple! Period!"

"Alex, don't let your enosiophobia confuse you. You're not like that."

"It might not sound right, but it still might be right. The only way to stop it is to finish it once and for all."

"Alex, you can't do that. It's your enosiophobia seeking a kind of grotesque gratification, so that now, finally, you would actually be *doing* something wrong. Alex? Alex, look at me—you're not listening. Alex. Your mind is elsewhere!"

*   *   *

Who's Who

Main

Dr. Alex Cole—psychologist/psychoanalyst/professor/author.
Rowdy—a.k.a. Rowan Quinn, a.k.a. Charles Rostmann Quinn.
Dr. Katherine Tess McFarland—psychoanalytic archivist.
Dr. Richard Martin—psychologist/psychoanalyst.
Marcus Rostmann—a.k.a. Roland Bremen.
Jeannie—a.k.a Gina Herrera, a.k.a. Jean Adele.

Police Contingent

Aldo Tancredi—Chief of Police in Milan, Italy.
Maria Oliva—One of Tancredi's special agents from his police department in Milan.
Sanford Garelik—First Jewish Chief Inspector of the New York City Police Department.
Dave Stein—New York City police department detective.
Jack McBride—New York City police department detective.
Inspector Jacques Grimand of Paris Secret Service; a French Jew of Italian descent.
Philippe Marcel—Genius type associate of Jacqaues Grimand from Paris.

Carl Persson—President of Interpol (International Criminal Police Organization).

Steve Marlow—Detective in charge of protecting Dr. Alex Cole.

Amy Hazen—From Interpol.

The Cabal

Marcus Rostmann—a.k.a. Roland Bremen. (See Nazi Squad Members).

Torsten Koppel—Caretaker of Bremen's Square St. Peter's Cathedral, Bremen, Germany.

Konrad—Minister of St. Peter's Cathedral in Bremen, Germany.

Frau Ilsa Krause—Guest at the hotel in Berlin.

Manfred Bauer—Chief Curator, German Historical Museum in Berlin.

Bishop Alois Hudal—Leader of Odessa, the underground railroad for escaped Nazis.

Supporting

Dr. Alex Cole's mother—one of the ghosts of dreams, speaking to Alex in his dream.

Nathan Kamen—Vice-President of the Simon Wiesenthal Center in Los Angeles.

Astrid Neumann—Hotel Concierge in Berlin.

Akilina—Waitress at the Seascape Café in George Town, Grand Cayman Island.

Ten Nazi Squad Members

Marcus Rostmann—Leader, Nazi Squad.

Hans Milch—Former Nazi soldier murdered by the assassin.

Horst Kapkow—Former Nazi soldier murdered by the assassin.

Klaus Gruber—Former Nazi soldier murdered by the assassin.

Heinrich Jaeger—Former Nazi soldier murdered by the assassin.

Gerhardt Eisler—Former Nazi soldier murdered by the assassin.

Alois Amsel—Former Nazi soldier murdered by the assassin.

Franz Hoch—Former Nazi soldier murdered by the assassin.

Wolfgang Kluge—a.k.a. Ludwig Aachen—Former Nazi soldier murdered by Minister Konrad.

Walther Koertig—Former Nazi soldier; died of natural causes.

Minor

Frau Fanken—The lady who kept Alex as a child at the farmhouse.
Young Austrian female student telling jokes.
Herr Hoepker—Administrator at Feller Industries (shipbuilding).
Renatta Kluge—Wolfgang Kluge's wife.
Cousin of Walther Koertig.
Rostmann's driver in Berlin.
Rostmann's driver onto the ship.

Individuals Referred to but Not Actually in the Story

Dr. Sigmund Freud—Known as the father of psychoanalysis.
Bishop Alois Hudel—Leader of Odessa, the underground railroad for escaped Nazis.
Dr. Louis Ormont—Primarily known as an important group theorist and practitioner.
Guiseppe Tomas di Lampedusa—The Prince of Lampedusa.
Baroness Alexandra Wolff—Wife of Guiseppe Tomas di Lampedusa; psychoanalytic archivist.
Dr. John Lilly—Primarily known for his ethological work with dolphins.
Dr. Alex Cole's parents.
Armand Calle—Police Chief in Paris.
Rostmann's contact in the Caymans.

Unnamed

Landlady who saved Alex as a child from the Nazis.
Elderly lady in apartment building in Paris.
Elderly lady answering questions in apartment building in Paris.
Woman on phone at the Wiesenthal Center in Los Angeles.
1st Unnamed New York Police detective shadowing Alex.

2nd unnamed New York Police detective shadowing Tess.

3rd unnamed New York Police detective stationed at the Waldorf Astoria Hotel.

4th unnamed New York Police detective stationed at the Waldorf Astoria Hotel.

5th unnamed detective from New York City Police Department to assist Detective Marlow.

Unnamed bodyguard from Interpol to protect Carl Persson.

1st unnamed man; a confederate of Rostmann and Bauer.

2nd unnamed man; a confederate of Rostmann and Bauer.

Unnamed docent of the German Historical Museum.

Unnamed two men who abducted Maria Oliva and later drove the trucks.

Several unnamed investigators from the German Secret Service.

Two workers at the Rothschld Bank in the Caymans.